Win Or Die

ALSO BY DARREN O'SULLIVAN

STANDALONES
The Night They Stole My Baby
The Husband
Win Or Die

WIN OR DIE

DARREN O'SULLIVAN

JOFFE BOOKS

Joffe Books, London
www.joffebooks.com

First published in Great Britain in 2025

© Darren O'Sullivan

This book is a work of fiction. Names, characters, businesses, organisations, places and events are either the product of the author's imagination or are used fictitiously. Any resemblance to actual persons, living or dead, events or locales is entirely coincidental. The spelling used is British English except where fidelity to the author's rendering of accent or dialect supersedes this. The right of Darren O'Sullivan to be identified as author of this work has been asserted in accordance with the Copyright, Designs and Patents Act 1988.

No part of this book may be used or reproduced in any manner for the purpose of training artificial intelligence technologies or systems. In accordance with Article 4(3) of the Digital Single Market Directive 2019/790, Joffe Books expressly reserves this work from the text and data mining exception.

Cover art by Nebojša Zorić

ISBN: 978-1-80573-065-1

To my dear friend John Shields, who is one of the kindest men I know, and one of the bravest.

PROLOGUE

I hoped I'd done enough to not be found.

I hoped I had been smart enough to not be caught.

I was wrong, because when I heard him shout, I knew he was close.

'We know you're here. No point running anymore.'

I hobbled further into the park, further from those pursuing, desperate for somewhere to hide. A huge willow tree stood in the middle, surrounded by a circular patch of grass that in spring boasted daffodils and bluebells. I rounded the tree, wondering if I could climb it, but knew I would fail. My body was too tired, my bare feet too sore and numb. My calf throbbed from the wound. Had it really only been twelve hours since I'd got it? If I tried to put too much pressure on it, my leg would buckle. So, I pushed on, in more of a limp than a run.

Finding a copse off the main path, I pressed myself into it. It was mostly brambles and bush, but in spite of the spikes digging into my skin, I lowered myself to the ground to take the pressure off my aching feet, and fought to keep my breathing calm and quiet. I hoped they would come through, assuming I'd left the park via the south side, their search fruitless.

Time would tell.

As my breathing fell into a steady rhythm, in and out, I heard a voice calling, and my breath snatched.

'Come out, come out, wherever you are!'

Then, silence. I counted in my head. *One, two, three, four, five, si—*

'No point hiding anymore,' he called again, a little closer. I could hear the excitement in his voice.

I huddled into the brambles, fighting the cold that had seeped deep into my bones from a night out in sub-zero temperatures. I kept as still as I could, and waited to hear him speak again to see if I could work out where he was — before he worked out where I was.

But everything was quiet. He didn't call out again, and that told me he was closer still.

Hiding wouldn't help. I had to move. I had to run.

Taking some deep measured breaths, I looked down at my bare, bloodied feet and my injured calf, and hoped they would carry me for just a little longer.

'Is there any sign of her?' the man shouted.

'Nothing,' the woman called back.

'Maybe she ain't here,' called the other man.

'She's here. Keep looking.'

Drawing in one final breath, I freed myself as best and as quietly as I could from the brambles, ready to launch into a sprint. Ahead of me, around 100 metres away, was the gate. If I could get to it without being seen, I could lose them in the warren of city streets, could hide in people's gardens until the time ran out.

If I could get to the gate, I might just stay alive.

I began to count down.

Three.

'Cassie, we are going to find you.'

Two.

'Come out, you bitch. There is nowhere you can hide.'

One.

Welcome to DareMe

There are three fundamental rules to follow if you want to be a profile user in the DareMe app.

1: Each dare must be completed in the time allocated by the DareMe DareMaker. A dare completion time can range from one minute to five hours in length. There is no cap on the value of the dare.

2: There are two types of dares in the app: open dares and closed dares. Any profile user can attempt an open dare and the first to complete the dare wins. Closed dares are specifically for one profile user. Only that individual can complete the dare.

3: In order to receive payment, each dare must be livestreamed in the app for proof of completion.

For a full list of our terms and conditions, please visit our website.

PART ONE

CHAPTER ONE

Seventy hours before...

My alarm sounded, telling me it was half past six, and time to get up. I had been awake for an hour already, staring at my phone resting in its charging dock, tapping the screen periodically to see the time, yet I still jumped.

Sighing, I snoozed the alarm and, not wanting to get out of bed, checked my socials. I didn't know why I bothered. TikTok wasn't for me, and my Instagram was private, with fewer than 100 followers. But still, I scrolled. When nothing interesting leaped out, I opened DareMe, so I could kill a little time watching people having fun. I watched a kid, maybe sixteen at most, jump off a bridge into a frozen river somewhere in Minnesota. I watched a woman, @krazyklaire, run into a church in just her underwear. I scrolled through people eating disgusting things, performing stunts with varying success and letting themselves be stung and bitten by different critters, all just to make a few quid. DareMe was a car crash on a screen. Bite-sized movies with amateur stars and huge dopamine climaxes. It was all stupid, sometimes reckless, occasionally illegal, but I watched anyway, as did millions of others.

My alarm sounded again.

'All right, I'm up!'

I rolled over and sat up, silencing the alarm in the process, then rubbed my tired eyes. As much as I wanted to go back to bed, I knew I had to get ready for work. Standing, I walked to the window, drew the curtains and looked outside. The night held firm, but there was a soft orange glow in the sky. Dawn was coming.

It was going to be another cold one. Thick frost covered the ground, shimmering in the street lights. It made outside look otherworldly, magical, full of cheer and promise and excitement. A Disney world where everyone's stories ended happily ever after. If only. Really, it was just a winter morning. Cold and bleak. People would be miserable, and walking to the bus stop would be treacherous. Even if I wore sensible shoes today, which I always did, I had to factor that in, so I'd not be late for work. Flicking on a light, I looked to my bedside table.

'Morning, Mum,' I said, kissing my fingers and placing them on the glass of the photo frame that had stood beside my bed for ten years. I looked at the two of us, smiling at the camera. Behind us was the town park, a huge green space north of Peterborough city centre. Despite it being only a mile away, I hadn't been there for far too long. The picture wasn't the most recent of me and Mum, I had plenty of us after I was a kid and before she died. I had another whole decade of my mum before she was taken. But this picture was my favourite of her, she looked the happiest I can remember her ever being, from a time that made the most sense, before puberty and hormones, before Sam was born. When it was just me and her. Maybe that's why I kept it over any other. Maybe I needed to hang onto that somehow. I knew every pixel of the picture. If I tried really hard, I could almost see it, the day itself, but it was more shadow that light, more shade than colour. It was almost lost in the grey. Soon it would be gone.

I wish I'd known back then how important the moment would be. I wish I'd paid more attention. I wish I had taken in more — the colours and sounds and smells. I wish I had focused on her laugh. But I was a kid, barely ten. The world didn't work like that for kids. They didn't reflect, they only were. They took it all for granted. Despite being not yet thirty, I knew that youth was really wasted on the young.

I took in Mum's smile once more, then slipped on my dressing gown and made my way out of the room.

Sam's bedroom door was open. My brother hadn't come home, again. Opening his door wider, I peered inside. His bed was untouched.

'For God's sake, Sam,' I cursed, before continuing into the bathroom. I should have expected it — he always acted up when it was close to the anniversary. I didn't know why I thought this year would be any different. I guess I'd just hoped that with each passing year, it would get easier. But who was I kidding? It never got easier. Never. I just needed him to find a way to accept it, or at least bury it, like I had.

After my shower, I checked my phone again, this time messaging him to ask where he was. As I blow-dried my hair and got dressed, applying a little make-up to cover the bags under my eyes and a spot which was begging to have its moment in the spotlight, I kept one eye out on the road, expecting to see him wandering down it, hands in his pockets, head down. But the street remained empty.

Down in the kitchen, I made myself a coffee and lunch for both me and Sam. Sometimes he would stay out all night doing God knows what, and still make it to work on time. Sometimes he didn't. I had to hope he would walk in, mumble something I couldn't discern, quickly get showered and changed and then head out to work. Sure enough, as I finished my coffee, my annoyance having fully morphed into worry, I heard the front door open.

'Sam?' I called out. 'Is that you?'

Getting up from the kitchen table I made my way towards him.

He was sitting on the stairs, struggling to get his shoes off. He was visibly hungover.

'Sam? Are you still drunk? Sam?'

'I'm fine.' His words were barely audible, his movements slow.

Rage boiled up inside me. He made me worry too much. He made me work too hard. 'For God's sake, you'll lose your job again.'

'Cass, don't.'

'Don't what, Sam? We can't go on doing this. Don't you understand how hard it is to stay ahead? Don't you understand it's just us?'

'Yes.'

'We have to do this together now. I need you to do more.'

'I'm trying.'

'Do you understand me? No one is coming to help us. No one. And things aren't cheap. The bills have shot up in the last year, food too. I need you to do your part.'

'I am.'

'Sam, you're going to get sacked again. How many jobs is that in the last year? Four? Five?'

He didn't reply, but lowered his head and began to quietly sob. I wasn't expecting that, and all of my frustration melted.

'Sam.'

His quiet sobs became louder.

'What's happened?' I lowered myself beside him on the stairs.

'Nothing. I'm fine.' He got up, brushing off the hug I had tried to give him.

'You don't look fine. Sorry, I didn't mean to rant — I'm stressed.'

'It's fine.'

'What's going on?'

'Nothing.'

As he looked up, I gasped. 'What happened to your face?' I tried to get a closer look, to see if there was any damage to his eye beyond the deep bruise.

'I said I'm fine.' He pushed my hand away, turned and made his way up to his room.

I wanted to call after him, to check he was all right, to find out what had happened, but knew my words wouldn't be welcomed.

Sam slammed the bedroom door so hard my heart almost stopped. I'd learned over the years that, sometimes, my brother needed space. And with us coming up to the tenth anniversary of our mum's death, I suspected the loss played heavily on his mind. She'd been dead exactly half the time he had been alive. I couldn't imagine how hard that would be. If my memories were fading, did Sam have any of her left? Were his completely gone? Did he remember her at all? He was just a kid when our lives had changed for ever. Just a little boy.

But he wasn't a kid anymore and his bruise worried me. My little brother wasn't so little. And it scared me. Caring for a kid was hard, a teenager harder still. But he and I always talked. We always shared, we only had each other. Now Sam was a man, and he had his secrets, just like I had mine.

'Sam? I'm going to work now,' I shouted up, hoping he would say something back, a curt 'fine', or even a huff. He was still my little brother who needed me for comfort. 'Sam?' I called again. 'I made you some lunch, for work. If you're not going to go in, I understand, but you have to call it in. Don't just not turn up? All right? Sam?'

He didn't respond, and I didn't want to press. I just had to hope he would do the right thing.

Putting on my warm coat, scarf and boots, I collected my bag and headed to the front door. As I opened it a wave of frigid air swept into the house.

I took one more look up towards my brother's bedroom, hoping to see him looking down at me. But his door stayed firmly closed.

CHAPTER TWO

I walked gingerly towards the bus stop, trying not to slip on the ice. I tried to work out when things had changed so much between me and my brother. We were close. We'd had to be — I'd become his legal guardian when I was only nineteen. Ever since it had just been the two of us. All we had was each other, and we were closer than any other siblings I knew, bonded by our grief, our trauma. But lately, I could feel him pulling away. He stayed out more and said less. He was up to something. Sam was reckless, and with only a sister to keep him in check, he didn't have a great understanding of the world; in the past he had done some silly things. But now I wasn't sure that silly hadn't been replaced with something else. Drugs maybe?

I'd have to talk to him. He needed to tell me what was going on. That bruise looked sore and his sobs told me he was in trouble. It was my duty to fix it. Yes, I was his sister, but I was also the closest thing he had to a parent. I had a responsibility. I owed it to him. I owed him more than he would ever know.

I was so caught up in how I would start that conversation that I wasn't paying attention to where my feet went. And even in my sturdy boots I slipped on a frozen puddle, which sent me crashing to the ground.

'Shit,' I said, rolling onto my side before sitting up. My heart raced, the fall having startled me. I looked around. Thankfully, no one had seen, and I got back to my feet. My left bum cheek ached, and would likely bruise, but aside from that I was fine. I set off towards the bus stop once more, this time with the necessary focus. I was within touching distance when my bus, the number three, passed me at pace.

'Shit,' I said again.

I had to wait almost twenty minutes for the next one, and I arrived at work cold, aching and five minutes late. I apologised profusely to my boss, who didn't seem to mind as, in his words, I was 'rarely late'. He was wrong, though. I was never late. Never. In almost ten years, I'd only had three or four sick days at most, even during Covid times. Even when Sam was at primary school. He was in breakfast clubs, and I was contracted to work less hours. Even when I was a grieving teenager, a struggling sister and a brand-new guardian, I was never late. But I didn't challenge him on it. I simply thanked him for his graciousness, took off my coat and sat down at my desk. Across the office, Mia caught my eye and gave me a thumbs up. I returned it with a smile and small nod. She knew I was never late either.

Settling into work, I tried to brush off Sam's sobs, that sore-looking bruise, the conversation I knew we needed to have, and the ever-widening gulf between us as he got older, by throwing myself into my workload. It didn't take me long to realise that it was going to be one of those days. Every customer who called in was either aggressive, argumentative or plain rude. As I tried to help people at their worst with submitting their insurance claims, I also checked my phone, waiting for a message from my brother to tell me he was all right. It finally came just after lunch.

Going out, back late, don't wait up x

I asked if he had called work like I'd told him to. He read my message, but didn't respond.

I was worried about him, of course I was, but I was also pissed off. I waited for him to get back to me all afternoon, as customer after customer shouted and cursed and verbally abused me. I was blamed for being corrupt and only wanting to help the rich. I was blamed for how complicated it was to submit a claim, like I was in charge of the policies and procedures for the entire multimillion-pound company. I was even blamed by one man for him dropping a can of gloss paint all over his new sofa. It was one of the worst days I'd ever had in the job. By the time five o'clock rolled round, and I disconnected from the call list, I wanted nothing more than a cup of hot chocolate and my bed. But Mia, my irresponsible bestie, who had spent the day watching me have the day from hell, had a better idea.

'Rough one?' she asked, when I dropped my headset to my desk.

'You could say that.' I massaged the bridge of my nose to try and rid myself of a burgeoning tension headache.

'Got anything on tonight?'

'Nope. Nothing.' Sam wouldn't be back until late. The talk wouldn't happen this evening, and after such an awful day, I didn't want to be alone.

Mia smiled. I could see she had an idea that would lift my mood, and relieve my worries. 'Let's get a drink.'

'That's literally the best thing I've heard all day,' I said.

CHAPTER THREE

Mia bought the first round in our favourite bar in town, and when she handed me the glass of wine, I drank it quickly. Too quickly. It barely touched the sides as it went down.

'Woah, Cassie, getting on it on a school night?' Mia's glass was only half empty.

'Sorry, I needed that.'

'Everything all right?'

'Yeah, yeah,' I said. 'It's just this time of year.'

'Guess it doesn't get any easier?' she replied.

'I mean, it's OK. It is what it is, can't change it, so we have to get on. Sam struggles though. Always has. He is younger, I guess. I was almost an adult when we lost her. Sam was only ten.' My mind flashed back to Sam, crying on the stairs. Something was going on. Maybe he had fallen in with the wrong crowd. Whatever was going on, I wondered if it would be happening if Mum was still alive.

Mia snapped me away from my thoughts. 'It's unfair,' she said.

'It's life.' I shrugged, trying to ignore the niggle that wanted to force its way out, the truth that I kept hidden.

'Cass?' Mia said, seeing my hesitation.

'I'm getting another, want one?'

'Why not?'

I knew Mia was worried for me. She was chaotic at times, permanently bouncing from crap relationship to crap relationship via a right swipe, but her heart was pure. She was a good person and she loved me as much as family. And I loved her too. I stood, and she watched me intently, concern plain to see, and I flashed her a smile before heading for the bar. While I waited, a man came and stood beside me, and he too tried to get the barmaid's attention, being more successful than I was. I expected him to say I was there first, as was bar etiquette, but he ordered his drinks, paid, and walked away. Another person did the same. After they left, Mia got up and approached the bar.

'Excuse me. Hello?' she called out to the barmaid, who came over.

'What can I get you?'

'Sorry, it's just, my friend was stood here, and you served two others who came after?'

'Did I?' She looked towards me.

I nodded. 'It's OK. Can I get two Pinots, please?'

'Sure thing,' she said, walking away to make our wines.

'Thanks, Mia.'

'I got you, girl.' She play-nudged me before going back to the table.

The barmaid returned with our wines. 'Sorry, I didn't see you waiting.'

'Nah, it's OK.' I waved her off, and went to join Mia once more.

As we continued to talk about things other than my mother or brother, we were interrupted by a young man, maybe around the same age as Sam, who had climbed up onto the table directly beside us.

Standing, he began, 'Ladies and gentlemen.'

'What the . . .' Mia said. He was drawing everyone's attention.

'I would like to begin with a sincere apology.'

'What is he doing?' I asked, and Mia shrugged.

'I am player Helter-Skelter, and this is me completing my DareMe challenge.'

'What on earth?' Mia said. Clearly, she wasn't on DareMe.

I looked behind the lad. His friends were giggling and getting ready to film him on their phones. Then, just as the man was being told to get off the table by staff, he pulled a Britney Spears mask out of his pocket and put it on.

'Are we streaming?' he asked.

'Yeah,' his friend shouted back, and he began to sing 'Hit Me Baby One More Time' as loud as he could, and barely in tune. He had just about scratched out the first line when he was lifted from the table by door staff. He continued to sing until he was carried out of the bar, his friends following, to the applause and cheers of the entire pub.

Through the open door we could see the bouncer put him down outside. The lad raised his hands in defence and the bouncer shook his head and walked back in, smiling. Helter-Skelter, with all his friends, shouted, 'Dare complete' before running off.

Inside the bar, people laughed before returning to their conversations and drinks.

'What was that about?' Mia asked.

'It was a DareMe challenge.'

'A what?'

'I swear, Mia, you are so cool, but sometimes you are so behind the times.'

'What do you mean?' She said, enjoying my teasing.

'You're the queen of Insta, the most successful human on earth on Tinder, but don't know DareMe.'

'I'm too busy trying to meet my future husband.'

I rolled my eyes. 'It's a new app, a game, you know, like that Pokémon one a few years back when everyone was running around catching monsters, or whatever they were.'

'What was he catching?'

'No, I mean, it's a new fad. This one is daring people to do stupid stuff. Loads of people are doing it.'

'Are you?'

'Loads of *young* people,' I corrected. 'But I watch on the app.'

'I see,' she said, but really, I knew she had no idea what I was talking about.

'I'm not playing, but it's fun to watch,' I continued, unlocking my phone to show her what I was talking about. 'Basically, people make up dares, stupid things, some a bit dangerous, and then the players can try to complete them.'

'Why?'

'For money. Each dare has a value and the person who completes it gets paid.'

'A lot?'

'Nah, a few quid here or there. Depends on the dare.'

'Right. Where does the money come from?'

'No idea. Where does any money come from? Bored rich people, entitled students, people wanting to get kicks. Disposable-income generation and all that.'

'Yeah, I guess.' She took a sip of her wine.

'Look here.' I gestured to the phone where a video was livestreaming. 'There's a player called MadMary who's streaming that she's about to set fire to a bin.'

'What?' Mia looked at the screen. A woman, her face covered with a mask, set fire to a newspaper and posted it in the bin. The paper ignited whatever was in there and as she ran off laughing, she cheered before shouting, 'Dare complete', and the stream ended.

'Why did she do that?' Mia asked.

'Says she made twenty quid.'

'But it's illegal?'

'Mia, come on.' I rolled my eyes once more. 'I mean, I won't be doing any of that, but people want to be famous, and they want money. That's it.'

'You sound like you'd play?'

'God, no, I like my quiet life, thanks. What about you, fancy it?'

'Aren't we a bit old for that stuff?'

I laughed. 'You'd be surprised. Some of the players on there are pensioners.'

'Well, I guess everyone wants their fifteen minutes,' she said.

I nodded. She was right. Everyone did want to be famous. Everyone but me. I could think of nothing worse. Maybe Sam was a player on DareMe though? Maybe he had done something stupid on the app? God knows many young men were at it.

I scrolled down, using the navigation bar to pin down all players and games in Peterborough. He wasn't on there.

The second glass of wine went down a lot slower than the first, and feeling beat from the day, Mia and I agreed it was time to go home. As we left the warmth of the bar, we both groaned.

'Jesus, I cannot wait for summer,' Mia said.

'Me neither. You gonna be OK getting back?' I asked.

'Yeah, I'll get a cab.'

'Message me when you get home.'

'I will. You gonna be OK, Cass? With Sam?'

'Yeah, we'll get through it. It's just a few days until the anniversary, and then it gets easier again.'

'Well, shout me if you need anything.'

'Will do.'

Giving Mia a hug, I put my head down and began to walk home. Despite it being a well-lit, well-trodden path down Bridge Street and over the river, I felt on edge, more than usual. Perhaps it was the amount of abuse I had suffered at work all day, maybe it was my worry about Sam and his black eye, but by the time I could see my road, I practically ran to my front door, relief washing over me as I heard the lock snap behind me.

Untying my boots, I wrestled them off and walked towards the kitchen to get a drink, but before I opened the door I heard Sam on the other side, quietly talking. The door was ajar, and I looked in. He was holding his phone in one hand, massaging the back of his neck with the other.

'I know, I understand, I just need some time. Please . . . No, no, you don't have to, I will get it. I will . . . Thank you. Thank you.'

I hung back, watching, listening, as Sam first lowered his phone and then his head. I thought he was crying, like that morning, and I was about to walk in to comfort him and make him talk to me, but as I moved to push the door he grabbed the chair, lifted it above his head and slammed it repeatedly into the floor.

'Fuck. Fuck. Fuck. Fuck. Fuuuuuuck!'

The wooden chair cracked, then split, then shattered into small pieces. Only then did he stop, drop to the floor, and sob.

CHAPTER FOUR

I let Sam finish sobbing. I knew he was aware of my presence. When he eventually stopped crying, there was no surprise on his face at seeing me. I didn't ask if he was OK. It would have been a stupid question, and I knew he would clam up. Like he always did. Instead, I began to clean up the broken chair around him.

'Leave it. I'll do that,' he said quietly, looking me in the eye. It reminded me of that night after we were told Mum was gone, and it was just us. I felt equally as helpless.

'No, it's OK.' I tried to force a smile as I continued to tidy.

Sam helped too and, in silence, we found all the bits of chair and dumped them in the garden. Sam took the final load out while I took a seat at the kitchen table. When he came back, he stood at the sink, his back to me, holding onto the edge of it, like he was holding on for dear life.

I wanted to hug him. I wanted to demand answers. But I waited, and waited and waited, until, without turning to look at me, he spoke.

'I'm in trouble, sis.'

I didn't respond. I wanted him to come to me on his terms. It was how he was. He opened the door, he let me in, but it had to be when he was ready. That night, when we found out Mum was gone, Sam locked himself in a toilet, and as much as I banged, kicked, begged, he didn't come out. It was only when I stopped, when I told him I was there and I wasn't going anywhere, and I would wait for when he was ready, that he eventually came to me. It took all night, but he did. I'd wait again, if I had to, but thankfully, this time, Sam started to talk.

'I was presented with an opportunity to earn a bit more money, you know, for us,' he continued.

'Doing what?'

'Just moving things.'

'What things, Sam?'

He hesitated.

'Sam? What things?' I said more forcefully.

'Cassie, don't be angry, OK?' He was unable to hold my eyes.

'What the hell have you gotten yourself into? And what did you mean you need more time?'

'I didn't ask questions. I just had to move things. It was a lot of driving.'

'So, you've been a courier?'

'Sort of. They paid me to take stuff places.'

I tried to sound calmer than I felt. 'What stuff?'

'I didn't ask questions.'

'Sam, what stuff?'

He opened his mouth to continue, but no words came. He turned back to face the sink.

'Sam, you need to talk to me. What do you mean you need more time?'

'I lost something.'

'What?'

'I had a bag. I was driving it to Dover.'

'Dover, that's like a hundred miles from here?'

'Hundred and twenty.'

'Why did you have to go to Dover?'

'To get on a ferry to France.'

'What? When did you go to France?'

'I've been a few times. That's where they send me.'

'You've been taking things across to France? How many times?'

'Six. I didn't ask questions, they paid me well.'

I thought about the times Sam didn't come home. I had assumed he was out partying, with a partner maybe, but it was neither — my little brother had been leaving the country, and I'd had no idea.

I was failing to do the one thing I'd said I would. I was failing to keep an eye on him.

'Why haven't you told me?'

'You would have told me to stop.'

'You know you were likely smuggling, Sam?'

'Yeah,' he said, completely defeated. 'The other night, when I came home, I was supposed to go again, but at the border the queue to join was huge and when I looked, they were checking cars. I panicked. I thought the border guards knew something. I was stuck in the queue to get on the ferry — I had no choice — so I threw the bag into a ditch.'

I paused again, waited again.

'I thought I'd get to France, then come straight back on the next ferry and get the bag and return it to those who'd asked me to take it. I thought it would work, and then I'd try again. But the bag was gone.'

'What was in it?' I asked, taking the risk that now he had partially opened the door, he wouldn't slam it in my face.

He nodded and took a deep breath. 'I went back to the man who told me to take it.'

'Who is he? The man?'

'His name is Mr Jamison.'

'Mr Jamison. Is that it?'

'That's all I was told. I don't know him. I was introduced, was told he was a good employer. It was easy money, no risk.'

'Sam, what was in the bag?'

'Cash,' he said, so quietly I could barely hear him.

'What?'

'Money, Cass, lots of it. I was taking money into France, to the address I had been told. I know it's dodgy, but I swear, I didn't know I had a bag full of money. Not until it was lost.'

'Why the hell would anyone want you to take cash to France?'

'I don't know. But I lost it, so now I owe it.'

'OK, where is he, this Jamison?'

'I don't know.'

'What do you mean you don't know? Where did you meet him?'

'Down by the river, by the old mill.'

'What? Sam, did you not think that meeting someone at the old mill for a job that's cash in hand is probably illegal?'

'Yes, of course I did. I just wanted to make some money, for this house. I hate that you carry the load. I'm an adult now and—'

'Then bloody act like one!' I snapped.

Sam almost snapped back, but he stopped himself, and instead nodded. 'I fucked up.'

'Is that how you got the bruise?' I asked quietly. I was angry, so angry, but I needed to stay calm. I had a duty to help.

Sam nodded. 'He wants the money back. I said I needed time. He's given me a week to pay what I owe.'

'OK, we can go to the bank. We don't have a lot, but my credit score is OK. I can try for a small loan. We can work out how we'll pay it back later.'

'No.'

'It would be in my bank account within minutes.'

'No, Cass. A small loan won't help.'

'Why? Sam? How much did you lose?'

'Nineteen.'

'Nineteen? Nineteen what? Hundred?'

'Thousand.'

'Oh, God,' I said.

'I'm fucked,' Sam said. 'I don't know how I'm going to find that kind of money.'

I wanted to say we could, that everything was going to be OK, but nineteen thousand? We'd never had that kind of money. I didn't need to ask the bank — they would never loan me that much. We barely scraped by as it was, without needing to find the monthly repayments on a loan that size.

Sam turned to me. 'Cass? What do I do?'

'We'll think of something,' I said, having no idea how I could help.

CHAPTER FIVE

Jamison

Jamison sat at his desk and didn't move. The call with the kid put him in an interesting position. He didn't speak for a long time, weighing up his options.

He looked up at his two subordinates, Harry and Mike, who had patiently been waiting for him to finish contemplating the next steps. He had worked with these two men for over two decades. They had been through it all together. They had waded through blood, shit and tears to get themselves where they were and that hard work was all about to pay off. Both men were in their fifties, like him, and both had families, paid their taxes and contributed positively to the community. Both were clean with no convictions, no criminal footprint, like him, and to the outside world, no one but them knew what they had been quietly planning for over three years. No one knew the enterprise they took part in.

The kid losing the money wasn't part of the plan. It had been designed to be a safety net over on the continent. But that was the only blip in an otherwise meticulously planned operation. And Jamison had known something like this might happen. Taking goods out of the country always came with a risk. It was just disappointing that of all the things the kid had ferried over, the cash was the thing he'd lost. He would need reprimanding for his mistake. Jamison came from a world where, unless you dealt with all your affairs, even the small ones, even ones that could be completely forgiven, none of them mattered. Forgiveness made you weak.

'Boss?' Harry asked. The look on his face told Jamison he had been quiet for longer than he thought.

'Do you believe he is good for the money?' Jamison asked.

'Honestly? No,' Harry said.

'And you?'

'No,' said Mike. 'He's desperately trying to buy time. But he knows he cannot repay.'

'What would you have done?' Jamison asked. 'If you thought the border guards were on to you?'

'Kid did the right thing. If he was stopped with all that cash, he would have been arrested for sure. It would have come back on us somehow,' Mike said.

'Yeah, I agree,' Jamison said. 'Kid's done well so far, several trips over. New passports, provisions, all waiting for us, so we don't have to do anything but get a ferry, like any other day tripper. This is just a blip.'

'It was a lot of money, boss.'

'I'm aware of that, Harry, but it's nothing compared to the payout we will get. It's unfortunate, but we'll still make it work. We just have to be more careful.'

Jamison sat back in his chair and took a deep breath. The plan had been in place for years — the scam of a lifetime. The kid losing the money wasn't ideal, but soon it would be insignificant. He wouldn't tell the kid.

For years, Jamison had been working away, collecting the most valuable thing on the planet to use when the time was right. Information. Now, he had enough to ensure he could retire somewhere in the sun. He had information about some powerful, influential, political people. Information that would ruin reputations and careers. Information that would cause arrests and scandal. Information that people would pay a lot to keep secret. Jamison had enough to know that nine of these people would pay for his discretion and silence.

However, powerful people were also dangerous. So, Mike and Harry, under the guidance of Jamison, had to time it perfectly. Utilising division of labour, the three of them each had a memory stick containing three targets. Jamison had already begun on his. The first person was blackmailed, an important celebrity figure with a liking for younger men. Boys, really.

Jamison had emailed them from a dummy email account from an internet café while on holiday in Spain, in case his target had the ability to trace the email to source. The email contained a snapshot of the information Jamison had uncovered, as well as the details of other evidence that would be released to the public unless they complied. A different demand was being made to each of the nine victims, based on their net worth portfolio.

When all nine agreed, Jamison, Mike and Harry wouldn't ever have to worry about money again. The money would sit in offshore accounts and filter through to them via dummy companies of which they were directors. It would be untraceable. They would be untouchable.

Harry was next. He was going to take his memory stick loaded with everything on his three subjects and disappear to France, where he would send all three threats from various locations over the course of ten days. When Jamison outlined his plan, both Mike and Harry had wondered why they all needed to leave the country — if the encryption software was good, surely they could send their terms from anywhere and never be found. But Jamison didn't like to take risks. His paranoia wouldn't let him. He'd worked too hard, for too long. So Mike would go to France too, shortly after Harry, and take a train across to Germany before sending his own. Jamison would hold off a little longer, then go further afield into Greece. Once all nine had been blackmailed, they would meet again and wait for their payday. It was foolproof. If any of their targets spoke to one another — which he doubted they would — they would never find the source of the blackmail. Or the people behind it.

Again, the kid's mistake was just a blip. A small, inconsequential annoyance in a grand, undefeatable plan.

As Jamison reassured himself that years of planning, research and preparation hadn't unravelled, his phone vibrated on his desk. Snatching it up, he opened it. It was an alert via the dummy email account. He loaded the account through his encryption software. He read the only message in its inbox, smiled and turned the phone to show his colleagues. The first target in their blackmailing campaign had finally reached out.

What do you want from me?

Jamison hesitated. If the encryption software was compromised, it would only signpost another location, another country for someone to search. The net was too wide for him to ever be found. Satisfied it wouldn't impact his hard work, he set the demand and hit 'send'.

A new email came back within a minute.

'That was quick,' Harry said.

'They are twitching, boss,' Mike said. 'What does it say?'

'Says what's to stop them going to the police.'

All three men laughed. Jamison replied telling them that before the police found them, the whole world would know exactly what kind of person they were.

A new message arrived. Jamison smiled again. 'Now they are saying they won't be threatened.'

'What do we do?' Harry asked.

'I think we need a show of force,' Jamison replied. 'He's afraid. Let's show him that not only do we have the information, but we also have the power. Let's make him fear us. Not only that, we'll leak his dirty secrets. Let's show him we will hurt him too.' He sank back in his chair and withdrew into a pensive silence once more. It lasted all of a minute before he received another email. The fight in their target dying already. The bravado fading, with a weaker statement saying, 'You won't get to me.' Jamison smiled, typed his reply and hit 'send'.

'What did you say?' Mike asked.

'I told them that tomorrow morning, at 8 a.m., they need to turn on the news. I told them that although this person wasn't anything to do with them, it illustrated that we are not to be fucked with. At any point, we can get to anyone we want, including him.'

'We need someone then?'

'Yep. Get the kid.'

'You mean Sam? I thought we agreed he did the right thing by dumping the money,' Harry said.

'He did, but he doesn't need to know that. He still fucked up. Don't hurt him too much. But it needs to be more than the black eye he's already received from us.'

'Got it.' Harry said.

'Hurt him, but don't kill him. Then, make sure he is displayed,' Jamison continued. 'Make sure our target knows it's for him.'

'You sure? The kid's, like, twenty,' Mike said.

'He knew what he was getting himself into. Make sure it's public, make sure people want to film it. Dress the kid in our target's merch, so when he sees the news, he knows it's for him.'

'Merch, boss?'

'He's a fucking movie star. Find a T-shirt or jumper with his fucking face on it or something. Just get it done.'

'Sorry.' Mike flashed Harry a look. A look that said he was worried. Harry looked back, mirroring his thoughts. Jamison didn't see. He was lost in his own mind, again.

'And after, they'll pay up. They'll all pay up,' Jamison whispered to himself before zoning back in. 'Harry, you ready?'

'Yes, boss. Suitcase is packed, USB is right here.' He waved his car keys with the small flash drive attached. 'We'll sort the kid, and then I'll wait for your call.'

'Good lad. Keep it with you, look after it — it's not time yet. Let's get this taken care of, get our first to see we aren't fucking about, and then we'll go. This time in a month, lads, we'll be done.'

'You got it,' Harry said, making his way to the door. Mike moved a little slower.

'You all right, mate?' Jamison asked.

'Tired, boss.'

'Well, don't worry. Pretty soon the money will come flooding in, and we can take a step back. We've worked hard, all of us. We are owed the good life.'

'Can't bloody wait,' Mike said, joining Harry's side.

'Oh, lads?'

Both men stopped and looked back.

'Take it easy, yeah, on the kid. He needs more than the shiner he's got, but don't get carried away. I know what you boys are like.'

Both Harry and Mike smiled.

'He's a message for our target. This isn't about the money.'

Mike nodded. 'Yeah, don't worry. We got this.'

Mike and Harry left and walked out through the office silently. Both men had noticed that, recently, their boss was acting different. His usual cool and calm composure was dimming. He was rattled. But then the plan was his idea, and he had dedicated years to what would happen in the next few weeks. They didn't say it to each other — they didn't need to. But it was there.

Jamison watched them walk away, sat back in his chair and smiled. The kid taking a beating would assume this was about his debt. He wouldn't question it. He'd try and find the money. But Jamison didn't care. This was about a much bigger fish. The plan he had been working on for years would finally pay off. His retirement plan was coming to fruition.

CHAPTER SIX

I couldn't sleep. Nineteen thousand just kept looping around in my mind. Nineteen thousand. Sam had taken himself off to bed after his disclosure, and even through the thick 1920s-built walls that made up our small house, I could hear him crying. My brother had been naive. He had messed up and I knew I was partly to blame for that. I was the one who had raised him from ten years old. It was my job to make sure he understood that some people weren't who they said they were. I had failed just as much as he had. I wracked my brain for something, anything that would help. Tentatively, I tried the bank.

Logging in to the app, I followed the tabs until I was on the loan page, where it asked how much I wanted to borrow. I knew if I went for the full amount, I would be rejected and they might not accept another application. I had to get this right. I figured if I got something from the bank, it might appease whoever it was Sam owed until we could work out what to do next. We just needed time, that was all.

First, I typed in £7,000, spread out over four years, but even that felt too high, so I deleted it and put in £4,000. Four grand would take a dent out of his debt. It wouldn't be all of it but it would surely help.

I applied, held my breath, and to my surprise, they accepted. I read the contract, agreed the repayment terms and completed the application. An hour later, the money was in my bank.

Getting out of bed, I ran to Sam's room and knocked on the door. He opened it quickly and I was surprised to see he was dressed. He looked terrible, his eyes were puffy, his face gaunt. I wanted to hug him so much but knew better.

'Sam?'

'I have to go out for a bit. They want to talk.'

'Is that a good idea?'

'It will be fine.'

'Let me come with you.'

'No, no it's OK.'

'I have four grand,' I said.

'What?'

'I got a loan. I have four grand, see.' I showed him the app and saw his face lighten just enough to make me feel hopeful. 'I know it's not enough, but it's a start. All we need is some time, and we can get it all ironed out. Tell him that the four grand here is his. I can wire it right now. It will help, won't it?'

'Thank you.' He gave me a big hug. 'Thank you,' he said again, mumbling into my dressing gown. He was hugging me tightly, tighter than I could ever remember. And he didn't let go for the longest time. When he eventually did, he kissed me on the cheek.

'Don't wait up, OK? I'll be back later.' He walked past me, not turning back.

'Please, let me come with you.'

'No. I have to go alone.'

'Sam, I don't want—'

'Cass, I have to go alone,' he snapped, spinning to face me and making me flinch. He saw this, and softened. 'I'll be all right. I'll tell them I can send four right now, it will help. It will. Thank you, Cass.'

I nodded, still stunned at his outburst. 'Be safe.'

'I will. I love you.'

'You too, Sam.'

He headed downstairs, put on his shoes and coat and, giving me one last smile that didn't quite seem authentic, stepped out into the night, closing the door behind him.

Running back into my bedroom, I watched as Sam stuffed his hands in his pockets and walked down the road until he disappeared from view. I hoped to God he was going to be OK.

I climbed back into bed, knowing I wouldn't be able to sleep. I grabbed a notepad and pen, and wrote in big letters:

How do I make 15k in a week?

Beside it, I wrote ways I knew people made a lot of cash, fast, but for most of them, you need cash to make cash. I did have four grand in the bank, but I couldn't dare risk it. OnlyFans was the only thing I could think of where you didn't need money to make money, but I didn't think I could bring myself to do it. I wanted anonymity. It was for maybe a last resort, but not yet. Besides, I wouldn't expect to make any money that way anyway. Then, I wrote down one word.

DareMe?

Once upon a time I'd had a brave streak. After, a few knew what had really happened the day Mum died: the police officer on the scene, and then Mum's sister and brother-in-law. I didn't want to remind them of what I had done. I didn't want to face them. I had no doubt that they hated me — I deserved it — and I had all but vanished from their lives. I didn't want them to see me playing, see me being careless and reckless again. They might speak out, they might tell the whole world of my mistake. And then, Sam would know too.

But the app didn't say you had to tell the world who you were. Most players wore masks or face coverings specifically not to be recognised. No one would know it was me.

I opened the app and a video sprung up, showing a person hanging onto the back of a bus while skateboarding. I didn't scroll like I usually would. Instead, I looked in the top left corner at a red tab I'd seen countless times. I'd always ignored it. It asked if I wanted to sign up to be a DareMe player. I didn't want to be famous — I didn't want anyone to know who I was — but Sam needed me more than ever. Still, I hesitated.

CHAPTER SEVEN

£4,000 raised

By the time my alarm sounded, telling me to get up, I had maybe slept two hours at most. All night I waited for Sam to unlock the front door, but the house stayed quiet, the front door shut, the lights off.

Sam hadn't come home.

I tried not to overthink it, an almost impossible task. Life seldom played out the way we wanted, and I wanted nothing more than Sam to be OK. I tried to dismiss my dread. Surely someone couldn't be that unlucky in life. Surely we had suffered enough. I replaced my fear with more optimistic thoughts. Maybe he went to speak to the man, it was all OK, and he'd gone out to a friend's, or to see a girlfriend, if he had one. He and I didn't talk about those things. Sam was a smart kid, deep down. He was OK. He was always OK. He and I had no choice. So, I got up, showered, dried my hair, had my coffee, made my lunch, just like any other morning and then set off for work. Sam would wake up, wherever he was, and message me, telling me he was fine.

Everything would be all right.

But I couldn't shift the elastic band around my diaphragm that felt so tight it might snap, so, even though it was cold, the ground slippery, I decided to walk into the city and catch a bus from there, hoping the walk and increased heart rate would calm my fraying nerves.

It seemed to help. The brisk stroll helped me get a handle on my anxiety, and loosened that band, but as I neared the city centre, people were screaming and running. I didn't know what was going on. I saw a black Range Rover take off, wheels spinning. I caught its number plate: AK03. It was an old car. Over twenty years old, but I didn't catch who was driving it.

I looked back to where the panicking and screaming was coming from, and could see in the distance a small crowd gathered around the steps to the town hall. I didn't want to know. I didn't want to get involved. I just wanted to get to work, speak with Sam and try to work out how to make a lot of money in a short space of time. But to get to the bus station, I had to go past the commotion.

I set off, keeping my head down. However, the closer I got to whatever had happened, the more my curiosity took over. It was like the videos I watched on DareMe — a morbid fascination.

So, I looked. And at first, what I saw, I couldn't make sense of at all. My eyes registered the reason for the chaos, but my mind wouldn't let me process it. I was paralysed to the spot, only for a beat, but just long enough for my brain to understand what I was looking at. When it had, I was almost sick.

But it couldn't be true, it must have been a trick somehow.

Then, I heard his voice, a small moan, distinctively his, before his head lolled forward.

Bound to the pillar of the town hall's entrance, battered and bloodied, was my little brother. A small crowd had gathered. A few of them were filming him.

Before I knew what was happening, my legs, hollow and close to buckling, broke into a run. I pushed through the crowd, shoving people so hard they stumbled and swore at me.

'The fuck you doing?'

I didn't reply, I didn't look back, my eyes solely on my brother. I wanted to see him move, moan again, but he was still, too still.

I'd seen someone this still once before, and that time, they didn't move ever again.

What had they done to him?

'Sam!'

By the time I got to him, two men were by his side, desperately trying to free him, and I grabbed at the thick black cord he had been bound with.

'Sam? Sam? Can you hear me?' I said.

He didn't reply. He didn't move. My brother wasn't moving at all.

We, me and the two strangers, continued to fight with the binds, unwrapping him and untying knots until he was released, and he fell onto the ground in a crumpled heap, his body limp on the cold stone.

For a horrifying moment, I thought he was gone. I dropped to my knees and rolled him over, expecting to look at the face of someone I loved who was dead at my feet, again. But he let out a weak, quiet moan.

I thanked God. He was bruised and bloody, but he was alive. His face was battered, both eyes swollen shut, his nose almost at a right angle, and, as he gasped for air, I could see several of his teeth were missing.

'Has anyone rung for an ambulance?' I said, not knowing what to do to help my brother. One of the men who untied him came to my side and helped me put him into the recovery position.

'The ambulance is on its way,' he said.

I thanked him and leaned in closer to Sam. 'Help is coming.'

Sam tried to say something I couldn't hear, and I leaned in closer, so the blood that covered his face ended up in my hair.

'Don't talk to the police, Cass, promise me,' he mumbled, his words slurring.

'You've been hurt. The police need to know what's going on.'

'Tell them nothing, Cass, please,' he wheezed, as his eyes began to roll.

'Sam? Sam?'

'Don't say anything, Cass,' he whispered. 'They'll kill me, they'll kill me.'

CHAPTER EIGHT

The ambulance arrived within ten minutes, and fifteen after that, Sam was stabilised and we were on our way to hospital. I sat in the back, holding his hand as the paramedics connected IV lines, administered pain relief and fluids, and tried to keep him comfortable until he was with the doctors. I was in shock, I knew I was, because even with my brother so poorly, the paramedics working around me, all I could think about was the jumper he was wearing. It wasn't one I'd seen before.

'It's not his, the top. It's not his,' I said. The paramedics rightfully ignored me. My shock kept me focused on it. On it, there was a print of the poster of a recent movie. The lead star, Jackson Hunter, holding a gun, looking like a typical Hollywood action star. I wondered where he'd got the jumper from. It didn't matter, though. It was just a jumper. My mind was simply trying to tether itself to something so I didn't pass out.

As we sped through the city, the paramedics worked on my brother. They kept using words I didn't understand, or couldn't process. As we got closer to the hospital, one of the machines that Sam was hooked up to began to beep loudly.

'What's that? What's going on?' I asked, but the paramedics ignored me. Whatever it was, it wasn't good, and both leaped up and began to work on Sam, one blocking my view. They spoke to each other, louder, and I moved to try and see him. His body was rigid, his hands curled into balls, his head thrust up at an almost impossible angle.

'What's happening to him?'

'He's having a seizure. Please, let us work,' one of them said. I moved back again. I couldn't even blink. I watched my brother's body convulse. I was sure I was watching my brother die.

As we arrived at the hospital, I was separated from Sam as they wheeled him into trauma. A kind nurse took me by the hand and led me to a room where I could wait, offering me tea. I heard my phone vibrating in my bag and, with shaking, bloodstained hands, I dug it out. It was Mia.

Cass? You're not at work. I've tried calling. Are you OK?

I started to message her back, struggling to type as my hands wouldn't stop shaking. Mid-message, my phone rang.

'Cass? Finally, are you OK? You've not come to work? You sick?'

'Sam was hurt.'

'What?'

'He was . . .' I started, but my words cut out as I began to cry. 'He was beaten, tied up. Mia, he had a fit in the ambulance. I think . . .' I couldn't finish my sentence. I couldn't say I thought my brother was about to die.

'Where are you?'

'At the hospital.'

'I'm leaving work now.'

'No, don't. Not yet, he's with the doctors now. I'll know more soon. I'll ring you, OK?'

'Cass, I want to be there.'

'Please, I just, I need a minute. And I might be with Sam anyway.'

'OK, ring me.'

I hung up without saying goodbye, and as I dropped the phone beside me, the nurse came back in with the promised tea.

'I've put some sugar in it — you need it,' he said.

'Is he OK?'

'He is with the doctors now. They are a good bunch. Have you rung your parents? Do you want me to?'

'It's just us, just me and Sam,' I said.

He nodded. 'OK, I know it's hard, but sit tight. I'll be back soon, and we'll go from there.'

'What's happening to him?'

'He's with the doctors. Lots of people are looking after your brother right now.'

'Is he going to be OK? Please, tell me.'

'He's in the best hands,' the nurse said, before leaving. We both noted how he couldn't say anything about my brother being all right.

CHAPTER NINE

For the longest hour of my life, I sat there nursing the same cup of tea and waiting for news. In the silence, punctuated only by a ticking clock that mocked my desperation, I thought of how my brother had changed after Mum died, how he struggled to fit in, how he trusted too easily, trying to fill the void of having no parent. I'd had to fight to keep him at home. Social services had wanted him to stay with me, but they'd needed to be sure I was up to the task. Being just nineteen when Mum passed, I was still a kid myself in many ways, but I'd insisted I could do it. So, my plans of university and getting away from Peterborough had been replaced with running the home and finding a job to support my brother. It wasn't always easy, but we'd got through. Together.

I didn't know what I would do if the worst happened.

A man walked in, wearing a white shirt, sleeves rolled up. Sharp eyes. Maybe around fifty years old, I assumed he was a doctor. He didn't come into the room fully, instead lingering in the doorway.

'Cassie Jones?'

'Yes?' I said, getting to my feet, my stomach in knots. 'Is Sam OK?'

'I don't know, I'm afraid. I'm Detective Sergeant Wakelin.' He offered his hand.

I took it in mine. His grip was firm.

'I wanted to ask you a few questions about today,' he said.

'Where is Sam?' I asked again, hoping he knew something, anything.

'I want to understand what happened this morning,' he replied, ignoring my plea.

'Can this wait? I just want to know if my brother is OK.'

'I know, and I'm sure someone who can tell you how he is will come soon. The reason I'm here so quickly is because of the seriousness of your brother's assault. I want to find the ones who did it, and in these things—'

'These things?'

'Assaults that are a statement of some kind.'

'What?' I asked, feigning that I didn't understand.

'Miss Jones, Cassie, I would like to get moving. It's important that we take accounts of what people saw and heard as soon as possible after an event like this.' He was intent on ignoring my distress. 'The way your brother was hurt, it's been shared all over social media. I need to find out who did it to him. I understand you found him?'

'Yes. I mean, no, I was there. But I wasn't first there. I was walking into town, to catch a bus to work, and came across . . .' I stumbled, the image of Sam tied, beaten, seemingly dead, came back and robbed my words. I looked down at the floor.

'It's OK, Miss Jones, take your time.'

I nodded, took two measured breaths, and then looked at him once more. He looked back, his expression neutral, like he'd seen trauma and grief and fear a thousand times.

'Are you OK to continue?' he asked, and I nodded. 'Miss Jones, did you see anything that might help? Anyone fleeing the scene?'

I thought about the Range Rover, and almost told him, but then Sam's words before he passed out came back to me. How he didn't want me to speak to the police. I wanted to say everything I saw, but I had failed my brother enough. I wouldn't do it again.

'No.'

'Are you sure?' He looked at me in such a way that I was sure he could probe my mind.

'No, I just came up Bridge Street, saw the crowd, and then Sam. I wasn't looking at anything else. Just Sam.'

As the detective opened his mouth to say something else, a doctor walked into the room.

'Cassie?' she said.

Wakelin was clearly annoyed by the interruption, but thankfully didn't push me anymore.

'I'll speak to you soon,' he said with a curt nod. 'Doctor,' he said, as he rounded the corner, and walked away.

Once he was gone, the doctor looked from where he had exited to me.

'Is Sam all right?' I asked.

'Please sit,' she said, and I did as she asked. 'I'm Dr Adams. I'm a surgeon.'

'A surgeon? Has Sam had an operation?'

'Not yet, no. We have been working on him to assess the damage he sustained in the attack. He is stable, and although it must have been frightening to find him in that state, his injuries aren't too severe. We did a CT scan to look at his brain—'

'Oh, God! He was fitting. Is he—'

'The CT looks clear. He was hurt, badly, but there isn't any damage to his brain. We do, however, need to operate. His left eye bone has been badly fractured, and we need to correct this by putting in a plate.'

I started to cry.

'We don't know the extent of the damage to his eye, but there is a chance his vision might be permanently altered.'

'But, he will — I mean, he is going to be all right?'

'Yes, we believe so. We are going to operate soon, but he is awake, and wanted to see you before he goes into theatre.'

'I can see him?'

'He keeps asking for you.'

'Thank you. Thank you, Doctor.'

I wanted to hug this woman, this stranger who was telling me my brother would be OK, but I stopped myself. Instead, I just followed her through the hospital, past several closed curtains, where people coughed, moaned, snored. I reached the end, where the doctor opened the curtain to reveal Sam in a hospital bed. The doctor nodded and walked away, leaving me to have a moment with my brother.

He looked awful. His eyes were so swollen that I wasn't sure he could see me at all. His left eye looked so bad I could barely look at him. His lips were bloody, his jaw black. If I'd not been told he was going to be OK, I would have thought he was going to die. I swallowed my grief and painted on a smile.

'Hey,' I said quietly, trying to hide my sadness and shock. He looked worse than in the ambulance.

'Cass?' he said.

'It's me, I'm here.' I took his hand.

'How do I look?' he said.

'You look fine.'

'Be honest,' he said, with a hint of a smile.

'Fine, you look like crap.'

He laughed, and then, with a hiss of pain, he stopped. 'They say I might lose my eye.'

I nodded. 'Try not to worry about that, OK? They are going to take you into theatre soon. After, we'll get you well, and we'll sort this out.'

'Have the police spoken to you?'

'Just now. I said I didn't know anything.'

He nodded. 'Thank you, Cass.'

The curtain pulled back, and the doctor smiled at us. 'Right, Sam, let's get you patched up, shall we?'

I gave Sam a gentle kiss on the forehead and told him I'd be waiting for him to come out, and he was wheeled away from me.

Once I was sure he couldn't hear, I put my head in my hands and cried until I was gently guided out of the trauma unit back into the waiting room to sit and wait all over again.

My brother got lucky. He could have died. Judging by the fact that he didn't want me talking to the police, I had to assume he didn't think this was over. The four grand I had borrowed as a promise to them wasn't enough to keep them off his back. If this is what they had done this time, I was worried that next time, if he didn't repay what he owed, they would kill him.

I needed to act.

Sam was £15,000 short, and he was in no fit state to try and make it. So, I would have to do it. I couldn't let myself think about what would happen if I didn't find the money.

Pulling out my phone, I went to the DareMe app. The home page was easy to navigate with its sleek black and red scheme. In the middle of the screen was a livestream of various players completing various dares. This was where I usually scrolled, watching people do stupid things for money. Below it was a tab you could expand to a list of all the open dares that had been posted onto the site. There were countdown timers on each, indicating how long was left to complete it. When one was claimed, it flashed with the handle of the player who had succeeded first.

But I didn't look at either of these elements of the app. I looked at that tab in the top left-hand corner, inviting me to become a player. This time I didn't hesitate.

I tapped 'yes'.

CHAPTER TEN

It took me about half an hour to create a profile, adding all my details and agreeing to the terms. The app said it was designed to be fun, and should not, under any circumstances be used to hurt others. It said the law was the law.

All my information would remain private. One of the things the app boasted about was that, like WhatsApp, everything would be encrypted. Finally, I had to add my PayPal details, as that was the whole point, and a profile picture. Having my image there, for all to see? I hesitated again.

It was my fault Sam felt the need to do more. It was my fault he was naive to what people could be like. It was my fault he didn't have a solid anchor to stop him doing things he knew he shouldn't. I'd had Mum to show me right from wrong. Sam only had me. I had failed to live up to the standard that Mum set. Even at the end, when she died, she was still trying to help me. Sam needed me to be like her. I needed it too.

Looking at other profiles, I saw that many didn't have a face: some had avatars, some dark screens, but most were of people posing for a selfie, with their face covered, like I had seen in the videos, so I rummaged through my bag and pulled out a black face mask. I kept a few still, a hangover from Covid times. I pulled out my yellow beanie, put both on and took a selfie. All you could see were my brown eyes. Everything else was covered. And brown was hardly striking. I was confident that even Mia wouldn't recognise it was me. As for the name, that was trickier. The app tried to give me a name linked to my email, but I didn't want anyone to work out it was me, so I went with my mum's initials, KJ — Kim Jones. The username KJ was taken, so I added the year she was born: 1974.

And then, just like that, there was a new DareMe player joining the app. Player KJ74.

With a profile picture, username, personal details, and my PayPal set up, I was ready to complete a dare, if I dared to of course.

Once registered, the app layout was different. Instead of just a timeline to scroll, watching people complete their DareMe challenges, there was now a new tab in the top left corner asking if I was ready to do a dare. I tapped it and it took me to a new landing page, where there were two choices: 'open' and 'closed'. In the 'closed' folder, there was nothing, but then, I had expected as much. No one knew KJ74 existed, so no one would be directly messaging her to perform a dare that wasn't open for all players to attempt. For me to help Sam, that would have to change.

In the 'open' tab, there were dozens of challenges, with scores of players trying to be the first to complete them. Each dare was listed in value order, with the low-reward items at the top. They were relatively simple, safe things, like 'Shout in a library' and 'Sing in public'. As I scrolled down, they increased in value — and risk. I saw one that was 'Jump through fire', another 'Climb onto a roof'. Beside them all were timers counting down the remaining time on each of the dares before they were cancelled and no money could be made. The amount of money varied wildly, from 50p to £50. A few went up into the hundreds, but all of them would get you hurt if they went wrong.

It seemed straightforward: accept a dare, complete it, film it and then the money would come via PayPal. I didn't know where the money came from. Maybe it was via advertising, as the site was growing, or maybe from those who watched. Likely it was a bit of both. I didn't really care. All I cared about was Sam, and making sure he got out of the mess he was in. I dreaded to think what would happen if he didn't pay back what he owed.

Sam told me he had a week to get it all back. Now, he had just six days. Once Sam was out of theatre, I would be allowed to see him, but then they would send me home, and I would get to work.

I waited for another hour, but this time I had a purpose. I scrolled through the list of open challenges, working out if I could do any of them. Some were simple and could be completed quickly. There was only a little bit of money in these challenges, but it would get me started, and could add up. My confidence would grow to take on the bigger things, or maybe I could just tick off thousands of trivial things to raise the money Sam needed. I wouldn't accept any challenges right now — I didn't want to leave the hospital — but I did see a few dares that would get me going. If they were still there when I had to leave, I would accept them.

The same surgeon from earlier interrupted my thoughts by clearing her throat.

'How is he?' I asked.

'He's in recovery. The surgery went well, and a plate has been grafted to his eye bone. There is still a chance he could have optic nerve damage, but the nerve itself is still attached. We won't know for a while.'

'So, he will be all right?'

'It looks that way, yes.'

'And the optic nerve? What does that mean?'

'It means that he will not lose his vision.'

'Thank you.' I lowered my head as a wave of relief and grief in equal measure washed over me. 'Can I see him?'

'He is still in recovery. Once he's awake and the anaesthetic has worn off, he will be taken onto the ward. You'll be able to see him then. Given the circumstances, we have given him his own room, and a police officer will be posted outside, just in case.'

'Really? Thank you.'

'If you would like to follow me, I can take you to his room, and you can wait for him there?'

'Yes, please. Thank you, Doctor. Thank you so much.'

I followed the doctor through the hospital towards a small room with two armchairs and space for a bed. A uniformed police officer was posted outside. He nodded as I entered.

'Take a seat. He won't be long.' The doctor smiled before turning and leaving, no doubt to go and help someone else. I felt a pang of guilt. Doctors and nurses did so much. This one had helped fix my brother's broken face, and I didn't even remember her name.

Soon Sam was wheeled in, fast asleep. His bed was placed in the gap between the two chairs. The porter then adjusted his wires, making sure he wasn't tangled in them before leaving.

Reaching over I took Sam's hand, and he stirred. Turning towards me he flashed a crooked smile. There were several stitches across his eye bone where they had set and added the plate, which made his face look worse still. But I didn't say anything.

'How are you feeling?' I asked.

'Like shit,' he croaked out. 'How do I look?'

'Like shit,' I said.

He gave me a weak, tired smile. 'Well, at least chicks dig scars.'

'Really?' I laughed, glad that despite it all he still had his stupid sense of humour. I thought about it all — the beating, the public display of his body, the fear he might be blinded — and my relief wanted to morph from laughter to tears, so to stop myself crying, I stood and gave him some water, just a sip. He swallowed hard.

'Thank you.' He lay back down, looking up at the ceiling.

'Sam, I'm gonna have to go soon,' I said, feeling guilty. If I stayed by his side, all I would do was watch him rest, and he needed me for more. Fifteen thousand things more.

'That's fine.'

'Will you be OK?'

'Yeah, I'll sleep it off.'

'We are going to find a way out of this mess,' I said, and he nodded.

'I'm such an idiot.'

'Yep,' I agreed.

Sam laughed, then abruptly stopped again with a wince.

'You were unlucky, Sam. You just trusted the wrong people. That's all. We can make this right.'

'I don't see how.'

'Have faith, little brother.'

'We need a miracle, Cass.'

Sam closed his eyes, and I blinked a tear onto my cheek. He was right, we did need a miracle. In our little world, miracles weren't a thing. I stayed with him, holding his hand for ten minutes, watching him drift off to sleep, and then I gently let go. Standing, I leaned over and kissed him on the head.

'I'll make this right,' I whispered, before collecting my things and making my way out of the hospital.

I was barely out of the elevator in the hospital's atrium before I had the DareMe app open.

I waited for a bus outside the main entrance, watching the sun begin to dip and give way to yet another long winter night. I'd been in the hospital all day. I knew I needed to check in with work, I needed to tell them I had to take some time, but it could wait. I was focused on DareMe. I scrolled the list of open dares until I found one, and I tapped it.

Welcome, player KJ74
Your DareMe challenge:
Swim across a river (£50)
You have 32 minutes and 16 seconds remaining.
Do you accept?

CHAPTER ELEVEN

As the bus slowly made its way from the hospital towards the city, I watched my phone, expecting at any moment to see that the DareMe challenge I had accepted had been completed by another player, but the timer kept ticking down. By the time I arrived at the bus station, the dare was still there, probably because it was cold outside, barely above freezing. The river would be colder still. Fifty quid clearly wasn't enough to tempt most people to risk hypothermia, but I needed to get going. I needed to make a start.

The River Nene was only a five-minute walk from my house. I could film myself jumping in and swimming across, and then, if I ran home, I'd be in warm clothes in no time and hopefully no one would see me complete the dare. I could get dry, warm myself by the radiator, and then get out and find another dare. Then another and another and another until I'd made enough to help my brother out of the shit he'd found himself in.

Leaving the bus station, I headed down Bridge Street past the town hall where I'd found Sam. I tried not to look, but I couldn't help myself. The image of his limp body, bound and broken, would haunt me for ever. But I didn't have time to think about that. That ghost could come for me once I had done what I needed to do.

I upped my pace towards the river. Even with my coat on and my scarf wrapped around my neck, I was cold. The water would be freezing, dangerously so, and for a moment I wasn't sure I could do it. But Sam said we needed a miracle, so I had to push through. I was a keen swimmer when I was younger. Fast too. I'd be in and out in a minute.

One minute. Fifty pounds.

Approaching the River Nene, I looked for somewhere I could set up my phone to film the dare. The side closest to the city centre was safest, there were more people around, and the theatre sat proudly on the bank, but the theatre car park was rammed with people leaving after enjoying the 2 p.m. show. I didn't want to draw attention to myself by getting out there. Besides, I needed to finish this swim on the side closest to where I lived. The side furthest away from the city. I would be cold, and having to get out of the river and then walk back over the bridge to head south to home seemed like a bad idea. Getting out on the south side would mean less people too. I could get out, go home and hopefully not be seen. I had to hope that no one saw me jump in. If they did, they would ring the police, assuming I was trying to hurt myself. Then it would be chaos, and it would be really embarrassing.

So I crossed the bridge to the other side of the river. The side closest to home. There were several office blocks being built that dominated the south bank, all in various stages of completion and all empty, along with a hotel still under construction. It was quieter on that side but felt a little more intimidating, like someone could be lurking in the shadows. I figured if I was quick, I could set up my phone, then run over to the other side, jump in and swim back towards it.

I found a spot where my phone would capture the dare and set it up. I checked my screen, opting to film on landscape to make sure as much of the river was in shot, just in case, and then happy the patch of river I wanted to film was fully in focus, I took off my coat, shoes and jumper and placed them neatly on the riverbank. Then, putting on my beanie and a face mask, matching my profile picture, I opened the app and began to livestream.

'I'm KJ74. A new player. And this is my first DareMe challenge. And it's going to be freezing. God, what am I doing?'

Walking away from the phone and leaving my belongings there, I ran back to the side of the river opposite. I stood close to the edge where I knew I was filming, and prepared to jump in. Foolishly, I dipped my toe in first. The cold was instant and painful, and I gasped. Taking one final look around to make sure no one could see me, I looked out into the cold, deep water, wondering what the hell I was doing. The gap was twenty metres, maybe a little less. In a pool, an easy swim, but out here, in the cold, in the dark. I hesitated.

Then I thought of Sam, and counted down.

'Here goes. Three, two, one!'

I jumped into the river, and even though I knew it was going to be freezing, the cold took my breath away. It pressed on my chest and snatched my diaphragm into spasm, which hurt so intensely I would have screamed if I could. My limbs went numb within a second. For a moment I wasn't sure my body would react and let me swim. The cold was so all consuming that it felt as though my body didn't belong to me anymore.

As much as I tried to get my brain to fire, to move me in breaststroke, I couldn't. I floundered, unable to tread water and catch my breath, my lungs having shut down through shock. I felt myself begin to sink. I looked up and the street lights above shimmered, but no matter how hard I tried, I couldn't swim to them.

My head dipped below the surface, the inky black water burning my eyes. They instinctively wanted to close, to protect my vision, but I forced them to stay open. I dared not close them. The water was dark and frightening. I had never liked deep water, imagining the monsters that lurked below.

I needed to fight them, somehow, even though they weren't real.

But fictitious monsters weren't even my main concern — the fact my body was numb, and sinking, was.

Despite my desperation to move properly, I continued to flounder and continued to sink. I was going to drown.

Then, as my feet skimmed the silty bottom of the river, my legs started working again, and I kicked as hard as I could. The adrenaline then reached my arms, and I dragged myself up to the surface. Gasping for air, barely keeping my mouth and nose above water, I began to move, swimming across to the other side. The width of the river wasn't huge, but it was as though my arms and legs were weighed down with lead.

I fought on, the current working against me. I started to panic. It was so much harder than I'd thought it would be. I looked towards the other side, to where my phone was recording, and saw that I was being pulled away from my destination. Digging deep, I swam hard, my arms windmilling, slapping the water in my uncoordinated effort to keep moving forward, and stay in shot. I kicked too, but my legs were all but useless. At last, when I was within a foot of the side, I reached for it.

I missed and slipped under the water again.

It was so dark, deathly dark, and as I began to sink, I reached out for something, anything I could hold on to. I managed to grab some sort of plant with my right hand, river kelp perhaps. But whatever it was, it was covered in algae and slipped through my hands. I grasped again, this time pulling myself into it, so I could wrap it in my arm, and pulled myself closer to the bank.

I threw my left hand forward, blindly grabbing at whatever I could. My hand hit something hard, and I grabbed it. it took me a second to realise I had grabbed a branch of a tree. I pulled with all my might, and lifted my face out of the water. I coughed so hard, I retched. Exhausted, I knew I couldn't stay in the water anymore — hypothermia would get me — so I half-heaved myself out of the river, my chest resting on the bank as I struggled to pull the rest of my body out with my numbed limbs. Finally, I rolled onto the ground and looked up to the new night sky, sucking in lungfuls of frigid oxygen.

Remembering I was still livestreaming, I pulled myself to my knees. Somehow, my hat had managed to stay on, but the face mask had snapped in the water and was gone. I didn't want my face to be seen, so, crawling towards the phone, I made sure only my soaking torso was in shot.

When I reached it, my teeth chattered as I spoke.

'D . . . d . . . d . . . dare complete.'

CHAPTER TWELVE

I hit 'end stream', and then, for a moment, I couldn't move. The cold was the most intense I had ever felt, and I shivered so violently I was almost sick.

Making sure I was alone, I pulled my hat off, the smell of rotten things from the dirty river stuck in my nostrils, and I retched again. I then peeled off my top and wrapped my coat around me, hugging my knees to try to slow my convulsing limbs and regain control of my body. It helped a little, but I needed to move before someone found me, so I collected my things, dropping my shoes several times as my fingers couldn't grip, and scurried off in the direction of home.

On the way, my phone pinged twice. One notification was from DareMe, congratulating me on the dare completion. The second was PayPal notifying me that £50 had been deposited into my account.

As quick as that. Despite the cold, despite the fear of thinking I could have drowned, I smiled. It was only £50, but I had done it. I had taken charge. I was helping my brother.

My phone pinged again, another from DareMe. I opened it and discovered there was a closed dare. A dare just for me.

Welcome, player KJ74
Your DareMe challenge:
Run down a busy road in just your underwear (£50)
You have 5 minutes remaining.
Do you accept?

I stared at it for a few moments, knowing exactly what this was. Some freak, some weirdo out there had seen me jump in the river and wanted to get their kicks. Pervert. I needed the money, but I declined and continued to walk home, carrying my sodden clothes.

Another notification pinged.

Welcome, player KJ74
Your DareMe challenge:
Run down a busy road in just your underwear (£100)
You have 3 minutes remaining.
Do you accept?

Whoever had set the dare had seen me decline and upped the money. They were persistent in their want to see me, and I almost declined it again, but it was £100. I could just run home, that would be enough to complete the dare, and home was only a few minutes away. £100 for three minutes. But still, it was degrading. I declined again.

The app pinged a third time. I was being goaded to accept.

Welcome, player KJ74
Your DareMe challenge:
Run down a busy road in just your underwear (£150)
You have 1 minute remaining.
Do you accept?

It was so much money. I wanted to say no, but I wondered how else I would make that much for just one minute's activity. It was undignified, it was wrong, but then images of Sam flashed into my mind — the way he'd hung there, bound to that post, being filmed by people, his face battered. That moment when I'd thought he was dead . . . I had failed someone I loved before and I was failing again. But I would not have history repeat itself. Sam needed me to do this, for him. So, against my better judgement, I accepted the DareMe challenge, and the clock began to tick.

Putting on a fresh face mask from my bag and my wet beanie, which smelled awful and was so cold it gave me a headache, I tapped to livestream once more.

'This is KJ74, completing my second dare. Ready for a quick run.'

I put my phone down so it could film me, and, making sure I could be seen on the livestream, I took off my coat, exposing my bra, and then pulled my wet jeans down carefully so I didn't catch my underwear. Once I had peeled them off, I put my shoes on, which were dry and warmed my feet quickly, before bending down and scooping up my sodden, stinky clothes, holding them against me as a barrier to try and preserve some dignity.

I picked my phone up once more. 'OK, let's do this!'

Before I could stop myself, I ran back past the unfinished hotel, up the steps away from the river and onto the main road. No sooner than I hit the well-lit, busy road, a car horn blasted, and a man hung out of the window.

'Nice ass!'

I wanted to curl into a ball and die, but there was no turning back now, so I continued to run, holding my phone in front of me and willing my numbed legs to get me home as fast as possible. As I ran, I saw the number of those watching increase by the second. Thirty, fifty, 100 . . . the number was climbing and I had no doubt that no matter how hard I was trying to protect my dignity, I had flashed boob, legs, stomach, pretty much all of me, on camera.

By the time I reached my front door, almost 1,000 app users were watching, and at least a dozen people had seen it in real life. Some laughed, some clapped, cheering me on. One asked what my DareMe username was, knowing exactly what I was doing. Some catcalled but, thankfully, no one tried to stop or grab me, either to help or hurt.

On my doorstep, I wrestled to get my keys out. When the lock finally gave and the door swung open, I fell into my house and slammed it behind me. Dropping my wet clothes, coat, shoes and bag on the floor, I lifted my phone, panting as I spoke.

'Dare complete,' I said and ended the livestream.

Oh, God, Cassie. What are you doing? What are you doing?

A wave of shame washed over me. After Mum died, I vowed I would be grounded, centred and sensible. I wouldn't fight or argue. But then, I thought of Sam again, the tears he had cried, the beating he had taken. If I didn't do something, I feared it would end up worse. And I couldn't let that happen. I *wouldn't* let it happen.

I drained a glass of water to wash down the taste of river that had flooded in through my nose and dropped my drenched and stinky clothes on the floor next to the washing machine. Then I moved upstairs into the bathroom and turned on the shower. Stripping off the few items I had on, I stepped in and let the water warm my aching muscles. I felt cheap for accepting the challenge from someone getting their kicks.

My phone pinged twice and I reached an arm out of the shower and grabbed it. There were two notifications — one from DareMe and one from PayPal. I logged in to PayPal to see the money sat there. £200 in total.

Still smiling to myself, I messaged Mia, knowing she would be packing up from another long day at work.

Sam is going to be OK.

She messaged back quickly, as she always did.

That's such a relief. Are you OK?

I'm fine. Have you been watching DareMe?

A bit, why?

Check out player KJ74.

All right????

Putting my phone down, I washed river water out of my hair. Once I was convinced I was clean, I got out, put on some fresh clothes and waited for Mia to message back.

As I was wringing out my beanie, she rang.

'No, fucking way!'

'Hi, Mia.'

'No fucking way, Cass! KJ74?'

'Yep.' I laughed.

'What the actual hell is going on? I cannot believe you jumped in the river.'

I laughed harder down the phone.

'You ran home butt naked.'

'No, no, I wouldn't do that. I had my underwear on.'

'Cass, you have to tell me everything.'

'Actually, I was going to ask if you wanted to grab a drink.'

'I thought you'd be with Sam?'

'I'll go back tomorrow morning, I'm gonna email work, say I need some time off. So I can be by his side. But he's resting right now.'

'I told them you had a family emergency. They know you'll not be in.'

'Thank you.'

'Cass, DareMe? You need to tell me what's going on!'

'I will. Come to town, get a drink with me. God knows I need one now. Besides, it would be easier with your help.'

'Help?'

'With the challenges.'

'You're doing more? Holy shit. OK. Give me thirty minutes! Cassie, I don't know what's going on right now, but you are a dark horse!'

Mia started to laugh and then hung up, and I couldn't help but laugh too. A mixture of fear for Sam, relief he would be OK, adrenaline from jumping in the river and then running home. It was all too much, and my laughter quickly turned to tears.

But I didn't have time to cry. It was almost 6 p.m. I swapped the contents of my shoulder bag for a rucksack, as it would be easier to carry, and made sure I had my beanie and several face masks. I pinged Sam a message, telling him I was thinking of him. Then I left to meet Mia.

However, as I left, I was startled to see a man at the end of the garden path.

'Jesus, you made me jump,' I said.

'Miss Jones, I was wondering if I could ask you a few more questions about your brother's attack,' Detective Wakelin said, looking at me in a way that told me he knew I hadn't told him the truth earlier.

'Um, sure,' I said.

'Can we go inside?'

'I was just going out actually.'

'Where to?'

'A friend is taking me for a drink. It's been a rough day.'

'I promise I'll be quick.' He smiled.

CHAPTER THIRTEEN

£4,200 raised

I pushed down a wave of nausea as I opened my front door again. I didn't want to lie to the police, nor to hold back any information that would help make an arrest. My brother had been beaten up and someone should be punished. But Sam had warned me if I said anything it would make it worse, and I didn't want to do that either. His words, 'They'll kill me', rang over and over in my head. I couldn't let my brother down.

As Wakelin stepped in, he looked through to my kitchen, and I cursed myself that the pile of sodden clothes were still on the kitchen floor.

'Sorry, the place is a mess.'

'It's fine,' he said, looking like a question was forming in his mind. Thankfully, he didn't ask it.

'Please, come and take a seat,' I said, offering the front room. I wanted him gone and out of my house, but I couldn't let him see that.

'I won't keep you long. I know you said you're off out.' He didn't look at me but instead took in the room without stepping over the threshold of the doorway, his eye trained and keen like a hawk trying to find something to grab with its talons. He took his time too, despite saying he wouldn't keep me long, and I watched as his gaze fell on our battered old sofa, rug, TV, the armchair that was gifted to us in the aftermath of my mum's death. Finally, his eyes focused in on the fireplace and a photo of me and Sam, drunk and smiling on his eighteenth birthday. I almost commented, but as I took a breath to speak, he got there first.

'Cassie, earlier, when we spoke, you were in a bad way,' he said.

'My brother had been hurt, badly. How else was I going to be?' I was sounding more defensive than I wanted.

'I'm sorry I didn't show more compassion,' he said, defusing me.

'It's OK.'

Wakelin took a step into the room, and perched himself on the arm of the sofa. I moved to the armchair and perched too.

'I'm here because I want to help him. How he was attacked, how he was displayed — it's not normal. I need to work out what's going on. Crimes like this, they always have a reason beyond bad luck.'

I nodded, but didn't offer any more. My phone pinged and I pulled it out of my pocket, thinking it might be Sam. It was a DareMe notification. I ignored it. It pinged again. And again.

'Someone's popular,' Wakelin said.

I quickly muted the notifications, locked my screen and placed it face down on the arm of the chair.

'Everything all right?' he asked.

'Yeah, just Instagram. Sorry,' I lied. Sam's words echoed. *Don't say anything, they'll kill me.*

Wakelin looked at me intently for a full second, then continued. 'I'm trying to find out who did this, and why. Can you tell me what you saw?'

'I was walking to work.'

'Why? I mean, I've just seen there is a bus stop not far from here. Why walk all the way into the city? Especially in this weather. It's pretty dangerous out there.'

'I was stressed, I needed to walk it off.'

'Why stressed?' he pried.

'Life, I guess. Just one of those days. I heard commotion, and then I saw Sam.'

'And you saw nothing else?'

'No, nothing.'

'I see,' he said, looking at me with such intensity that I had to look away. 'Did your brother ever suggest he might be in any kind of trouble?'

'Trouble?'

'In with the wrong crowd, owed someone some money.'

'No. No. Nothing.'

'Nothing?'

'No. Not that I know of.'

He nodded and looked around. 'Is it just you two here?'

'Yes.'

'Nice house.'

'Thank you.'

'Cassie, how do I get hold of your parents?'

'Why?'

'I want to ask them the same things. I want to understand what happened.'

'We don't know our dad.'

'And your mum?'

'She passed.'

'Oh. I'm sorry,' he said, and I believed him.

'It's OK, it was a long time ago. It's just me and Sam.'

'And he didn't tell you he was in any kind of trouble?'

'No.'

'No?'

He knew I was lying about something, so I made sure to hold his eye. 'No.'

'All right, well, if you think of anything, be sure to ring me.' He stood and pulled a card out of his pocket.

'I will.' I took it and looked down at it, just to make it appear that I would.

'Look, Cassie, if your brother is mixed up in anything — we can help. I want to help,' Wakelin said.

'I don't know anything.'

He nodded. 'Your brother. He's twenty, right?'

'Yeah.'

'Same age as my son. I get that you want to protect him. But that's not just your job. Not for this. It's mine.'

When he was gone, I closed the door quickly and took a series of deep breaths. Lying didn't come naturally to me. I hated doing it. I had lied about one thing, one big thing for a decade, and that lie alone had made it almost impossible to lie about anything else.

I had just lied to a police detective. I wanted to stay in, hide away, but I needed to carry on, so I left the house and made my way to find Mia.

CHAPTER FOURTEEN

As I walked towards town, my phone buzzed with a message from Sam. I stopped on the bridge, right near to where I had jumped into the river only an hour before and opened it. He told me he was bored, and I cried with relief. Bored meant he really was OK. Bored meant he wanted to be at home, meant we could put this awful day behind us. As long as I could raise the money needed in time.

I messaged him back.

> *Get some sleep, Sam. I'll be with you tomorrow as soon as I'm allowed. I'll bring snacks. Love you.*

Hey, I might be less bored now. A cute nurse has just come on shift. Love you too.

> *As you said, chicks dig scars.*

I hit 'send', smiled, then, I quickly emailed work, stating I needed time off and would provide a doctor's note if needed. Then, I put my phone away.

By the time I reached the bar, I felt exhausted. It had been one of the roughest days I'd had since Mum passed, but

I couldn't complain. Poor Sam would be feeling worse. He joked but I knew he would be sore for a long time. So, I shook off the tiredness that ached in my bones and walked inside.

The bar was filled with lots of drinkers laughing and chatting. The tables around the room were mostly full too, with groups of friends and couples enjoying a meal. I scanned for Mia and saw her sitting in the corner at a small table for two, with two glasses of wine.

'Hey,' I said. 'Thanks for the wine.' She stood and I gave her a hug, and she squeezed me tightly.

'OK, so before I get going, have you spoken to Sam?'

'He messaged just now. He's pretty busted up, but he will be OK. Thank God.'

'Yeah, thank God,' she echoed. 'His assault was on the news.'

'Was it?'

'Yep. People filmed it, it went everywhere.'

I felt sick all over again. My poor brother, as he was, being displayed like a Victorian circus attraction. I needed to sit, and as I lifted my wine to take a sip, Mia sat back down too.

'You need to tell me everything!'

I took another sip, a larger one, to steady myself, and then told her about what was going on — Sam's debt because of his stupidity in taking a dodgy job, the assault. I told her about the amount he owed. About the loan I had taken out, but I didn't tell her I had lied to the police to protect Sam.

'What will they do if you don't get the money?'

'I dread to think,' I said quietly.

'When you messaged saying you were—'

I cut her off. 'Mia, I don't want anyone knowing about DareMe, not even Sam. This stays between you and me. OK?'

'OK.' She nodded. 'When you told me, I thought you were just blowing off steam.'

'This is hardly how I blow off steam.'

'I know. A book and a bath is more your vibe. But this isn't about that, is it?'

'I just want to help my brother.'

'OK, how long has he got to find the money?'

'Six days.'

'That's not a lot of time.'

'No. No it isn't.'

'Right,' she said, taking a big drink of her wine. 'We need to get cracking. Get your phone out.'

I did, and Mia dragged her chair to sit beside me. We loaded the DareMe app and opened my profile.

'Jesus, you have over seven hundred followers already.'

'Yeah,' I said, not sure how else to respond. My closed-dare inbox had seventeen dare requests in it. There were dares to strip, to streak, to do other things that were awful and offensive, and illegal. I didn't care how much they were offering, I declined them all.

'What about open dares?' Mia said. Most of the ones available were clearly geared up for young men to complete, almost a spin-off of the *Jackass* generation that I was a little too young for, but could remember from my youth. Stupid things that would no doubt end up with me visiting the hospital, too. I couldn't help Sam if I was in a bed beside him.

'What about this one?' Mia said, pointing at my screen.

'No way.'

'Why not? Seems like an easy one.'

'But...'

'And the money is pretty good, look — £50.'

'Yeah but...'

'No one will know it's you.'

'Mia, I don't do that sort of thing. What would it say to the people sending me closed dares? I've already stripped to my underwear.'

'Before you do it, say why you're doing it. Say you want to help someone you love, you don't want sleazy messages, say you want this to be fun for everyone.'

'But...'

'It's £50.'

I thought about it. £50 for a few seconds. £50 for something less risky than the swim. Sam needed me to do all I could, and Mia was with me. I was safe as long as she was close.

I drained my wine. 'Screw it.'

Taking the phone from her, I hovered my finger over the dare.

CHAPTER FIFTEEN

Welcome, player KJ74
Your DareMe challenge:
Kiss a stranger (£50)
You have 3 minutes and 12 seconds remaining.
Do you accept?

'I can't believe I'm about to do this,' I said, and Mia grinned at me. 'Right. Here goes.'

I hit 'accept', and immediately felt sick. 'I think I need another wine,' I said.

'No time, you've got about three minutes. Come on, I'll film it discreetly.'

'Is this even OK? I mean, kissing someone without consent? Isn't it against the law?'

'Cass, we've seen someone setting bins on fire. A kiss is hardly a criminal act.'

'But, still.'

'Come on.' Mia stood and we both began to walk through the bar, looking for someone I could complete the dare with. I didn't want to ambush a person, so I smiled, trying to catch someone's eye. I hoped I didn't appear nervous, or like a maniac, but I wasn't sure I was convincing. My heart galloped in my chest, my palms sweated, and butterflies hovered in my stomach. Not the kind that were gentle and romantic. These were as big as sparrows and frantic, like those in a Hitchcock movie. I looked to Mia for support, but she wasn't looking back. She was focused on someone at the bar.

'What about him?'

A man was sitting on a bar stool, reading something on his phone. I looked around to see who he was with, but he appeared to be alone.

I turned back to Mia. 'No. What if he is waiting for his date? Or wife?'

'I don't think so,' Mia said, gesturing for me to look once more. The man was looking our way, smiling. 'You gotta go for it.'

'Oh, God, OK.' I opened my bag and pulled out my hat and mask.

'Wow, sexy.'

'I don't want anyone to know it's me. Don't film my face when I do it.'

'I'll stay here, so I'm filming from the back.'

'OK, here goes.'

I nodded and, using my phone, Mia hit 'stream'.

'Hey, it's KJ74, about to complete my third dare. But to those out there sending stuff into my inbox, keep it clean, keep it fun.'

I turned and walked with purpose towards the man. Once I was sure the camera couldn't see my face, I pulled down the mask and, just as the man went to say something, I grabbed him and placed my lips on his. It lasted for less than a second before he pushed me away.

'What the fuck?'

'I'm so sorry.'

'No, it's — you caught me off guard.'

'I'm sorry, I really am.' I pulled my mask back up, turned and walked away. When I joined Mia again I looked at the camera and said, 'Dare complete.'

Mortified, I grabbed my bag and walked out of the bar, Mia chasing after me. As I opened the door, the man was staring my way, a shocked look on his face. I held his eye for a moment, and then stepped out into the night.

Only when I was far enough away to not be seen by him, or anyone else in the bar, did I pull off my beanie and mask.

'Oh my God, Cass, that was hilarious.'

'It was awful. That poor man.'

'He'll be all right.'

'I don't wanna do anything like that again.'

'OK,' she said, handing me back my phone just as it pinged, telling me the £50 had landed. 'So, what now?'

I looked at the time. It wasn't late, but I felt terrible for violating that poor man. My fatigue felt even worse. I was doing this for Sam, but I didn't want to hurt anyone else in doing so. It didn't feel right. It didn't feel like me.

'Cass?'

'Sorry.'

'Shall we find another?'

'OK.' I looked at the app. My inbox was full again, of people wanting me to do crude things, and again, I deleted them all. 'This isn't going to end well.'

'So, speak to your followers, tell them more.'

'I doubt it would work.'

'Worth a try?'

'Mia, I feel awful now. This isn't me. I'll find another way to help Sam.'

'What? No, this is great! How much have you made already?'

'£250.'

'In one evening, and you've not even got going. Cass, you said you wanna help Sam.'

'I do.'

'Then keep doing dares.'

'But people are so filthy. I'm not gonna compromise who I am.'

'So, tell them.'

'All right.'

Tucking around the corner, slightly off the main street, I put on my hat and mask again. Once I was sure no one could make out it was me, I hit 'livestream' and began to record.

'Hey, it's player KJ74 here. I've just completed my third dare, and I wanna tell you why I'm doing this. Someone I know, someone I love, needs money, and I'm doing this to help them. This isn't for fame. In fact, I don't want fame. Not now, not ever. This is because I care. So, if you see this, if you are watching, send me dares, things to do. I won't take my clothes off, I won't engage in anything depraved, but I will be brave, and give you something good to watch. So, hit me up — if you dare.'

I hit 'end stream', and Mia clapped. 'If you dare. I loved that!'

'We'll see if it helps,' I said, lowering my face mask.

Within seconds, a new DareMe notification pinged; a closed dare just for me.

'Well, open it! What does it say?' Mia asked.

Welcome, player KJ74
Your DareMe challenge:
Meet a man on London Road for a good time (£500)
You have 10 minutes remaining.
Do you accept?

'People are disgusting,' Mia said.

'Yeah, they are,' I replied, hitting 'decline' on the dare.

'I'm sure there are decent people out there. Let's look for another open dare.'

I nodded and went to the open dare list, scrolling it with my thumb to find something that leaped out as doable, and worth it. As I did, Mia leaned close.

'What about that?' she asked.

'I'm not gonna steal anything.'

'It's just a pub chair.'

'Mia, no, and it's only for £15. It's not worth it.'

'What about . . .'

Before Mia could finish, we both became aware that someone was close. A man, around the same age as us, tall, lean, like he hadn't had a proper meal in years. When he spoke, there was a slur, alcohol induced. 'No fucking way? KJ74?'

I turned my back, so he couldn't see my face, and pulled my mask up.

'Hi?'

'I'm a player too. You heard of me? StretchDareStrong. Like Stretch Armstrong, but dare, cos of the app and the fact I'm so fucking long.'

'It's a great name. But sorry, no.'

He waved it off. 'Fuck, it is you. Man, it's really you — you're, like, getting famous now. I follow you on DareMe. That river thing, that was wild. I was sure I was gonna watch you drown.' He broke into a laugh. 'Give me a selfie.'

The man came close, taking his phone out and, before I could protest, he put his arm round my shoulder, almost pulling me into a headlock. I tried to calmly free myself, but his sinewy grip was strong. He stank of stale beer, and as Mia attempted to usher him away, he began to stream.

'Hey. It's your boy, StretchDareStrong, with my main girl, KJ74. Say something, KJ.'

'Um . . . hi.'

'You guys out there, dare me to do something with KJ. Anything. Let's blow up on DareMe.'

He ended the stream, and sure enough, his inbox pinged. He opened it and looked at what the dare said.

'Fuck. That's a lot of money,' he said, glancing over at me.

'What?' I said.

Stretch didn't speak. Instead, he turned the phone to me, and I read the closed dare in his inbox.

Welcome, player StretchDareStrong
Your DareMe challenge:
Rape KJ74 (£1,000)
You have 15 minutes remaining.
Do you accept?

My eyes shot up to the tall, drunk man in front of me. I wanted to tell him that if he touched me I'd kill him. I wanted to cry for help, to grab Mia and run, but I couldn't move.

'What does it say?' Mia asked, and neither me nor Stretch spoke. 'Cass?'

I took a small step back, and as I did, the man looked around, making sure we were alone.

'Cass?' Mia said again, but I couldn't take my eyes off the man.

He stared back at me.

'Get out of here,' he said, his voice suddenly sober. 'I don't know what this sick game is, but I'm not fucking playing. Get out of here, KJ, before someone else is dared to do this.'

'You're not going to hurt me?'

'This is supposed to be fun. Make us famous. This is so fucked up.'

'Yeah,' I said.

'Get out of here. Don't let anyone find you. Fuck this app, man.'

'Thank you.'

'Go,' he said again, a little more forcefully.

I didn't hesitate. Grabbing Mia's hand, I started to run, taking off my hat and face mask so no one else could recognise KJ74, and I didn't look back.

CHAPTER SIXTEEN

Jamison

Sitting in his office, Jamison scrolled on the DareMe app, his adrenaline so high that he needed distraction. The app had come to his attention earlier in the day. One of his kids was talking about it over breakfast before he left for work. The rare sit-down time together with his children that seldom happened anymore. They only visited once every two weeks, stayed one night, then he would leave for work, come home to an empty house. Begin the countdown until they next visited. They didn't come because they loved him, or missed him, they came because they were duty-bound, and usually needing money. But Jamison didn't mind, he had made his bed, long ago.

His eldest kept talking about it, DareMe, and he wanted to see what the fuss was all about. He knew he wouldn't be a player. That would be ludicrous, but it was interesting to watch what people would do these days for a quick buck. He watched young men jump from stupid heights, lots of people streaking, some smashing things they owned, another kissing a stranger in a bar, all for a few minutes of fame. It was a little pathetic and, having seen enough, he closed the app. He then messaged his eldest kid back. He told him it was OK to watch, but Jamison's would not be players in this stupid fad. His boy replied by sending a thumbs up emoji, just as Harry and Mike walked in.

'You wanted to see us?'

'Take a seat, boys.'

Mike and Harry exchanged a nervous look, then Jamison broke into a smile. 'I have some news.'

'OK?' Mike asked, shifting in his seat.

'Our first has complied.'

'To all of it?' Harry asked.

Jamison didn't reply, but instead unlocked his phone and showed his screen. On it were three separate accounts for banks in the Cayman Islands. Each with a hundred grand deposited.

'Where's the rest?' Harry asked.

'Coming. It has to be done over a period of time. It's our time, lads. Let's tie off our loose ends here and leave all this shit behind. That beating seems to have done the trick.'

'What's the plan?' Mike asked.

'I've heard the police are gonna go and talk to the kid.'

'Who?' Harry asked.

'Wakelin,' Jamison replied.

'I can't stand that fucking prick,' Mike said.

'I'm gonna do some digging. Find out if he says anything but, lads, I don't want him thinking that just because he's in hospital now with a copper at his door that we can't get to him.'

'What do you want us to do?'

'Just in case he feels safe and thinks it might be better to talk, go and show him he isn't.'

'Do you think he will talk?'

'Probably not — the kid isn't stupid.'

'I feel sorry for him,' Harry said.

'He was paid well for his work. He knew the risks.'

'Boss, you know if we fuck him up, he'll never be able to clear his debt.'

'That's not my problem,' Jamison said. 'Again, the kid owes small change. It's about the message we are sending more than the money. Pay him a little visit. Make him know that we can get to him anywhere, anytime. This is about making sure we finish what we started. We need people to know we can get to anyone.'

'Sure thing,' Harry said.

'And Harry, get ready to leave tomorrow night. Keep that USB with you. When you're at the safe house in France, ring me from the burner. Mike, you head to Germany the day after tomorrow. I then want you both working on all your targets from the off.'

Both Harry and Mike nodded. It wasn't the plan they had agreed, but the situation with the kid had upped the stakes. They trusted their boss. He'd not steered them wrong before. Speeding up the process couldn't hurt.

'Once you two are out of the country,' Jamison continued, 'I'll manage it from here. Keep the heat away and then I'll go to Greece for the final two. We are almost there, lads. Just these loose ends to tie.'

CHAPTER SEVENTEEN

£4,250 raised

Despite my exhaustion, sleep didn't come easily. The moment with the tall DareMe player who was offered £1,000 to assault me played heavily on my mind. The man who called himself Stretch was decent, but I knew many out there weren't. DareMe was dangerous, but then, wasn't it just emulating life? People wanted to see these things. So, the app itself wasn't the problem — it was us, the people playing. We were the wrong in this world. At what point would it all stop? How far would it go before the site was shut down?

Less than forty-eight hours ago, my life was routine. The scariest thing to happen was me slipping on some ice. Now I had a brother in hospital, I'd nearly drowned in a river and I'd narrowly escaped being assaulted. I didn't want to leave the house ever again.

But I had no choice. At least for now, I had to push my fear down. I had to bury the last two days and help my brother.

Although DareMe was an app that anyone could access at any time, I found from my early morning scrolling that more happened in the evenings. People worked, had lives, families and commitments, so even though my account had hundreds of closed requests, and I had over 2,000 followers, there was no need to rush to play. Not yet. I needed to see Sam, to make sure he was OK first. I checked my emails, my boss telling me to take whatever time I needed. Sam's assault was all over the local news pages on social media, and a doctor's note wouldn't be needed. It made me feel sick to think of my brother being newsworthy that way. But it had happened, I couldn't change that, all I could do was focus on my promise.

The bus journey to the hospital was quiet. I didn't know why I expected anything else. The small dares I had done were unremarkable in the scheme of things, especially compared with what I had seen, and what I had read on Stretch's phone. And nobody would be able to ID me anyway.

I had nothing to do but sit alone with my thoughts as the bus rumbled through town towards the city hospital. I missed my mum. If she were alive, none of this would be happening. If she were here, Sam would be OK. We'd fought so much in those final months before she died. If only I had known then that her life was going to be cut short because of me. If only I had known the mistake I was going to make.

But life didn't work that way. 'If only' were the cruellest two words.

When the bus finally reached the hospital, the driver swore and beeped his horn. A car had parked in the stop.

'Bloody arseholes,' he said, having to pull up beside it, blocking the road to the cars behind. I walked around the problem car and made my way towards the entrance.

But something about the car nagged me.

Turning, I looked again — a black Range Rover. I looked at the number plate. It was the same one I had seen in town, when Sam was hurt.

'Oh, God.' I ran into the hospital, ignoring the volunteer who shouted for me to slow down as I made my way to the elevator. The doors opened and several people got in, filling the lift. I headed for the stairs.

I climbed to the fourth floor, taking the steps two at a time, and burst into the corridor that led to Sam's room.

'Hey!' a nurse shouted but, just like with the volunteer, I ignored them and ran down the corridor. Once again, I was running on hollow legs, my body moving without my control. I needed to be with Sam, and the image of him tied, that image where I thought he was dead, flashed into my mind once more. Outside, I heard a horn blast, and my stomach dropped. I looked out of the window and saw two men climb into the Range Rover. They had barely closed the doors before they sped away.

'Sam?' I said, upping my pace. The police officer wasn't outside his room but a nurse was. She held up her palms to slow me down.

'Woah, woah, I need you to calm down.'

'Where is the police officer?'

'On a comfort break.'

'Have you been here the whole time?'

'What? No, I've been doing rounds.'

'Then who's been watching my brother?'

Pushing past the nurse, I ran into Sam's room, but he wasn't in the bed. 'Sam?'

Then, I looked down and saw my brother on the floor. He was biting down on a pillow, muffling his cries. He was holding his right hand. My stomach turned. His fingers were broken so badly they stuck out like gnarled branches from a tree.

'Help! I need some help!' I shouted.

The police officer ran into the room.

'He's been attacked. Where were you?'

'Shit,' the officer said, running out of the room again. He was no doubt trying to find Sam's attacker, but I knew it was too late. They were long gone.

I took the pillow out of his mouth and Sam moaned. I lowered myself to his side, trying not to look at his hand.

'A doctor is coming,' I said gently.

'The police visited,' he said through gritted teeth. 'I didn't say anything, but they knew the police came.'

'But why did they do this?'

'As a warning, Cass, so I don't speak. You need to be careful, sis — they know where we live. They are going to kill me, I just know it. Please, don't talk to the police.'

'But, Sam—'

'I know these people, please. Promise me. Cass, promise me.'

'I promise,' I said. 'We'll find the money. I need to contact them.'

'Cass, no, I can't drag you into this.' Tears streamed down his face.

'Sam, I need to tell them the money is coming. I need their number.'

Violently shaking, Sam grabbed his phone and unlocked it. He held up the screen for me to see and, scrambling, I punched the number on it into my own phone.

'I'm fixing this,' I added, as a desperate afterthought, cradling him in my arms. Sam started to cry harder, and I held him, stroking his hair, like I did when he was young after a bad dream. Only this wasn't a nightmare. The monsters were real, and they drove an old black Range Rover.

'How, Cass? How can you fix this?' Sam said, just as a doctor ran into the room. Pushing me out of the way, they tended to Sam, and when another doctor joined, they were told to prep him for X-ray. Sam was then helped into a wheelchair.

'Cass, don't do anything stupid. Don't get involved.'

CHAPTER EIGHTEEN

As soon as I was alone, I looked at the number Sam had shown me. He hadn't said whose number it was, but I had to assume it was the Mr Jamison he'd mentioned. I saved it as such, and then wondered how I could even begin to talk in a calm and considered way to a man who had hurt my brother. I wanted to call him a monster, a villain. I wanted him arrested. I knew I couldn't call. My voice would betray me immediately, show him I both wanted justice and was lost, afraid. It would say I didn't know how I was going to fix this mess and save my brother. I messaged instead.

> *This is Sam's sister. I'm sorting things. You will get your money. The police know nothing. Please don't hurt him anymore, he's just a kid.*

I hit *'send'*, then wanted to throw up. My chest felt tight, like it had when I'd jumped in the river. I needed to walk to try and ebb the flow of panic wanting to escape out of every pore.

Sam had gotten lucky with his eye, but the same couldn't be said about his right hand. The doctor told me he had multiple fractures, massive tissue damage, nerve damage too. I didn't ask questions, didn't say thank you. I just sat on the edge of his empty hospital bed, numbed. These men, whoever they were, were not messing around. They planned to cause permanent damage. They wanted to make sure Sam would never forget his mistake. But it was just that — Sam hadn't intended for any of this to happen. He'd simply been foolish. He'd wanted to help me. I was the one always talking about how stressed I was about money. He had only been trying to help me. It should have been my hand that was maimed. But it wasn't, and for the second time in as many days, my poor brother was in theatre. This whole thing was a mess, and I suspected because of it, Sam might struggle to hold a pen ever again.

The message was clear though. No police.

I waited for Sam to come out of theatre, unable to cry, or move. I didn't hear the door to Sam's room open and jumped when Wakelin spoke.

'How are you doing?' he asked.

'Shit. You scared me.'

'Sorry.'

'Not very well.'

Coming in, he closed the door behind him. 'Is Sam OK?'

'His hand is a mess. I thought your people were supposed to be looking out for him.'

'We are, we were. It seems that whoever attacked your brother was here in the hospital, waiting for their moment.'

'He shouldn't have been left alone.'

'I agree.' He took a seat in the chair opposite me. 'Cassie, look. I know I come across really brash, and a little unlikeable.'

'A little unlikeable,' I said, trying to lighten the tension I felt at the way he looked at me.

He smiled. 'I know you know more than you're letting on. I know you saw something. I can see it on your face every time I ask you, or him. I want to help your brother.'

I wanted to tell him everything I knew about the debt and the car. But Sam was under police protection, and still they'd got to him.

'Cassie, you can trust me.'

'I don't know anything. If I did, I would tell you,' I said.

'Cassie, if you are hiding information, you could be interfering with a police investigation. It could get you in trouble. I just want to help him.'

'I don't know anything,' I said more forcefully. 'Sam and I don't talk like we once did and I didn't see any more than I've told you. Now, it's been a shit couple of days, can you just leave me alone? I don't want Sam to worry about me when he comes out of theatre. He's been through enough.'

My phone vibrated beside me, and I snatched it up quickly. It was an unknown number calling. It had to be him, the man Sam owed money. Wakelin must have seen the panic on my face.

'An unwanted call?'

'It's just work. I'll call back later.' I put the phone down, pressing the screen into the bed.

He nodded, and got to his feet. 'I'll need to talk to your brother.'

'I'll tell him you stopped by,' I said, holding his eye. I couldn't get a read on this man. At times he appeared like he cared, others like he held me with mild contempt. But I wouldn't talk to him. Sam needed me to keep my promise.

Once Wakelin had gone, I lowered my head and took deep, measured breaths, picked up my phone, went to my missed calls and dialled.

CHAPTER NINETEEN

Jamison

'Why didn't you pick up?' Jamison asked, insulted that he was ignored.

'The police were here.'

'What did you tell them?'

'Nothing, I swear. Look, I know my brother messed up, and owes you now.'

'Do you? He shouldn't have talked.'

'He didn't. I don't know who you are, or what you do, I only know he owes you, and that's why he was hurt. Please, I can get the money. He said he had a week. Give me a week and I can repay you. I can.'

Jamison didn't reply, but once again fell into one of his pensive silences. She sounded sure she could repay the money, but it wasn't about the money. Not now. Right now it was about keeping her quiet. If she spoke to the police, it would only complicate matters further. He had to maintain her silence, just long enough for Harry and Mike to get out of the country. He had to keep her busy. A week was too long — he needed her to be fixated, focused, only thinking of her brother.

'Hello?' the sister said on the other end.

'I don't like that you know of your brother's predicament.'

'I swear, I only know he owes you, that's it. I can fix this.'

'You have twenty-four hours.'

'What? No, you said a week.'

'That was then, this is now. Twenty-four hours. Once you have it, I will tell you how to repay it. Good luck, sister.'

Jamison hung up the phone. She would be so preoccupied trying to fix her problems, she wouldn't dare speak to anyone. He was confident the kid issue was resolved. He had served his purpose. In reality, Jamison had made a lot more money than the kid had lost, and the sister being aware meant little. Still, he wanted to be sure so, picking up his phone again, he rang Harry.

'Boss?'

'You ready?'

'Yes, boss.'

'Good. There is one more thing I want you to do.'

CHAPTER TWENTY

Locking my phone, I fought to keep my composure. Speaking with the man had scared me. I could sense he wanted me to fail, that he wanted to cause more harm. As much as I wanted to stay and wait for Sam, I was no use to him sitting here. Time was not our friend. I had less than a day to save my brother.

Sam would forgive me for not being there when he woke, maybe not straight away, but one day, when this was all behind us.

As I stepped out of his room, I smiled at the nurse at the station.

'I'm just getting a coffee,' I said, but I wasn't getting a coffee at all. I was going to get the money my brother needed.

When I opened DareMe again, it told me I had just over 1,500 followers. There were scores of open dares, and over thirty closed dares in my inbox. Most were what I had now come to expect. Among them though were some dares that weren't about sex. It seemed my message about helping someone I loved had resonated a little. I was going to exploit it.

One dare stood out. It was risky. It could land me in trouble, but I had no choice. I would risk it all for my brother to be OK.

Welcome, player KJ74
Your DareMe challenge:
Steal something from a museum (£250)
You have 2 hours remaining.
Do you accept?

I hadn't stolen anything in my life. But then, I hadn't ever worried about Sam losing his.

I tapped 'accept'.

CHAPTER TWENTY-ONE

I made a quick pit stop at home to grab my rucksack before heading to the museum.

£250 was a good chunk of money, a small but definitive step to helping Sam. But really, when I thought about it, it was also a tiny amount for committing a crime. Less than a week's wages for something that could potentially put me in a lot of trouble. I had never understood criminals before, always believing I was above that.

Funny how things can change.

I would deal with how I felt about being a thief after. However, as I walked back over the river towards the city, drawing closer to the Georgian building with the reputation for being the most haunted place in Peterborough, I realised I didn't have to be a thief at all. The dare didn't say I had to keep what I had stolen. I was merely borrowing a museum item. Once the dare was complete, I would return it.

Reaching the entrance, I double-checked I had what I needed, and then, forcing down the knot of anxiety that was beginning to grow, I walked inside and smiled to the museum worker who greeted me.

'Hi,' I said, trying to sound relaxed, nonchalant.

'Welcome,' he said.

The man looked like someone I would want to be friends with. He had a kind smile, bright eyes. I could tell, even before I saw the book on the desk, that he was a reader.

'What are you reading?' I asked, not knowing why I didn't just walk away and remain as invisible as possible.

'It's called *The Day She Disappeared*.'

'Is it good?'

'Yeah, really good,' he said, his face lighting up. 'I love a whodunnit.'

'Me too. I'm just . . .' I hesitated. 'I'm just going to look at some things.'

'That's what we are here for.' He smiled before serving a customer who was buying something from the small shop to the left. He put the book down, and for a moment I thought of stealing that. The dare said only to take something, it didn't mean an artefact of some kind. But, I didn't want to lose out on £250 due to a technicality. I knew what the dare maker intended, and I had to play the game properly.

I walked into the museum, pausing to drop a few pounds in the donation box and then, once I passed the threshold, I headed for the stairs to take me up to the exhibits.

On the first floor, I walked around the Jurassic and Ice Age gallery. I'd forgotten how brilliant it was. As a kid, we came to the museum all the time with Mum. After she died, I hadn't come again. Sam had missed out on so much that was designed for a child to enjoy. It was yet another example of how I had let him down.

As much as the galleries were wonderful and nostalgic, I didn't see anything I could easily take, so I headed up another level. At the top of the stairs was the Victorian operating theatre. Historically, the museum was a hospital, and a single room was now dedicated to that bygone era. I remembered being afraid of this room when I was a kid, Mum having to hold my hand to go inside. It was designed to look and smell like it was a functioning operating theatre. It made me feel a little sick. And it made me think of Sam, who might still be on the operating table even now.

Opening the door, I stepped in, and part of me was whisked back to maybe being eight or nine years old, before Sam was born, holding my mum's hand as she read me the facts about the room.

I stopped myself from remembering too much. It wouldn't help.

There was a hospital bed on the other side of a low barrier, set up to look like an operation had just taken place. There were tools, fake blood and bandages strewn across it. It was the thing that had scared me when I was young. It still scared me now. I turned away and looked behind me. A huge display cabinet stood laden with old surgical tools and descriptions of what they were and how they worked. All of them were small enough to steal, if it weren't for the fact that they were behind glass. I wouldn't smash the glass — that would be going too far — so I turned my attention back to the bed, and as I looked, I could see that some of the tools displayed weren't pinned down in any way. They were just props. But the dare didn't say I had to steal something of value from a museum. Just that I had to steal something.

Slinging my rucksack off my back, I crouched to unzip it and pulled out my hat and face mask. Leaving the bag on the floor, so I could quickly stuff something inside, I stood to put my hat on and film my crime, but just as I started to do it, the door opened and a young dad with two children walked in.

The dad noticed I was off straight away. It must have been how I was stood, how I looked at him. He knew I wasn't quite right. I'd not been a thief before, and I must have been shouting it with my body language. He didn't say anything, but in the way he creased his brow, it told me he knew I was up to no good.

I didn't run. I held onto my hat and turned to look into the display cabinet, reading about the various tools and what they were used for. As the man began to answer his children's questions, I watched them through the glass. One of his girls was about the same age I was when I used to come with Mum. She didn't like the room either, and begged to leave. The man agreed, and as he left with his two children, he gave me another puzzled look.

As soon as the door closed, I pulled on my hat, mask, and hit 'livestream'.

'This is KJ74. About to complete my fourth dare. What I'm about to do is wrong, but I am doing it to help someone I love, so, yeah, I don't really have a choice. Right. Here goes,' I whispered.

Making sure I caught it on film, I jumped over the barrier, and grabbed a hacksaw from the table. It was heavier than I first imagined. I cursed. It wasn't a prop at all, but a real surgical tool from the Victorian times.

'Shit.'

Fearful the man or someone else would walk in, I jumped back over the barrier and stuffed it in my bag. Securing it on my back, I left my hat and face mask in place, even though it made me look like I had something to hide. I quickly made my way down the stairs. As I hit the bottom, the man with the children was at the entrance. He was talking to the museum worker. They both looked my way, and I knew I'd been caught.

'Excuse me,' the museum worker said, walking towards me.

I had two options — I could explain what I was doing, hoping the kindness I'd sensed in him meant he would understand and didn't call the police. It would mean failing the dare of course as I'd have to hand back the saw. And lose the £250 I needed to help Sam.

Or I could make a run for it.

'Can you take your mask off, please?' the man said, getting closer.

I looked at my phone. I was still streaming. Hundreds of people were watching.

'I've been caught, but I'm not giving up,' I said into my phone, and before the man could get to my side, I ran towards him. I saw the panic in his eyes as I approached, and he lunged to grab me. I sidestepped and made for the door. The dad of the two children was blocking my way, but his only concern was his children, and he ran to their side, shielding them from me. With no one in my way, I ran from the museum, shouting that I was sorry. I turned left and headed away from the city centre and towards the bus station. Slipping down a smaller road, I ran until it broke out into a busier street. Confident the museum worker hadn't followed me this far, I slowed. Ahead of me, a group of teenagers watched a phone, and I heard one of them call out.

'That's here, I'm telling you. That's this road. KJ74 is here somewhere.'

They looked up and saw me. I thought they were going to try and stop me. After all, I had committed a crime, but instead they clapped.

'KJ74,' they called, and I waved awkwardly towards them. They approached and jumped onto my livestream, waving to my camera and congratulating me.

'You smashed it,' one of the lads said.

'Thanks, listen, I gotta run,' I said.

'Yeah, no problem. Listen, if the fuzz come, we'll tell them you went down towards the river.'

'Thanks, lads.'

Continuing away from the group, I turned a corner, and stopped. Leaning against a wall to catch my breath, I looked at the camera once more. 'Dare complete.'

Putting my phone away, I took off my hat and mask and then my coat too, just in case. I stuffed them all into the bag and, trying to look casual, I walked back the way I came. If anyone was trying to find me, they wouldn't suspect someone who looked like they could be casually shopping. I just had to keep my emotions, my fear, in check. As I passed the group of lads who had just been congratulating me, they didn't give me a second look.

A minute later, £250 landed in my bank account.

A minute after that, Mia messaged.

Cass? What the fuck are you doing?

CHAPTER TWENTY-TWO

£4,500 raised

I didn't know how to explain to Mia what I had done, as I still hadn't fully processed it myself. I'd tried to live a good life, a quiet one. Now I had committed a crime and, looking at the DareMe app, watching my followers climb to over 3,000, I wasn't so invisible anymore.

The adrenaline of my DareMe challenge began to ebb and, feeling tired, I stopped at a coffee shop, ordered a latte and found a seat in the corner, where I could watch the world walk by. I found comfort that although KJ74 had been recognised, Cassie was still anonymous. As long as I kept it that way, everything would be all right.

Sipping my drink, I felt my rucksack. The blunted saw felt conspicuous, damning, and I waited for someone to say something, point a finger at me, call me a thief, but no one did. No one looked at me. No one saw me. People had their own things going on. The older I got, the more I realised this fact. No one cared, no one looked because the torch was shining on their own lives too.

I kept looking at the DareMe app, kept watching my followers increase and my inbox fill up. There were over thirty closed dares and, going into the folder, I saw that there weren't as many unsavoury requests. There were some, which I declined, but most were requests to pinch something new. It seemed people liked watching a reluctant thief.

It made me feel uncomfortable.

As I scrolled the list, my phone rang. It was Mia. The idea of talking to someone who knew I was KJ74, caused a ball of panic to rise in my throat. But I knew she wouldn't stop calling so I picked up and forced myself to speak. 'Hey, Mia.'

'What are you doing?'

'They got to Sam this morning,' I said, feeling the ball force its way further up. It wanted to spill out as a cry, or a scream, or hyperventilation, but again, I swallowed it down.

'What? Shit, is he OK?'

'They hurt him again, and reduced the time we have.'

'Shit,' she said again. 'How long?'

I looked at the time on my phone. 'I've got about twenty-one hours.'

'Cass, I think you need to go to the police.'

Despite being on a call, Mia's voice channelling straight into my ear, I looked around to make sure she hadn't been heard. 'No, no. I can't do that.'

'Cass, you have to.'

'Sam had a police officer guarding him, and they still got to him. I can't. They won't help. The only thing that will is to get their money back.'

'I'm worried.'

'Me too. But I have to keep going.'

I heard her take a deep breath. 'OK, how can I help?'

'I guess I need help to become famous. The more followers, the more dares, and maybe the more money for each dare.'

'Makes sense. Let me message around, see if we can create even more buzz.'

'Don't tell anyone it's me.'
'I won't, I promise.'
'Thanks. Now, I've just got to work out what to do next.'
'Want my advice? Keep showing them you're versatile. You've jumped in a river, run home in your underwear, kissed a stranger and stolen something. What was it, anyway?'

'An old surgical saw.'

'Gross.'

I couldn't help but laugh, despite it all, and felt the tension lift.

'Do something fun, silly, something that takes a while so the livestream lasts longer, and we get to watch you more.'

'I'm not keen on being watched more.'

'But it will help. Trust me. If they can see you then they'll want to help you.'

Saying my goodbyes, I hung up and looked at the list of dares — spotting one that might work.

It was something I had secretly wished for, for years, and had never had the nerve. But before I could accept, I needed to make sure it was possible.

On Google, there were three places that could help, and I rang the first, a place called Lost Time, only a few minutes' walk from me. I spoke briefly, told them what I needed, and when they asked for my name, I said KJ.

'Wait, KJ, as in KJ74?' the person on the phone said.

'Um, yes?'

'*No* way, we fucking love you. Your last dare, that was cool.'

'Thanks, so do you think you can fit me in?'

'Fuck yeah! Come in half an hour. And don't worry, we'll make sure no one sees it's you. Do you know what you want?'

'It says to let someone else decide.'

'Love that! Great, don't worry, KJ, we got your back.'

CHAPTER TWENTY-THREE

Welcome, player KJ74
Your DareMe challenge:
Get a tattoo, place on body and image decided by a stranger (£150)
You have 1 hour and 30 minutes remaining.
Do you accept?

I had always wanted a tattoo, something for Mum, but the pain had always put me off. However, a dare was a dare. And although the amount was less, it would stream for longer than any other challenge. If Mia was right, it would help raise my profile.

Internet famous. Two words I had always hated, and now I was pushing to become it.

Once I had accepted the challenge, the waiting was hard. I tried to ring Sam, but his phone went to voicemail, so I rang the hospital. It took a while to connect, but when I finally reached his ward, I was told he was out of theatre and in recovery. The police were there too and this time there were two officers instead of just one, which made me feel that Sam was at least slightly safer than before. But I didn't doubt that Jamison meant his threat. They would find a way to get to Sam if I failed.

Finishing my coffee, I looked at the time and reasoned if I was a few minutes early, they wouldn't mind, so, making sure I had everything, I left the coffee shop and walked towards the tattoo parlour. I wanted it over with. The only thing that made me want to stop was that it was up to a stranger to decide the tattoo's placement and design. If they decided to tattoo somewhere intimate, the whole world would see. Running home in my underwear was one thing, exposing myself to countless thousands, something else entirely.

Outside, I paused and donned my beanie and face mask. After opening the DareMe app, I hit 'stream'.

'Hey, friends, it's KJ74 and I'm about to complete my fifth dare.'

I walked into the tattoo shop and closed the door behind me. A receptionist, a young man covered in tattoos, who must have been Sam's age, saw me and jumped out of his chair.

'She's here,' he said, coming around the counter to wave to the livestream. From behind, I saw three people being tattooed and the artists paused and waved my way.

'Hey, everyone,' I said.

A man stepped out from a side room to my left. He was tall, with long, dreadlocked hair, his face covered in tattoos and piercings. His arms were completely black with ink, as was his neck and chest, from what I could see over the top of his shirt. My first thought was that I found him intimidating, but as soon as he opened his mouth to speak, I was ashamed.

'Hey, KJ. I'm Dan. This is my shop,' he said with a grin.

'Hey, Dan.'

He looked at the camera livestreaming. Then back to me. 'So, you need a tattoo?'

'Yeah. A stranger has to decide what and where,' I said, the fear of being compromised leaping forth once more. Thankfully, Dan looked at me with compassion, and I felt safer for it.

'Great, well, I'm a stranger.'

'Yep,' I said, my nerves beginning to kick in with a sick feeling in my stomach and an involuntary twitch of my muscles.

Dan showed me into his room and asked me to take a seat. As he chatted to me, getting me to sign consent forms, I kept one eye on the livestream. He noticed and offered to set my phone up, so I didn't have to hold it. I handed him the phone and he placed it on a shelf, so the whole room was in shot.

'Have you had a tattoo before?' he asked.

'No,' I said, my voice beginning to betray me and show my fear.

'Right, so we can do anything. Tattoo anywhere?'

I felt a rise of panic again. I wanted to leave, but as I looked at my phone, I saw there were over 6,000 people watching, and the number was climbing. Most were hoping for the thing I feared most, I suspected.

'Yeah.' I swallowed hard, my mouth dry.

Dan spun in his chair and started to prep. He hadn't said where he was going to ink me, and I felt dread slowly sink into my bones. To distract me, he asked why I was a player, and I told him, without saying any real details, that I need to help someone I loved who was in a jam.

'So, none of this money is for you?' he asked.

'No, none.'

'And this isn't about you getting famous?'

'No, no, I don't want any of that. I just want to help.'

He spun back to me, and nodded. 'Well, KJ, shall we?'

I nodded, and as Dan sat and fired up the gun then dipped it into the ink, I felt my fight or flight response kick in.

'What are you going to do?'

'You'll see.'

'Please don't make it too big,' I said, looking at him, trying to see where he was going to tattoo.

He looked me in the eye, then at my face, and I thought I was going to be sick. 'I — I don't know if I can do this.'

'It's all right, KJ. You said the tattoo could be anywhere, right?'

I nodded, unable to speak. The livestream continued, the number of viewers climbing steadily.

'OK, can you pull down your top a bit?' he said.

I nodded and did as he asked, and he helped, exposing my collarbone.

'Deep breath,' he said, calmly. As I inhaled, he put the tattoo gun on my skin. The rattle of it on my collarbone reverberated into my teeth and I fought not to cry out in pain. Dan chatted to me lightly and he scraped the needle over me, making small talk to distract me. Time ticked on, and I watched the views on DareMe continue to climb.

He looked and saw it too. 'Seems you're pretty famous now,' he said quietly, his attention turning back to his work.

'It's not what I want.'

'Yeah, I get that vibe about you. Just trying to help someone you love, right?'

'Yep.'

'I like that,' he said.

As he began to shade the tattoo, I gripped the chair and focused on my breathing. Another ten minutes, and he put the gun down.

'There, all done. You did good, KJ,' he said, turning to clean up.

I leaned forward, so I was closer to the livestream, and looked at my new tattoo. Dan had inked a small angel on my shoulder. It was delicate, pretty, and as close to perfect as I could have wanted.

'Bloody hell that hurt,' I said.

'Yep, it's not comfortable.'

'Dare complete,' I said, ending the stream.

I sat back in my chair, feeling sweaty, and Dan turned back to me. 'Thank you,' I said.

'My pleasure.'

'No, I mean, thank you for only doing a little one, somewhere where I wasn't going to be exposed.'

'I wasn't gonna do anywhere else, not while you were streaming.'

'Why an angel?'

'You're doing this for someone you love — an angel seemed the most fitting thing,' he said, and I could have cried.

I nodded, thankful that there were some good men still. 'How much do I owe you?'

'This one is on me,' he said.

'No, I can't accept that.'

'You wanna help someone you love, I completely get that. We all gotta try to help those in need, haven't we?'

'Thank you,' I said again. 'Can I quickly say something to my followers?' I asked, cringing at the fact I had just said, 'my followers'.

'Be my guest.'

Grabbing the phone, I hit 'livestream'.

'Hey, friends. Dare five is done. Keep them coming — I can do this all night. And thanks to Dan here at Lost Time. You'd be in good hands coming here.'

I ended the stream and stood up. 'Thanks, Dan, I really mean it.'

'See you soon, KJ. Happy healing,' he said.

Before leaving the shop, I was given a small card on how to care for my new tattoo, and then I stepped outside, glad for the cool air that hit my skin. The tattoo stung and my skin felt clammy.

I paused in a nook of a closed café and took off my hat and mask. Stuffing them in my bag, along with the old saw, I joined the thrum of people on Bridge Street, once again becoming anonymous.

My phone pinged. The £150 was there. I had made £650 in just over twelve hours. More than I made in a week's work.

As I moved effortlessly, invisibly, through the town, I passed the museum and saw a police car parked outside. Tentatively I approached, hoping I would be able to drop the saw back without being seen, but as I got close to the front, I saw a police officer inside talking to the employee I had dodged on my way out. It was too risky, so I kept walking.

My phone rang. It had no caller ID, and, thinking it might be my brother, I answered. 'Sam?'

'Miss Jones, it's Detective Sergeant Wakelin.'

'Detective Sergeant Wakelin,' I said, my voice quivering. 'Can I help?'

'The question is not can you help, but *will* you help?'

'Sorry?'

'Miss Jones, it seems you and I need to chat. I don't think you're being honest with me. Where are you?'

'I'm at home,' I said. I don't know why I lied but as soon as it left my mouth, I knew it was a mistake.

'See, I know that not to be true.'

'What do you mean?'

'I'm outside your house right now, Miss Jones, and nobody is home.'

CHAPTER TWENTY-FOUR

£4,650 raised

I fumbled my excuses, telling him that I had been home not too long ago but had nipped out to the city centre, but knew Wakelin wasn't buying it. I told him I would be home within ten minutes and, hanging up, cursed myself. Wakelin would want answers, and I didn't have any for him.

Walking towards my house, I saw Wakelin on my doorstep, and I hung back and watched him. He looked pissed off. I took a deep breath and slowly advanced, trying my best to look like I was only stressed because I had nipped out, nothing more. That was when I saw something that stopped me in my tracks and forced me to hide behind an overgrown bush. Further down the road, parked on the opposite side to my house and hidden from sight of Wakelin, sat an old black Range Rover.

I wanted to dismiss it, as there must be loads of old black Range Rovers in the city, but even from afar and partially obscured by leaves from the bush I was hiding behind, I could see it was *the* Range Rover. They were watching my house.

I felt my rage build. Not that I could or would do anything about it. If I approached and they saw me talking to

Wakelin, watched me invite him into my house, like before, they would assume I had told him something, and Sam would be killed.

I backed away, and walked towards the city again. I wouldn't be going home anytime soon.

My phone rang. I knew it was Wakelin, but I looked anyway. *No caller ID.* I hit 'end call'. Wakelin rang back, and when I ended the call again, a voicemail notification pinged. With my hands starting to shake, I listened.

'Miss Jones, I'm going to assume you're not coming home and failing to answer my calls is a sign you know a lot more than you're telling me. Just so you're aware, I know you have lied — we have CCTV footage from the main road. It shows you walking — and watching a car leave the scene quickly. What I don't know is why you would choose to hide that information from me. Now, your options are to come in and talk to me, or I will have to assume you want to be arrested. The choice is yours. You need to ring me, my number is—'

Ending the voicemail, I took a shaky breath but didn't turn back. Instead, I messaged those Sam owed and told them the money would be coming soon. Then, I rang Sam. I needed to hear his voice, to know he was OK. He was the one hurt, but I needed the comfort of talking to him. I needed my baby brother.

The phone rang and rang, and just at the point where I was going to give up, he answered. 'Cass,' he said, his voice barely a whisper.

'Hey, Sam, how are you feeling?'

'I'm OK,' he said, but I could tell he was putting on a brave face for me. 'Cass, they are outside.'

'Who?'

'Them, who I owe.'

'How do you know?' I said, wanting to say they couldn't possibly be outside the hospital, because they were currently outside our house.

'They messaged, told me I was being watched, in case I decided to run.'

'How on earth do they expect you to find their money?'

'They said someone else was sorting it — is that you? What did you tell them, Cass? These people aren't to be messed around with.'

'I'm fixing it,' was all I said.

'How?'

'Don't worry about that right now. You need to keep yourself safe, OK?'

'I feel like a prisoner here. Cass, I'm scared.'

'It's OK, Sam.' I bit my lip to stop me telling him I was scared too. 'I'm working on it. I'm fixing it. I gotta go.'

'Cass, what are you doing?'

'I gotta go, Sam,' I said, hanging up. I wanted to tell him I loved him, that I would come to him soon, but if I did, I would have cried, and Sam was hurting enough.

Finding a bench, I sat down and, despite being in a public place, let my emotions wash over me. I didn't care who saw.

'Cheer up, love. It can't be that bad!' a voice said. I wanted to tell them to mind their own business. That it was 2025, and telling someone to simply 'cheer up' wasn't OK anymore, that mental health issues were valid, that I was allowed to cry, and own how I felt, that putting on a brave face wasn't the right thing. But when I looked up, I saw it was a homeless woman. 'Things always get better,' she added as I wiped my eyes.

'Do they?' I asked.

'Yep, if you decide they do.'

'Decide?'

'Yeah, sometimes you gotta embrace the change, to find a way through.'

'You think?'

'Yep. Speaking of change, have you got any?'

'Um, sure.' I reached into my bag to pull out my purse and handed the woman a fiver. She smiled a toothless grin. 'See, my day is already getting better — you just gotta decide!'

The woman wandered off, with the five-pound note wrapped in her palm. I didn't know why, but having someone who was clearly struggling tell me things could get better somehow helped. Crying wouldn't help my brother, raising the money would. Embrace the change. That was what I needed to do. I needed to be like that woman, moving, finding, hoping, asking.

I looked for my next dare. It needed to be something big, something that would result in a huge step forward. As I scrolled I didn't look at the challenge itself, but the amount it would pay. High-ticket open dares were being snapped up. The money for these dares was ramping up as was the danger running alongside. I scrolled and watched people jumping through fire, crashing bicycles into moving cars. Punching strangers. One man got beaten up on his own livestream for £200. DareMe was becoming a lawless place.

Seeing nothing that would suit, I streamed anyway. I begged for someone to give me a big dare, something wild, something that would help who I needed to help.

Within minutes, a new message landed in my inbox. The dare was terrifying, and risky, but it was exactly what I had asked for.

It was also worth £5,000.

CHAPTER TWENTY-FIVE

Welcome, player KJ74
Your DareMe challenge:
Steal a car (£5,000)
You have 3 hours remaining.
Do you accept?

I stared at the screen. Five grand would take my total, including the loan that sat in my bank account, to almost £10k. It was more than half of what Sam had lost. I could use it as a peace offering, a deposit of intent. Maybe it would buy us a little more time or, at the very least, ensure they left Sam alone until I could raise the remaining money. But, stealing a car was extreme. I could still feel the weight of the saw I had pinched, a heavy burden in my rucksack. I intended to return that. If I stole a car, I could return that too — but I knew this was on a whole new level. There would be no going back. No undoing it. I could end up with a criminal record, lose my job, if caught, I could go to jail.

However, I needed to do it. If I was careful, they would never link KJ74 back to Cassie Jones. They would never find me. KJ had only existed for a day, and she was already someone very different from me. My Mr Hyde.

I had more pressing matters. Before I could accept or decline any more dares, I needed to charge my phone. My battery was down to fifteen per cent, and if it died, I wouldn't be able to livestream the dare. It would be completely pointless accepting it. I needed a power bank. I needed to go home.

Turning back on myself, I headed towards London Road, and before I got too close to my home I turned left, then right so I was on a road parallel to mine. I didn't think Wakelin would still be outside my house. I suspected he might have officers looking for me in the city, but I knew that Range Rover would likely be there, watching. I needed to be careful.

Each garden on my street was packed with tall conifers and fruit trees. It made it almost impossible to see if I was adjacent to my house or somebody else's. So, I had to guess. I would need to climb over the back fence of someone else's garden. It was drastic but so was the situation. I had seen what those men had done to Sam. If they did the same to me, we would never get the money. And, like that homeless lady told me, I needed to embrace the change.

Making sure I wasn't being watched by a curtain-twitching neighbour, I slipped up the drive of a house to its side gate. Thankfully, it was open. I walked in, closing the gate behind me. For a moment I paused, listened and, feeling confident no one had seen me walk in, made my way down the side of the house into the garden. If anybody had seen me then they must have assumed I lived there. Like mine, this garden was long and thin, and I looked over the back fence, through a gap in the conifers, and saw my home. My guess had been right. All I had to do was climb into my garden.

Peering around the corner, I looked towards the back door of the house whose garden I was in. It was closed, but that wasn't a surprise. It was so cold. I counted down from three, like I had the night before, in preparation for jumping in the river, and then made a run for it.

Three.
Two.

One.

As soon as I started to run, I knew I had made a horrible mistake. I wasn't alone. I knew one of the houses behind mine had a dog. I should have checked before bounding in. The bark was deep and loud. There was nothing I could do but run as fast as I could, and hope it didn't catch up.

I didn't look back as I charged towards the fence, but I could hear it barking angrily as it gained on me. Launching myself at the fence, I began to scramble up. I threw my right leg over — but then felt the pain. The dog had latched on to my left leg, biting in just above my ankle. I bit back the scream. I couldn't afford for those in the Range Rover to know I was home. I pulled. The dog tried to clamp down harder, adjusting its grip — and in that moment my leg came free.

I landed heavily in my garden. Scrabbling to my feet I hobbled towards the back of my house and unlocked the door that led into my kitchen. Once inside, I locked it behind me, and slumped to the floor. I started to cry. I didn't want any of this, none. I wanted a quiet little life. I didn't want to do stupid dares or be accosted by strangers or steal. It wasn't me. My leg throbbed. I was scared to look, knowing it would be bad, but Sam came back to me. How badly he was hurt. How I was partly responsible for not doing my job as his guardian. His face, his poor face.

Fuck's sake, Cass. Get a grip.

I rolled up my trouser leg and looked at my ankle. Blood ran over and dripped onto the floor. I shuffled towards the stairs and up into the bathroom. I lifted my leg into the bath and ran the tap. The freezing water soothed the pain. As it washed away the blood I could see the dog had only punctured my flesh with one of its teeth. Thankfully, despite it hurting like hell, it wasn't as bad as the pain suggested. Lifting my leg out of the bath, I reached to the bathroom cabinet and grabbed a first aid kit. I began to clean the wound, trying hard not to cry out when the alcohol wipe came in contact. The bleeding continued, but looked like it was slowing. I covered it with a dressing and applied pressure for ten minutes. Then, using a fresh dressing, I bandaged my leg tightly.

By the time I was done, I was sweating despite it being cold in my house. My hands were covered in my own blood. Standing, I placed my foot down; pain shot up my leg. To help, I washed down some painkillers, chucking several more in my bag. I still had a challenge to complete.

As I moved through the house, I kept the lights off. Once I was in my bedroom and had gathered my power bank, I looked out of my window at the car parked just down the road. It was closer to our house now than when DS Wakelin was here. They intended to be seen by me. Intended to scare. There was only one man, the driver. He was scrolling on his phone, his face lit eerily from the screen, but I couldn't see his features. I wanted to see exactly who he was. I wanted to see the man who had attacked my brother. One day, I wanted to be able to point him out in a police line-up. I wanted him to pay for what he did to Sam. I wanted him to go to jail for an extraordinarily long time.

While I had to continue with my current plan, I began to hatch another, so that once Sam's debt was repaid, justice would be served.

Looking at DareMe, I saw I had just over two hours and fifteen minutes left to complete the challenge — which I still hadn't accepted. Taking a breath, I hit 'accept'. As I watched, my followers increased once more. I had time to wait for the night to draw in. Then, I intended to get close enough to get a good look at the man then I would sneak away, find an old banger of a car, and steal it.

CHAPTER TWENTY-SIX

The waiting helped. The pain in my leg eased because I had stopped moving. I had managed to top my phone battery up, and with the power bank fully charged and in my rucksack I knew I would be OK until this was over.

I looked out onto the street below. The car was still there. The driver, still sat on his phone.

I didn't let myself think about how crazy it all was. If I did, I was sure to start hyperventilating and then have a panic attack, and that wouldn't help Sam. I had to keep moving, keep doing. If I stopped for too long, I would fail to do the one thing I promised Mum just before she died. I tried not to think about it, but I was tired, stressed. I didn't let myself remember that day, and how Mum died because of me. Ever. But sometimes it forced its way back. It would come in flashes, a jump that woke me, a smell or noise in the real world that reminded me of that night. I rarely saw Mum in these glimpses, never heard her voice. However, now, somehow, her final words leaped forward.

Look after each other.
Mum, stay awake.
Promise me.

Mum.

Promise me, Cass.

I promise. Mum, Mum, Mum.

I clapped my hands, snapping them together so hard my palms stung. It popped the memory. Brought me back.

I got ready to leave my house. I hoped that when I returned, I would have over half of Sam's money and a plan for how I would get the rest.

I just had to not get caught.

I stuffed some warm clothes into my rucksack in case I had to walk home from wherever I ended up tonight. I put the rucksack on, and the weight of the saw felt too much. The guilt was heavy too. I had no idea how weighed down I would feel after taking a car. But, needs must.

Sneaking through my house in total darkness, I made my way into the living room and ensured my lamp beside the bay window was switched on at the wall, while remaining unlit — for now. Then I continued to the back door, walked outside, and closed it behind me. I wasn't going to go the way I came — there was no way I would face that dog again — so I walked down the side of my own house and, before I got to the end, scaled the fence and climbed into my other neighbour's garden. They didn't have a dog.

Keeping my head low, I walked through their garden and out into the street, then I headed away from the car, walking a long loop around the city streets so I would approach the Range Rover from behind. The walk took me ten minutes, but I didn't want him to see me coming. As I approached the vehicle, I took my phone out and went to my Alexa app. It was time to trigger my plan.

The lamp in my living room had an Amazon bulb. Mia had bought it for me on my last birthday, because I kept telling her I got spooked walking into a dark house at night. She got me the gift so I could turn on the lamp as I approached and feel less afraid. It felt laughable that I used to be afraid by that. So much had changed so quickly. Now I was going to turn it on in the hope the man in the car would investigate. I would walk past, get a look at him, and then I'd keep walking to complete my DareMe challenge. It was risky, but I needed him to pay for my brother's eye. I needed him to be punished for what he had done to my brother's hand.

When I was within spitting distance of the car, I paused behind a parked van, to turn on the lamp. I couldn't see the car anymore, but was close enough to hear if the door opened. I waited for a moment, but there was no movement. He wasn't taking the bait. Then I realised that if he was there to simply watch, he wouldn't react. He would just wait. Maybe note I was home. My plan wasn't as great as I'd thought. I needed to do something to get his attention.

Opening the app again, I turned the lamp off and then on, repeatedly. The constant flashing would surely be enough to make him need to see what was happening. I kept doing it until his car door opened. I watched as he walked calmly across the road and up to my house. I turned the lamp off one final time, to make it look like I'd been caught, then I quickly took photos of him crossing and walking up my path.

I continued to walk. As I drew level with the car, I heard him knocking on my front door, persistently, to get my attention. Glancing in the car, I paused. His car key was hanging in the ignition. There were other keys attached to it, various locks for places unknown. And in the passenger seat, a thin brown file. I quietly opened the door to grab the keys. Their loss would cause him no end of issues. I could run, knowing he wouldn't be able to follow. Then, overcome by curiosity, I flicked open the file.

On the cover page of the document inside was a photo of my brother, and on the next page, one of me.

'Shit.'

I closed the file, wanting to be sick. I looked at the car key once more.

I had opportunity. I looked and saw that the man was still at my house.

I weighed it up. They would no doubt hurt me if I was caught. But they were going to hurt me anyway. They would do worse to Sam if I failed to make enough money and there was a little irony in those I owed actually helping me make the money back.

Fuck it.

Swinging my bag off my back, I quickly threw on my beanie and face mask and, before I could stop myself, hit 'livestream'.

'This is KJ74,' I whispered. 'About to complete my sixth challenge.' I jumped into the car, scooting over to the driver's seat where I turned the key in the ignition. Nothing happened and for a moment I panicked, until on the dash I saw a symbol telling me to press the brake pedal. I did so, turned the key again and the car came to life. Dropping it into drive, thankful it was an automatic as I hadn't driven in years, I put my foot down and the car lurched forward.

The man was heading back and saw me driving away in his car. 'Hey!'

He ran towards me, but I managed to get past before he could block my escape. I turned left and headed out of the city, towards the dual carriageway where I headed south. Once I was sure he wasn't coming for me, I dared to look at the camera. There were over 7,000 people watching me drive away in a stolen car.

If anyone worked out who I was, there was no way I'd be able to stay out of trouble. However, I didn't let myself think about that. As I slowed and headed out through Hampton towards the quieter villages south of the city, I heard my phone ping — PayPal telling me £5,000 had just been deposited.

I didn't know where I was heading. I didn't know what I would do with the car when I stopped, but I did know I needed to get off the beaten track. I needed to hide away, if only long enough to compose my thoughts.

I could think of only one place. When I was young, when Mum was alive, we would often go to a small woodland area in the village of Holme. It was always so peaceful, so quiet.

The only people who used the road that led to it were those visiting the woods. At night, no one would be there. I would be safe, if only for a while.

Looking at my screen once more, I saw there were almost 10,000 people watching now, 10,000 people enjoying the crime I had committed. I almost said something about it, but knew if I did, I would alienate the people I needed, Sam needed.

'That was wild,' I said instead, faking that I was enjoying myself for them. 'I'm gonna go off-grid now, but keep the dares coming. See you soon, watchers.'

Ending the livestream, I put my phone down and focused on the road ahead.

'Shit, Cassie, what are you doing?' I said as the tarmac rushed past.

CHAPTER TWENTY-SEVEN

Jamison

Jamison sipped his wine, a 2018 Châteauneuf-du-Pape, and allowed himself to daydream of what his life would be like in just a month. For thirty years he had slogged, taken the shit that comes with crafting a career, and for what? A divorce, two adult children who came over once every few weeks and always took their mum's side. An empty house with no personality of its own and shitty neighbours. He had tried to do the right thing once, be a good person. But in this world, the good get shit on from a great height.

Soon, the divorce and shitty neighbours wouldn't matter. He would be in Greece, sipping on scotch, and watching the money roll in. He'd spend it on women who only wanted him for the cash and he wouldn't care less. He thought about how he would see out his days: spending, drinking, fucking. Anonymous, happy and without a care in the world. His boys would visit, enjoy the high life. His ex-wife could die for all he cared.

He allowed himself to smile, thinking about the look on her face when she realised he'd won life's lottery.

He took another sip. This time the wine tasted smoother. His phone vibrated on the coffee table, and looking down, he saw it was Harry.

Picking it up, he smiled. 'Harry, spoken to the girl? This your farewell call?'

'We have a problem,' Harry said.

Jamison sat forward on the sofa and put down his wine. 'What do you mean "we have a problem"?' His tone was no longer light and inviting.

'A light in the girl's house was flicking on and off, so I went to find out what was happening, and I left the keys in the car and—'

'Harry, get to the fucking point. What do you mean "we have a problem"?'

'Boss, some little fucker has taken the car.'

'What do you mean?'

'I was gone for, like, less than a minute, and some fucker stole the car.'

'What about the USB?'

'It's on my car keys, in the car.'

'Fuck! Fuck!' Jamison shouted, picking up his wine glass and throwing it against the wall. Crimson splashed across the neutral paintwork like a piece of modern art. 'What the fuck were you thinking?'

'Boss, I fucked up. I'll fix it.'

'Why didn't you keep it with you?' Jamison said, his voice growing quiet, his rage seething.

'The lights were flickering, I didn't know what was going on. You said to find the girl, to make sure she stayed quiet.'

'The whole point of all this is for what is on that memory stick. We've worked on this for years, Harry — what the fuck were you thinking?'

'Boss, I know, I know. I'll fix it. I'll get it back.'

'You'd better, Harry. If anyone looks on the memory stick, we are fucked. Where did they go?'

'I don't know, boss, they just took it.'

'I cannot stress enough the importance of finding that USB.'

'I know, boss. I'll make it right.'

'You'd fucking better.'

Jamison hung up the phone and paced his living room. The daydreams of hot young women and a big 'fuck you' to his ex-wife were vanishing faster than a rock dropped into dark water. Installed on the USB was software that sent a notification when the USB was accessed. It hadn't pinged, so whoever had it hadn't opened it yet, which offered small solace. If the information on there made its way to the police it would bring all his dreams, his years of hard work, crumbling down. Harry had said he would get it back, but without involving the police, which wasn't an option, he wasn't sure how. Still, Harry would fix it. He had no choice.

'Just a blip,' he said to himself, walking into the kitchen to get a fresh glass of wine. 'Just a blip.'

He poured the rest of the bottle, this time drinking to calm himself rather than find pleasure. His phone rang again, and he snapped it up without looking at the caller ID.

'Harry?'

'It's Mike.'

'It's not a good time, mate.'

'Boss, has Harry called?'

'Yeah.'

'His car's been nicked, hasn't it?'

'Did he call you?'

'No.'

'Then how do you know?'

'Have you heard of DareMe?'

'Yeah, what about it?'

'I just watched a black Range get pinched, thought it looked like his.'

Jamison went to the DareMe app. He typed in the search bar 'stolen car' and, sure enough, there was a video posted not long ago by someone calling themselves KJ74. He loaded the video and watched as the girl in the yellow hat drove away in Harry's car.

He needed it back and quickly. He had an idea of how he could get other people to do the work for him.

'Boss, are you still there? What do you want me to do?'

'Stay watching the kid. I've got an idea. We'll get help finding the car.'

'How?'

'We'll dare people to do it.'

Jamison hung up and took a long drink of his wine. He was confident that, for a few quid, someone would find the car for him, and it would be sorted before any issues arose. Harry had still fucked up though.

Harry had to be reprimanded for his carelessness. He couldn't be forgiven. Not in this world. Forgiveness made you weak.

CHAPTER TWENTY-EIGHT

£9,650 raised

By the time I arrived at the narrow single-track road that ran parallel to Holme Fen, I was a wreck. The lane was in complete darkness. Only when the thick clouds overhead parted did the moon come through and cast the forest in a haunting silvery glow. In the summer, Holme Woods was a haven, a safe and wonderful ancient space that breathed deeply along with you. It was calming, centring. The forest was kind. In winter, it was eerie, too quiet, too lifeless. It was like the woodland had been sucked into a timeless void. Life seemingly gone. At night, it was something terrifying. It was the place where the monsters from our childhood hid, waiting for that moment to pounce. But as scary as it felt, I knew I wouldn't be found.

Turning on the interior light, I reached for the file with Sam's name on and opened it. Inside was everything about my brother — his name, age, bank details, with statements attached. They knew his job, our address, they knew his ex-girlfriends and people he hung out with. They knew more about Sam than I did. Turning the next page, I saw my name. They knew everything about me too. The file felt hot in my hands. They had it all. Even things about Mum.

Sam, who have you got yourself mixed up with?

These weren't just ordinary criminals. They were connected. They had our entire lives in a file, everything, and I didn't know how that was possible.

And I had just stolen their car.

The only thing I could do to end this was get the money. If I left the car, they would find it, and they would never link it back to me. KJ74 did the dare, not me. KJ was daring, brave, famous. I was just boring old Cassie Jones who jumped when her morning alarm sounded.

I needed to be seen so I could stay above suspicion. As a new plan began to form, I looked on DareMe, and saw an open challenge that featured my name. I tapped it and read.

Welcome, player KJ74
Your DareMe challenge:
Find KJ74, and get the car back (£2,000)
You have 2 hours remaining.
Do you accept?

There was £2,000 up for grabs for a DareMe player who found me and the car in the next two hours.

Then, my inbox pinged, and I saw a closed challenge just for me.

Welcome, player KJ74
Your DareMe challenge:
Do not let yourself or the car be caught (£2,000)
You have 2 hours remaining.
Do you accept?

It was a game of hide and seek. I didn't have a choice. I didn't want them to find me so I hit 'accept'. I wanted to know who had that kind of money to throw away watching games, but it wasn't the time. DareMe was wild. People were swept up in it and, for some, money didn't matter.

I stopped myself wondering. I had a job to do — I had to disappear. However, the rules were I had to livestream. So, putting on my hat and mask, I took a deep breath, and began recording.

'This is KJ74. Just hiding out. I'll be back at the end of the challenge as I don't want any of you finding me. See you soon.'

I hit 'end stream'. I hoped it sounded like I was having fun with this new game of cat and mouse, but really it was anything but. I was tired, afraid, and now that other DareMe players were looking for me, I was frightened that players and watchers of DareMe would all soon know who KJ74 really was. Even though I was quite isolated, it would only take someone to know this was a good hiding spot or recognise the trees behind me for them to know where to come. I needed to be more discreet.

Firing up the car, I drove slowly along the lane and looked for somewhere to hide. The road felt endless, but I knew there was a small group of houses ahead, and beyond that the main road led to a village. I didn't want to get that far, so when I saw a gap in the trees big enough, I pulled the car off road and drove into the woods.

Once I was far enough in, I got out. I grabbed fallen branches and tried as best I could to hide it. It was difficult as all the fallen branches were leafless, but the car was black and the night was complete, and I reasoned that, unless someone literally walked into the woods, they would not see the car, not even from the road. But I didn't want to take any chances. The people Sam owed might have set the dare to find me. To flush me out. They would likely know I had stolen the car — thousands had watched me take it. They had an incentive to find KJ74 as they needed their car back. If they succeeded, they would learn KJ74 was me. Then both Sam and I would pay.

I could ride out two hours. After that, I didn't know what would happen, but I could ride out two hours. I locked the car, kept the keys firmly in my hand.

I wanted to stay with the car, where it was safer, but the car would be easier to spot if someone came across me, so I moved further into the dark woodland. I sat and waited, one eye on the road, one eye on my phone, counting down the time.

It didn't take long for the cold to set into my bones, making me shiver so much I thought I was going to be sick. But I didn't dare move. After ninety minutes in one position, I wasn't sure I could walk if I needed to. I still didn't move.

Each rustle in the woods sent my senses into overdrive. I tried to look into the darkness, to see something, but there was no light pollution and the clouds had thickened, blocking out the moon. It was pitch black. And in the darkness, the monsters loomed. My mistakes and regrets manifested as shadows that morphed and moved silently. I closed my eyes so tight it hurt, making them vanish.

'Yeah, piss off.'

I looked at my phone. There were only ten minutes left. I began to let myself think I had succeeded. I had added another two grand to my target. Just as that thought had settled and relief was beginning to flood through me, I saw car lights. I hoped it was for one of the few houses further along, but the car was driving too slowly. It was like they were scanning, looking for me.

Someone had worked out where I was, and when a beam of torch light shone directly into my face, I knew I was in trouble.

'There she is,' a voice called, followed by a whoop from who I assumed was the driver.

I stood up, the effort hurting like hell in my cold and seized-up muscles, and began to run. The dare wasn't to not be seen. It was just not to get caught. Reaching the car, I unlocked it and jumped in. Firing up the engine I put my foot down and the car pushed through the makeshift camouflage and rumbled onto the road.

I didn't dare look back. The road was so narrow, so dark and, in the beast of a car I was in, I was sure at any minute

I'd lose it in a ditch. But I needed to stream, so I set up my DareMe and glanced towards the camera as I drove.

'Shit. Someone found me,' was all I managed to say, knowing I needed to entertain somehow. But I was unable to give any more attention to the phone, as I was so scared of crashing.

I reached the end of the lane and the main road, I turned right and continued to drive as fast as I could handle. Another turning took me out into the fens, endless flat roads and land that stretched as far as the eye could see. It didn't help me hide, but with clear and long roads I could push the Range Rover further and, hopefully, lose my tail. However, whoever was driving was braver than me, and they gained. They were so close I could see the woman driving. Then the Range Rover lurched, and I wasn't sure why. It lurched again, and I realised she was ramming me.

'What the fuck!'

I looked at the phone screen. 14,500 people were watching.

She rammed again, this time so hard the back end of the car swung to one side, the tyres screeching with the friction, and I had to fight to stop the car from spinning. It was exactly like that night with Mum, and I was sure the car was about to roll. I managed to correct it before I crashed. Then, I put my foot down harder.

My phone began to ring. It was an unknown number. It could be Sam, or Mia, but it also could be Wakelin or Jamison, so I didn't answer. I was streaming, and I didn't want anyone to work out who I was.

The phone rang again, and again I hung up. I pushed on. I glanced at the speedometer. It was pushing almost 100 miles an hour. I should have been losing my pursuer, but whoever it was, they were determined. I couldn't shake them. However, a mile further along, they began flashing their lights at me, and when I looked I saw they were slowing. At first I didn't understand why, until I looked at the DareMe app.

The time had run out. They had failed to complete the dare in time. I had won the challenge.

I slowed too and, seeing that they had come to a stop, I dared to do the same.

Getting out of the car, I looked back at them on the road.

'Nice driving, KJ74!' the woman shouted towards me. 'That was a rush.'

'You could have killed me.'

'But I didn't. I would say sorry for denting your car, but it's not yours anyway.'

I opened my mouth to speak, but no words came.

'We'll get you next time,' she said, laughing and waving towards me.

I waved back, dumbfounded at the fact that what had just happened was nothing more than a bit of fun to her. DareMe was fucked up.

Even though the challenge was over, I needed to get tucked away again. With my hands still shaking, I got in the car and drove off in the direction of the fens, hoping to find somewhere I could ditch it before finding a way home.

Behind me, the car went the other way.

Realising the phone was still streaming, I picked it up, and looked down the camera.

'Another dare complete. I just need a few more, to help who I love. Keep them coming.'

Ending the livestream, I saw I had almost 21,000 followers, and almost 100 closed dares. I hoped that whatever they were, I could do some, and achieve my target. I hoped it would be over soon, and I could give the money to those Sam owed, and they would forget we ever existed.

I hoped.

CHAPTER TWENTY-NINE

£11,650 raised

I rattled through the fens on the endless roads for another ten minutes until I saw an old barn on my left. Slowly I pulled up in front of it. It was dilapidated and empty. It was likely used for sugar beet, or other root vegetables at harvest time but, in the middle of winter, it was unused. The perfect place to hide a car.

Driving right up to it, I stopped and got out, leaving the headlights on so I could see inside. There was an old tractor, a pile of rotting vegetables at the back, but little else. It wouldn't be long before someone found it.

I drove the car inside and tucked it against a wall, hiding it from the road. I turned on the interior light, grabbed my things and climbed out. Realising my prints would be all over it, I tried to wipe down everything I had touched using one of the gloves from my bag. I didn't like it, but what choice did I have? I couldn't keep driving it around and I couldn't give it back. As I cleaned, I opened the glove box, and immediately wished I hadn't.

Inside was a gun, one with a cylinder, like in the old movies.

Who were these people Sam was mixed up with?

Who were these people *I* was mixed up with?

I rounded the car and opened the boot. Inside was a suitcase. I didn't open it. Not after what I'd found in the glove box.

Wiping down the final things I thought I had touched, my phone rang. I was relieved to see it was Mia.

'Cass? Are you OK?'

'Yeah, I am.'

'Where are you?'

'I'd better not say.' I was sounding completely paranoid. 'But I'll message you in a bit. Could you come get me?'

'Yeah, of course. Cass, this is getting out of hand.'

'Only a few more to go, and I'm done.'

'How much do you still need?'

'About seven and a half grand. But I'll get there.'

'Cass, I spoke with my dad. Not about this, no one knows about this. I said I needed to borrow a bit of money. He gave me three grand.'

'What? Mia? No, I can't take that.'

'I've put it in your bank already. Once this is over, you can pay me back, OK? Will that help?'

Putting her on speaker, I logged in to my bank and, sure enough, my current account had almost seven and a half grand in it. The four from the loan, three from my best friend and what was sitting there before.

'Mia. I can't,' I said, my conviction gone, replaced with a wave of grief and joy rolled into one.

'Will it help?' she asked again.

'Yes, it will. Thank you, Mia. I promise I will pay you back.'

'I know you will. Cass, how much do you need now?'

I roughly added it all up. The loan, her kindness, and my DareMe challenges. 'About five.'

'OK.'

I could hear the worry in her voice. She'd hoped I would be closer.

'I've managed, with your help, to get to fourteen and a half in a day. It will be over soon.' I was trying to lift her spirits — and mine.

'Promise?'

'Yeah, I promise.'

'OK, I'm waiting by the phone. Let me know when it's done.'

I hung up and took a moment to compose myself. Then I continued to rid the evidence of me from the car as best I could. I hated that Mia had given me so much money. But, I reasoned, if it was her in this mess, I would have done the same. I once thought my family consisted of only me and Sam, but really, Mia was family too.

My phone pinged again. It was DareMe, telling me my inbox had over 150 dares in it and asking if I wanted to look. I tapped it open and scrolled through. The dares were now reckless — someone was daring me to rob an ex's house. Another dared me to attack a stranger. Someone wanted me to hurt an animal. Someone wanted me to murder a parent.

People were sick. I couldn't wait to become anonymous again.

As I scrolled, despairing at the state of the world, only one dare leaped out at me. It was for five grand, and it was connected to what I had just done. It was wrong, illegal, but most things in the app now were, and for this one no one would get hurt. No one would be traumatised. No one would be a direct victim. I felt sick knowing that, despite it being awful, criminal, and immoral, I had fully validated it in my own head.

Getting back into the car, realising it was pointless me trying to wipe it down, I drove out of the barn, and headed in the direction of the nearest town. I wanted to do the dare where I was, but then I would be stuck in the middle of nowhere. I needed to get home after.

On the outskirts of Ramsey, a good half an hour's drive from Peterborough, I found a supermarket car park and parked the Range Rover at the furthest corner from the store.

I killed the engine, took out the keys. And for a moment sat in silence. Was I really about to do this? I checked there were no nearby trees, I checked the direction of the wind, and, satisfied it would be OK and I wouldn't cause more damage than necessary, I readied myself for the next dare. Thanks to Mia, this would be the last one I would need to do.

And then I would transfer the money from PayPal to my bank account, and my brother would be safe, and I would get my life back.

CHAPTER THIRTY

£14,650 raised

With the livestream running, I looked once more at the dare I was about to accept. It was the dare to end all dares.

> *Welcome, player KJ74*
> *Your DareMe challenge:*
> *Set fire to the car (£5,000)*
> *You have 30 minutes remaining.*
> *Do you accept?*

 I hoped by reading it again, I would find a loophole. I had intended to return the car. Like when I stole the saw, to absolve myself from the guilt of being a thief. These words were hard to interpretate any other way. I had to torch it. I could try to set it on fire, and put it out, but again, like in the museum, I didn't want to fail on a technicality. The car had to burn.
 There was one problem. I needed a spark and an accelerant. The interior needed to burn until the flames reached the fuel, which would take care of the rest. I had neither — I didn't even have a lighter. So, going back to the car, I rummaged around, trying to find something.

When I looked in the glove box again, seeing the gun for the second time was no less terrifying. I pulled it out and dropped it on the seat. With the gun out of the way, I saw a zippo lighter in the glove box and considered whether to pull it out. I felt mixed. Without the lighter, I wouldn't be able to torch the car. It would be found and I'd probably get away with stealing. But having the lighter meant I could burn it, and I had no doubt the owner would come for KJ74 and want her dead. Burning it would also mean I was done. Sam would be out of debt. Between the money I had borrowed from the bank, Mia and the DareMe challenges, this would be over. Sam needed me to end this.

As I got out of the car, I looked at the gun. Soon, the police would come. They would find the gun, and they would know KJ74 had stolen the car. I had to hope they didn't link me to it or think that KJ was the owner. Part of me knew I should pick the gun up, keep it with me until I could find a better way to dispose of it, but I couldn't. I just couldn't. I wiped it down with my sleeve and put it back in the glove box.

I picked up a few dead, dried-out branches and twigs from the green area that lined the car park and put them in the passenger footwell. I then accepted the dare, and began the livestream.

'This is KJ74, and I know this is wrong, really wrong, but I am doing it for the right reasons. I cannot condone my actions. Nor should anyone copy this. What I am about to do, what I have done, is terrible. I just hope people understand.'

Putting the phone down against a kerb so I could be seen, I knelt down, sparked the lighter and watched as the dead leaves caught, then the twigs, then the branches, until flames licked the car's interior. I stepped back and filmed the car glowing brighter and brighter as the flames grew in strength, until the bonnet was totally consumed by fire.

Turning the camera so I could be seen in front of the car, I spoke. My words, thick with regret for my actions, and relief that this was the last thing I had to do. 'Dare com—'

I was cut off by a cracking sound, sharp and loud. At first I didn't know what it was, then it cracked again and glass exploded. It sounded like a banger, those awful cheap fireworks kids throw around on bonfire night, but when I heard a third crack, followed by the sound of metal being punctured, I realised it was the gun going off. Lowering my head, I ran. More cracks sounded and I dropped to the ground and rolled into the treeline. The cracking happened twice more, and then, as the car became an inferno, it stopped.

I looked at the camera. Almost 40,000 people had just seen that happen.

'Shit, shit that was close. Dare complete.'

I ended the livestream and, before anyone could see me, I ran away from the car, heading for the town centre. And even though Mia had said to call her, I couldn't. As soon as I found a taxi rank, I got in and asked the driver to take me home, and as he did, trying his best to make small talk, I looked out and saw an orange hue in the sky. The fire I had caused, marking the night.

Just as the guilt set in, just as I was about to cry, my phone pinged twice — DareMe congratulating me on the challenge, and then PayPal, telling me five grand had just been deposited. I requested the transfer, which would happen within thirty minutes for a fee which I happily paid, and then I wanted to cry all over again, for a very different reason.

It was over. I had enough to repay Sam's debt.

And KJ74 would vanish. For ever.

CHAPTER THIRTY-ONE

Jamison

Jamison threw stones into the river and watched a homeless man wander along the other side of the bank, mumbling to himself. The only thing Jamison could clearly understand in the slur of words were punctuated expletives. Fuck. Wanker. Beyond that, he could hear the sound of the city. People, noise, the occasional siren.

He smiled, enjoying the spectacle, appreciating the nice distraction. There was something about watching someone on the fringe of society, broken by life, that was therapeutic. It could happen to anyone, at any time. Even him. But fate had dealt him another hand, one of riches, decadence. Loose women in tight dresses. As the homeless man paused to swipe at nothing in the air, trying to swat whatever demon or imp that tormented him, Jamison picked up another stone, a larger one that was the same size as his palm. He didn't throw it this time but held on. He would throw it soon enough.

As the tramp wandered off, his voice trailing into nothing, Jamison's mind switched back to the problem in hand. The fucking girl and his USB. Jamison had watched on DareMe after posting the dare to catch KJ74. He didn't expect someone to counter the dare and make it a game. His plan had failed. He had underestimated how resourceful she was. Now the car had been torched and there was no good outcome from that. Either the USB had been incinerated with the car, and all that valuable information was lost for ever, or she had kept it and could still open it. If she did, she could go to the police and jeopardise everything. If Harry had found her as he said he would, if he hadn't been so fucking stupid in the first place, Jamison wouldn't have the headache that now pressed into the back of his eyes, squeezing into a migraine.

As soon as Harry came back to his mind, he heard a cough. The man himself was walking in his direction. Jamison had told him to meet him down by the old mill. Looking at his watch, he smiled. Harry was on time. He'd fucked up, but he was always on time.

'Harry?' Jamison said, when his subordinate joined his side.

'Boss.'

'I need an update.'

'The USB hasn't been opened. But she might have it still. I'll find her, boss. She was at Holme Fen, and the car was torched near Ramsey. I'll get her.'

Jamison held his eye and could see that Harry truly believed he would. He nodded. Then he pulled out a packet of cigarettes, bit one and drew it from the packet, then offered one to Harry. He lit his first, then held the lighter Harry's way.

'Thanks,' Harry said. 'Look, boss, I'm sorry about this stress. I'll sort it.'

'It's OK,' Jamison said, as Harry took a deep drag on the cigarette, the flame lighting its end. As he exhaled, Jamison swung his hand that still held the large stone, and it caught Harry on the side of his temple, sending him crashing to the ground with a dull thud.

Harry moaned. He wasn't quite unconscious, and Jamison dropped on top of him, hitting him once more, this time in the middle of his forehead. It knocked him out cold.

Jamison dragged Harry to the edge of the water and then, grabbing more large stones, like the one he had just bludgeoned Harry with, he stuffed them inside his friend's coat pockets. He filled them up and rolled him into the river.

The splash was drowned out by the orchestra of the city night. There was nothing to suggest anything had happened. Harry simply sank, vanishing into the inky black water.

Jamison sniffed, smoked more of his cigarette. Without giving it a second thought, he walked away.

Forgiveness made you weak.

Harry had paid his dues.

Now, KJ74 needed to do the same.

CHAPTER THIRTY-TWO

£19,650 raised

I had one more thing to do, and then it was all over. Going to my messages I sent one to the man Sam owed.

I have the money, how do I pay Sam's debt?

I didn't want to engage them in small talk. I didn't want them to ask questions. All I wanted was to pay them then disappear from their radar, for ever. I hoped that they would see it immediately and message back. But they didn't reply.

I rang my brother.

'Hey, how are you feeling?' I asked.

'I'm OK,' he said.

'Sam?'

'They have to do another operation on my hand, try and get it working a bit better.'

'When?'

'Tomorrow morning.'

'I'll be there.'

'Thanks, Cass.'

'Sam, I have some news.'

Sam paused, no doubt worried for what I was about to say, so I didn't linger. 'I have it. I have the money.'

'What? How much?'

'All of it.'

'Cass, how the hell . . .'

'It doesn't matter. I've messaged them, asking how they want to collect it. It's over, Sam. It's done.'

My brother began to cry, and, hearing him cry, I too burst into tears.

'Thank you, Cass. Thank you. You've saved my life.'

I struggled to speak after hearing that.

After we'd both calmed down, I told him I loved him, and that I was coming to see him. It wasn't visiting hours, but I didn't care. I wanted to hug my brother.

Instead of going home, the taxi dropped me off in the city, and from there I got a bus. I could have got the cab to take me all the way in, but the driver had insisted on trying to chat and I'd felt my anxiety climb. I needed air, a little time to compose myself before seeing Sam. I had stolen a car, found a gun, committed arson. I smelled of smoke and looked like shit. I needed the thrum of a bus journey to calm me.

It had been a shitty few days. The worst since Mum died by far, and, despite the things I had done, I smiled to myself. Everything I had done was so unlike me.

The heating from the bus warmed my feet, and I couldn't help feeling pleased. I had done it — I had proven I could look after someone I love. It wouldn't vindicate my crimes, my mistakes, but it did show me I could be a stronger person than I once was.

My smile didn't last long. My phone buzzed with a message from Mia. I felt my stomach lurch.

Cass, where are you? Have you seen DareMe?

No? Why?

There is a new open dare. Seems you're now really famous. And you've pissed someone off. I'd keep a low profile for a while. Cass, I'm scared.

I looked in my inbox on the DareMe app. There was nothing that stood out. I then went to the open dares and was shocked to see someone had posted a dare for £10,000. Then I read what the dare was, and I nearly threw up.

Welcome, player KJ74
Your DareMe challenge:
Find and livestream the exact location of KJ74 (£10,000)
You have 1 hour remaining.
Do you accept?

CHAPTER THIRTY-THREE

I knew exactly what was happening. The man who had attacked my brother, the man whose car I'd stolen and then torched wanted me. No — he wanted KJ74 so he could make her pay. He had come close with the car chase but now serious money was at stake. Ten grand? It seemed excessive. They were willing to give away over half of what my brother owed, just to catch me? And even though I was confident that KJ74 couldn't be linked to me, it still sent a shiver up my spine. Sam had taken a beating, had had his hand broken. I had no idea what they would do to me.

As I stared at the screen, I became aware that the person to my left was also staring at theirs, watching DareMe, and, noticing I was watching also, he smiled. 'You been seeing this?'

'Yeah. It's wild,' I said.

'KJ74 is an animal but, man, she has messed with the wrong people.'

'Yeah.'

'Would be the easiest ten grand anyone could ever make.'

'How do you mean?' I asked.

'They only want a location. Whoever finds KJ74, doesn't have to do anything but watch, stream in where they are, and wait to get paid.'

'But, it's pretty clear they want to hurt her,' I said. 'People like KJ74.'

'People like money a whole lot more.'

'I don't think I could do it,' I said.

'I know I could, in a heartbeat.'

He laughed, and I laughed too, but inside I wanted to cry. Putting my phone away, I turned to look out of the window, watching the street roll by. The bus came to a stop and a woman got on. She too was on her phone. She could have been texting, or watching memes, or any number of other things. However, as she sat down in front of me, I could see DareMe was open on her screen.

I tried to keep my cool and remain composed, but as I returned to looking out of the window, it reflected back into the bus, and I could see the man who had said he would take the ten grand looking at me. I tried to look like I wasn't aware, and opened my rucksack. In it was the Victorian surgical saw I hadn't yet managed to return to the museum. If the man tried to grab me, I would hit him with it. Beside the saw was the folder with all the details of me and Sam. I gripped the saw and looked at the man through the reflection. He was engrossed in his phone, but I could feel him watching. His body was twisted towards me, his head down, but I sensed he was looking at me out of his peripheral. I needed to leave.

Trying to remain neutral, I pressed the button to alert the driver I wanted to alight and, when the bus began to slow for the next stop, I stood, flashed a half-smile to try and seem calmer than I was, and got off the bus. As it pulled away, the man watched until he disappeared on with his journey.

'Shit.'

Despite living in Peterborough all my life, I didn't know exactly where I was. The hospital was close by, maybe a mile or a mile and a half away, but I knew I couldn't go to Sam. If someone managed to find out I was KJ74, Sam would be punished for it. I needed to keep a low profile. Walking with my head down, I passed people on the street. Some of them were on their phones, their faces lit up like Frankenstein's monster. Any one of them could be looking for KJ74 — anybody could be searching for me. I had to find somewhere to lie low until the hour ran out. I needed time to think.

Ahead, I could see a pub. As I drew closer, I realised it was a working men's club. It was one of the few remaining in the city and its patrons were all older people. I reasoned that it was unlikely any of them would be on DareMe. It was safer than walking alone on the streets. So, taking a deep breath, I opened the door and walked in.

People stared as I entered. I understood why. A young woman walking in on her own was possibly a rare sight, but nobody bothered me. They quickly returned to their loud conversations.

Approaching the bar, I smiled to the bartender, who smiled back while chewing gum.

'Can I have a glass of white wine, please?'

'Sure thing,' she said, grabbing a bottle from the fridge.

After I paid, I found a table in the corner, where I could watch the room, and quietly sipped, watching the DareMe timer count down. Just over half an hour to go. Then, my bank app notified me the money from PayPal had successfully landed in my account. I wanted it gone, it felt dirty.

Halfway through my glass, my phone pinged. It was from the man Sam owed, the same man who was likely now hunting me through the DareMe app. I opened the message, and it had four different bank account numbers and sort codes. Beside each one, a specific amount to deposit. The total, £19,000. I took a screenshot of the account details and set up the transfers. It took me fifteen minutes to confirm it all, and after, I messaged one word.

Done.

The message came back from them shortly after, telling me it was finished. Sam's debt had been paid, and it was over. Knowing my brother would be OK, I began to cry, my head turned to the window so no one could see. The mess Sam was in, I had fixed. Now, I just had to get myself out of the mess *I* was in.

It wouldn't be so hard. I had created KJ74. I could uncreate her too. I would wait out the remaining time on the dare, leave this pub, bin the hat and face masks, and then I would delete the DareMe app and pretend none of this had ever happened. I would go back to being boring, quiet, cut-off Cassie Jones. I would go back to work, watch box sets in the evenings, maybe go out on a date every now and then. I would return to quiet drinks with my friends and my biggest stress would be Sam eating us out of house and home and not replacing the food.

And I couldn't wait for it all.

My wine tasted better than before the debt was cleared. I slowly finished my glass, watching the timer tick away. I counted with it in the final few seconds.

Three, two, one.

It was over. The dare was off. Now, KJ74 had to vanish.

Feeling relieved and, consequently, exhausted, I realised there was one more thing I had to do. I had made a mess of it with the police. I had to talk to Wakelin. So, listening to the voicemail he left again, I made a note of his number and fired off a text.

Detective Wakelin. It's Cassie Jones. I'm sorry I've been avoiding you. I'm ready to talk.

Hitting 'send', I tried to come up with a reasonable explanation of how I had managed to raise Sam's debt in such a short time without incriminating myself as someone who had committed criminal acts. If I told them of the debt, I would have to show my bank account, and they would link me back to KJ74. I needed another reason for my silence, my hiding from Wakelin, and for why we didn't need to worry anymore.

But the more I thought about it, the more I knew there would be no way of digging myself out of this. Wakelin would find out what I did, what I had to do. I would have to face the law for it.

I needed another drink.

Getting my second glass, I sat back in my chair. My phone, upside down on the table, began to ping with one message after another. It vibrated again and again. Someone was trying to reach me in a hurry. I assumed it was Wakelin, but when I picked it up and turned it over more messages pinged across all of my socials.

The phone rang again and I snatched it up.

'Mia?'

'Cass. Shit, oh, Cass,' Mia said, her voice tight, afraid. She sounded so panicked that my heart rate leaped.

'It's OK, it's over. I've paid Sam's debt, the DareMe is off,' I said, hoping her voice sounded the way it did because of anxiety over what I was doing. 'I'm done with it. I'm going to delete it all now.'

'You need to look, Cass. You need to run.'

'What? Why? What's going on?'

'Just look.'

'At what?'

'DareMe.'

'OK, OK.'

Keeping Mia on the line, I went back into the app. I must have gasped or choked or something, because people turned around to look at me.

'Oh, God,' I said.

'Cass, get to the police. Get help.'

Mia didn't say she would come to me. She didn't offer to help me, and I understood why. She was afraid.

I was too. I thought about what the man on the bus had said about what he would do for ten grand. I knew someone would accept the new dare. Most people, I'd like to think, wouldn't. Most people were good, and knew that there was a line that couldn't be crossed. Most, but not all — and it only took one.

Welcome, player KJ74
Your DareMe challenge:
Kill player KJ74 (£100,000)
You have 5 hours remaining.
Do you accept?

PART TWO

CHAPTER THIRTY-FOUR

Wakelin
9.32 p.m. — 4 hours and 58 minutes remaining

Wakelin tried to call back Cassie Jones three times. Each time it went to voicemail. He didn't know what to make of her message. She seemed ready to talk, and yet, was now avoiding him. But that had to wait. The Range Rover beside him was still smouldering, long after the firefighters had finished putting out the flames. The ruin of the car matched the description of the Range Rover that was linked to the serious assault of Sam Jones. Yet, as he watched dark smoke rise into the sky, he couldn't connect the dots. There were many old black Range Rovers, but his instinct told him this one was their one.

When he had been instructed to take on the case by his DI, Wakelin had been less than pleased. An assault was hardly something he was jumping at the chance to solve. But the DI was the DI, well respected, long serving and Wakelin's friend. So, he accepted it without complaint. Even though it would be a waste of his time. The city was rough. Young men got a beating all the time. He had reasoned the lad would be OK. In all likelihood it was to do with drugs, and no one would speak. With budget cuts and rising crime in recent years, most small crimes cases were dismissed after the initial investigation. It wasn't right, but it was what it was. It presented as a mundane case. However, he trusted his gut, and the way the poor boy had been re-assaulted, as well as the sister's apparent knowing of the truth meant it was anything but the dull file he first read.

The kid had been hurt, taught a lesson for whatever stupid thing he was mixed up in. That should have been the end of it, but the kid had been hurt again, and the suspected car that was identified as being connected to the initial attack had been torched. It couldn't be a coincidence. Wakelin had been in the game for too long. Coincidences didn't exist. Something else was going on. Something bigger than what had first been presented to him.

And still Cassie, who had lied about being at home, who knew about the car and had failed to tell him, wasn't returning his calls despite her apparent readiness to talk. His gut told him she knew what was going on with her brother, and he wondered if she was trying to protect him. She fitted into all this somehow, but he couldn't work it out. He'd done some digging on her. A tragic past but, aside from that, her life was unremarkable. Vanilla. Cassie Jones was not a woman who avoided the police and, yet, she had.

Watching the car smoulder wasn't going to help. Wakelin turned to leave the crime scene, entrusting PCs to deal with the clean-up of the wreck. He would return to the station and talk it over with his DI. As he made his way back to his car, a young officer stopped him.

'DS Wakelin?' the PC asked.

Wakelin had to look at his shoulder to get his name. 'Yes, Peters?'

'Sir, I think you need to take a look at this.'

The young PC handed over a mobile phone and, showing his annoyance at the cryptic way it was handed over, Wakelin pulled out his glasses so he could focus on the screen. On it was an app, one he didn't know, but then, he didn't know any of them anymore.

'What am I looking at?'

'DareMe,' Peters replied.

'The thing we were briefed about last week?'

'Yeah, have you seen what's happening on it?'

'Let's pretend I'm too tired and too old to even have the faintest idea how to watch it,' Wakelin said.

'Yes, sorry, sir. There is a player called KJ74.'

'What about him?'

'Her.'

'Her, what about her?'

'She is the one who torched the car.'

'What?' Wakelin asked. 'Who is KJ74?'

'We don't know. The app protects people's identity.'

'How do you know this KJ74 torched the car?'

'Here.' Peters pointed to the screen. 'Press play.'

Whereas before, Wakelin was annoyed and uninterested, now he was fixated on the phone's screen. A video sprung to life.

'This is KJ74, and I know this is wrong, really wrong, but I am doing it for the right reasons. I cannot condone my actions. Nor should anyone copy this. What I am about to do, what I have done, is terrible. I just hope people understand.'

Wakelin watched as the woman wearing a bright yellow beanie and black face mask set fire to the car and filmed it burning. He watched as she had to dive for cover as the cracks of bullets discharged in the flames, before the livestream ended. Once it had, he looked up at Peters.

'That sounded like gunshots.'

'Yeah, it did.'

Handing back the phone, Wakelin moved towards the car and, despite it still smouldering away, covered his mouth and nose and looked inside. The glove box hung limply open, most of it melted, but he was sure he could see a hole in the side of it. He wanted to reach in and see if there was in fact a firearm in the car, but it was still too hot to touch.

'Someone get me a stick,' he called, and Peters arrived by his side with a stick in hand.

'Should we wait for Forensics?' Peters asked.

Wakelin didn't reply. He poked the stick inside the glove box and felt something heavy. He twisted the stick, trying to hook the heavy object. After a few attempts, he managed to move it just enough to see the handle of a revolver. He didn't pull it out. Seeing it was enough for him to determine there was indeed a gun in the Range Rover.

'Get this car cooled down, and get Forensics to look at that gun,' he said. 'Ring me once you have it.'

'You're leaving?' Peters said in surprise. A gun was something a DS would usually hang around for.

'I think, the people who owned this car badly injured a lad, and now we have proof they carry firearms. I need to find out who they are, and also who this KJ74 is. If they find her before me, someone is going to die.'

Wakelin turned on his heels and began marching back to his car. He pulled out his phone. His shift was due to end, but he knew he wouldn't go home. He rang Jen, his wife, who picked up on the third ring.

'Hey, love,' he said. His apologetic tones were enough to relay what he was calling to say.

'Late one?' Jen said.

'Yeah.'

'You're OK though, right?'

'Yeah, I think so. Weird one with this thing called DareMe.'

'Let me guess, KJ74.'

Wakelin stopped in his tracks. 'Yeah, how did you—'

'Because everyone is talking about it.'

'Really? It's only a car.'

'A car? Greg, have you not seen?'

'What?'

'Someone wants her dead.'

'What?'

'A dare has been put on, a hundred grand for her dead.'

Wakelin looked back at Peters, whose face was white. He had just seen it on his phone too.

'I gotta go. Don't leave the house tonight, OK? Ring Tom, tell him to stay in.'

'Tom? His uni's like a hundred miles away.'

'If there is a bounty on that girl's life, there is going to be chaos. Ring our boy, tell him to stay in. Tell him if he goes out anywhere, I'll arrest him myself.'

'You think it's gonna get bad?'

'I think people only need an excuse to kick off. There will be riots. It feels like London in 2011, and that spread everywhere.'

'That was a long time ago.'

'It was, but now, young people are struggling even more, and are more pissed off. A spark can cause a fire. I think this is that spark. I hope I'm wrong. But, tell our boy to stay in tonight. Don't answer the door to anyone. I gotta go.'

'Be safe.'

Wakelin hung up and walked back towards Peters.

'Sir, I—' he began.

'I've just heard. Let me see.'

Peters showed Wakelin the screen. Wakelin pulled his glasses out once more, and, sure enough, there was a massive amount of money staked on the girl's life.

'How do we get this taken down?' Wakelin asked.

'I — I don't know,' Peters said. 'I guess the DareMaker—'

'DareMaker?'

'The one who set the challenge — I guess they could stop it.'

'What about the one who set this up, that Zuckerberg fella?'

'It's not his.'

'Then whose is it?'

'I don't know. I'm not sure anyone does.'

'Find out.' Wakelin paused and looked at his watch. 'Just under five hours. That takes us to about 2.30 a.m.'

Without saying any more, he walked to his car. Before he got in, he turned back to the now bewildered police officer. 'Peters?'

152

'Yes, sir.'

'What do you think she means when she said she was doing it for the right reasons?'

'I don't know.'

'Yeah. Yeah,' he said, lost in thought as he closed the car door, fired up the engine and drove away.

Less than five hours to find KJ74 and work out what the hell was going on. As he left the outskirts of town, and headed down the long flat roads, he rang his DI.

'Sir, it's Greg. Something big is going on. I need to have some of your time.'

'Yes, I've just seen. Come now, brief me on where we are. My office is open.'

'I'll be there in twenty minutes.'

Putting his foot down, Wakelin sped towards the office. His phone pinged with a message from Jen.

Spoken to Tom, he will stay in. Be careful, Greg, I'm watching the news. A lot of people are heading out to try and find that poor girl.

CHAPTER THIRTY-FIVE

9.44 p.m. — 4 hours and 46 minutes remaining

I had read and reread the new dare countless times, hoping that it could be interpreted in a different way. My heightened state was seeing something that wasn't true. It was making me more paranoid. But there was no mistaking it, no confusing it. The person who owned that car, the one who'd had my brother beaten, now wanted me dead.

I knew they would be pissed off. Anyone would be if they had their car torched, but cars were insured and no one was hurt. They would get their money back. I had suspected that if they ever caught me, I would get hurt, but to offer £100,000 to have me killed? I didn't understand, and I didn't want to play anymore.

My only saving grace was that no one knew who KJ74 was. No one knew that I was her. They wanted KJ74 to be killed. I could get rid of her for them, without the need for bloodshed. She simply had to disappear.

None of the patrons in the pub had their phones out. No one was looking online. I felt confident that no one knew of the DareMe challenge posted asking for my life. But I still didn't feel safe. I was aware that there was only one clear way in or out. If anyone was playing and decided to kill me, all they would need to do is block the door and I would be stuck. It would only take someone to look inside my bag, see the hat and face masks, and the connection would be made. I needed to burn them all.

The woman who served me my wine wasn't behind the bar anymore. Instead there was a middle-aged, heavy-set man, who, judging by his complexion, clearly smoked. He saw my glass was almost empty and came over my way and asked if I wanted another drink. I said no, and he nodded, but there was something in the way he looked at me. He lingered too long. I could see he wanted to say more, to engage in conversation, and I didn't know why. Maybe he was being polite. Maybe, as I was younger, female and not the usual clientele, he wanted to try and instigate conversation for other reasons. Or maybe, somehow, he knew who I was, and was trying to make sure of my identity before he acted. He might have seen into my bag and spotted the hat. He looked too old for the kind of app DareMe was, but who was I to say at what age you should and shouldn't engage with these things? Maybe he wanted to talk to me to keep me there and had offered me another wine so I wouldn't leave. Maybe he was planning how he would do it. How he would kill me.

I needed to be outside. I needed the night to hide me.

Taking a final sip of my wine, not daring to drink it all as it might go to my head, I thanked the barman, grabbed my bag, and left. As I hit the wintry night air, I looked back into the bar. The man was watching me walk away. When I turned a corner, I broke into a run. I needed to create as much distance as possible from him, from everyone. But despite needing to hide away, I didn't want to be alone.

Taking out my phone, I rang Mia, and the phone rang for so long I was sure she was ignoring it. Then, she picked up.

'Mia. What do I do?'

'Where are you?'

'I'm . . .' I hesitated, hating myself for it. 'I'm not home, but I'm going that way. I'm going to hide away and let this dare run down.'

'Yeah,' was all she said in reply, but in that word I heard the question I was also thinking. This dare might run down, but what then? They could just set a new dare, worded differently. They could keep going and going and going for ever until I was dead.

'Cass?' Mia said when I didn't respond.

'I never meant to get caught up in this.'

'I know.'

'I just wanted to play some stupid games to help my brother.'

'I know,' she said again.

'Mia, what do I do?'

The line went quiet for a long time, so long I was sure she had hung up.

'Mia?'

'You're right, Cass, it's just a game.' She said it in such a way that I knew she had an idea.

'What?'

'It's a game, don't you see? Everyone watching and playing DareMe is playing a game.'

'But my life is hardly a game.'

'Exactly.'

'I don't get it?'

'People forget that social media is real life, people's lives. Christ, DareMe's whole success is because it's like watching a bunch of miniseries.'

'What's your point, Mia?'

'Tell them it's not a game. Show them that you are a real person.'

'I'm not going back on there,' I said. 'I'm done with it.'

'You have to. There is a dare against you. Like it or not, you have to be seen. Do it on your terms, tell them to stop. People will listen.'

I nodded. My attention was drawn to a couple walking towards me. I turned my back to them, but kept my eye on their movements in my peripheral vision. They didn't seem to care I was there, but I held my breath anyway until they had passed.

'You still there?' Mia asked. The couple walked further away, laughing at something the woman had said.

'What if people don't listen?' I asked.

'I . . . I don't know. But it will help. People will be on your side. Post something to your page, go home and, when you get there, tell me and I'll come over.'

'OK,' I said. 'OK.'

Hanging up the phone, I looked for somewhere I could hide and film a video as KJ74 to post on my page. Ahead of me was a housing estate. There would be alleys between houses like most estates built at a certain time in Peterborough. If I could find an alley that looked just like everywhere else, it would be impossible to know where I was and I could post a plea.

I loaded the DareMe app as I crossed the road. Once I was on the other side, I scrolled the timeline, looking at all the stupid shit people were doing to make some money. Mia was right — I was watching it like it was a miniseries. None of it seemed real. As I scrolled, I saw that loads of players, all wearing masks, were livestreaming the hunt for KJ74.

Maybe Mia's idea would work. If I could make KJ74 real, maybe it would all just stop. I still had my face glued to my screen and jumped as I walked straight into the path of an oncoming man. At first glance, he was exactly that, a man, but as I looked at him I realised he was maybe sixteen, at a push.

'Sorry.'

'Nah, it's good, my bad,' he said, then glanced down at my phone. 'You watch DareMe too?'

'Yeah,' I said nervously.

'Have you seen that massive dare for a hundred grand?'

'I have,' I said. I wanted to leave the conversation, but I wanted to see what he thought about it. 'I mean, it's a lot of money, but to kill . . .'

'Easy,' he said quickly. Frighteningly quickly.

'But KJ74 is a real person.'

'And a hundred grand is a real load of money,' he replied.

'I don't think I could do it,' I said.

'Then there is more chance for me — less players playing, odds of winning go up.' He laughed.

I laughed too, but only to hide the fear that was shooting through my body. I wanted to run, but I reminded myself he was talking about KJ74, and I was not her. Not to him. However, his statement dashed my hope. He'd said, 'the odds of winning'. He talked like it was a game, despite me trying to make him understand KJ74 was real, that I was real.

He then pulled out a balaclava and put it on. When he smiled, I feared him.

'I'm gonna go get rich,' he said excitedly as he turned and walked away. He held his phone up as he streamed. 'Yo, this is your boy, Hunter, and just like my name, I'm going for KJ74. Make sure you hit that follow button.'

He then ran off to try and find me.

CHAPTER THIRTY-SIX

9.56 p.m. — 4 hours and 34 minutes remaining

I took a deep breath to steady myself. Despite Hunter's views, Mia was right. I needed to stream. If I was going to get through this, I needed allies. I needed people to speak for me. I needed people to say it was wrong when I couldn't. Hunter was just a kid.

It didn't take me long to find a quiet area I could stream from. I found an alley between two houses that ran from the front of a cul-de-sac to a different street. The houses were mostly lived in by young families with swing sets and trampolines that poked over the top of the six-foot fencing. It was so late, and the dead of winter, that I felt confident no children would be out playing. Families would be in, children in bed, parents watching TV. I quietly pined for a life like that.

But I didn't have time to think about things that could be. I needed to focus. I needed to speak. So, making sure I was alone, I squatted beside a wall and opened my bag. Pulling out the hat and mask, I had one final check before putting them on and, once they were, I felt the clock ticking. I needed to stream, to speak fast and then burn it all.

I went to my DareMe page, where I now had a staggering 94,000 followers. A flashing notification across the top of the app congratulated me on being the most watched DareMe player in the region. I dismissed it, checked my mask was in place properly, and hit 'stream'. The number of people watching leaped into the thousands in seconds, and kept climbing.

'This is KJ74,' I whispered. 'I know I have done wrong by torching that car for money, and I know that, for most of you watching, this is entertaining. I also know that there has been a substantial amount of money, a life-changing amount of money, placed on a dare against me. But this is real life. This isn't a game. Not anymore. Yes, the money is real, but so am I. I am a person, I have a family, a job, I have friends. I enjoy movies and books. I love Spanish food. I am looking for love and one day hope to be a mother. I am real. For all of you watching this, this is not a game, despite how it's being presented to you. I am not a prize, and if you come for me, you will be committing a serious crime. I'm begging, do not engage with the dare. Do not feel tempted because you think you will be anonymous. If you kill me, you will get caught, and you will go to prison, and no amount of money is worth that. I know taking that car was wrong, but it was just a car, no doubt insured and easily replaced. I am a real person. Please, look out for me?'

I ended the recording and, within seconds, comments were being thrown up by people who had watched. Some sent hearts, some said they would never want to hurt me, some said they were going to delete the app altogether. And some called me a bitch, a whore, some said they were excited to hunt me. That I was worthless. That I was better off dead. One even said they would not only kill me, but everyone I loved. And although it sent a shiver up my spine, I dismissed it.

Fucking keyboard warrior.

I wanted to delete the app, vanish but, again, Mia was right; I needed to keep an eye on this until it was over. I exited my post and scrolled the timeline.

Something caught my attention. The video was a livestream. It was dark, the person filming as they walked down a path lit by street lights. In the video, I could see something in the distance, on the ground. As I watched it get closer, I saw a bright yellow hat. Bile rose in my throat as I realised that the thing I was looking at was me, and the person streaming was Hunter.

I snapped a look to my left and saw the shape of the kid at the end of the alley I was squatting in.

'Hey, KJ74,' he said, his voice coming through my phone a second after. 'Mind if we talk?' he added, his voice echoing again because of the delay from real life to the app.

I didn't answer. I jumped up and, before he could advance, bolted. I didn't call for him to stop, I didn't beg. I knew it would be a waste of energy. I just ran as fast as I could, my calf screaming at me to stop because of the dog bite, hoping my relative level of fitness would ensure my survival.

As I ran, I looked at my screen. Hunter was still streaming. I could see myself running away on my phone. He was calling out to me, but I couldn't hear what he was saying. His voice was dulled under the sound of my own heart thumping through my ears. Running out onto the main road, I didn't look back as I darted out in front of a car.

The driver blared his horn as he screeched and swerved to avoid hitting me. He called me a wanker, but I didn't slow down, and I scaled a fence into someone's back garden, hoping there wasn't a dog this time. I ran across a perfectly manicured lawn and into another, knee-deep in grass with rusting bikes. Only when I climbed into a third garden did I dare to look back and listen. I crouched among the dozens of potted plants filling a mostly concrete outdoor space. I couldn't hear him, but that didn't mean he wasn't close. Looking at my phone, I could see from his livestream that he was still on the main road. In the chaos of nearly being hit by a car, he must have lost sight of me. Keeping against the fence, in the shadows, I watched the stream as Hunter ran left down the main road.

I closed my phone, caught my breath for a few moments and then felt my leg throb. I lifted my jeans. The bandage around my wound was crimson. Running had opened up the cut from the dog bite. It hurt like hell, but I didn't have time to fix it. So, rolling down my jeans, I took a deep breath and walked alongside the fence until I found a gate that led me out onto the street.

I removed the mask and hat, stuffed them in my bag, and went onto Uber to get a cab. There would be one at the end of the road in five minutes, so I stepped out of the shadows and walked as though I was just another woman on her way home from work. As I reached the end, I looked to my right to see Hunter running towards me.

Shit.

If I ran, he would know I was KJ74, so I slowed down and crossed the road, still walking towards him, but on the other side of the street.

As he drew level, he shouted across, 'Hey, have you seen someone in a yellow hat?'

'Sorry?' I said, wanting to sound like I wasn't expecting him to talk.

'A yellow hat. A woman in a yellow hat?'

'No.'

'You sure?'

'I've not seen anyone.'

'Fuck,' he said, continuing to run past. Once he was gone, I dared to breathe again. My Uber said it would be another few minutes. All I could do was lean against the street sign, pretend to be relaxed, and wait. I only hoped my pounding heart and frayed nerves didn't give me away.

CHAPTER THIRTY-SEVEN

Jamison
10.02 p.m. — 4 hours and 28 minutes remaining

'Boss, you need to see this,' Mike said, bursting into Jamison's office without knocking. He didn't do that — nobody did that. So, Jamison knew it was something important, and the fact that Mike didn't see Jamison had company said even more.

'Oh, boss, I'm sorry.'

'It's OK. We were just wrapping up, give me a few minutes will you?'

'Of course.'

Apologising again, Mike backed out and Jamison wrapped up his meeting, watching Mike pace outside the office. He was anxious, tense and glued to his phone. Jamison knew it could only mean one thing. Someone was taking on the dare.

Once Jamison's meeting was finished, and the man was gone, Mike re-entered the office, closing the door behind him.

'Sorry, boss, I should have knocked.'

'It's OK. Grab a seat. What's going on?'

'We had a near miss.'

'She wasn't caught?'

'No, but someone came close. We think she's in the Bretton area. I've tried to reach Harry, can't get hold of him.'

'Harry isn't part of this anymore,' Jamison said, holding Mike's eye, unblinking.

Mike didn't press. He knew exactly what his boss meant. Harry had fucked up, and paid the price. He looked towards the floor, taking a quiet moment of grief for his work colleague and friend.

'We all know the risks,' Jamison said quietly, his eye twitching.

'Yeah, yeah we do,' Mike agreed, still unable to look his boss in the eye.

'So, you saw the girl. Did you see if she had the USB with her?' Jamison asked.

Mike shook his head. Cleared his throat and then looked at his boss once more. The grief, the fear previously visible on his face, now buried. 'Sorry, boss. Do you want to see the chase?'

'Yeah, I'm curious.'

Mike loaded Hunter's now finished livestream video and Jamison watched the chase unfold.

'How long ago was this?' Jamison asked.

'Just under ten minutes ago.'

'So, she is likely to be somewhere in Bretton?'

'That's what we think.'

Jamison continued to watch as the car skidded to a halt and KJ74 was lost.

'That's about it, sir. He doesn't find her again.'

Jamison nodded but continued to watch as Hunter ran and called for KJ74 to come out. He was about to hand the phone back when, on the screen, Hunter asked a woman if she had seen anyone, and she said no.

'Wait a minute. How do you zoom in?'

Mike took the phone and zoomed in on the woman before handing it back. When he did, even he understood Jamison's excitement.

'What the fuck? Isn't that . . . ?'

'Yeah, the kid's sister.' Jamison stared at the screen like a lion stalking its prey.

'What the fuck is she doing there?'

'On this app, can you load other videos on this, from the past?'

'Yeah, it's all there.'

'Show me those of KJ74.'

Mike did as he was asked, and Jamison watched all the videos featuring their target. He watched her jump in the river, kiss a stranger and steal his car. He listened as she said she was doing wrong for the right reasons.

'How much money has KJ74 made?' Jamison asked, and Mike looked at her 'dare complete' list.

'Just over twelve and a half grand.'

'And what was the kid's debt?'

'Nineteen.'

'KJ74 starts playing, and miraculously the kid's debt is cleared.'

'Could be a coincidence?' Mike said.

'You and I both know there is no such thing. Find her.'

CHAPTER THIRTY-EIGHT

10.16 p.m. — 4 hours and 14 minutes remaining

It was an agonising wait for the taxi, which was delayed by a couple of minutes. When I climbed in, the driver, an older man with a thick London accent, told me that there were dozens of people on the street.

'Looks like some sort of game of hide and seek? God knows what kids get up to these days,' he said.

I didn't offer a comment back, but obviously I knew exactly what they were doing. Hunter would have passed so many identifiable landmarks, a pub, a street sign, a particular building. All the players looking for me were flooding into Bretton.

As we drove towards the city centre I saw a group standing by the side of the road, trying to get cars to slow down.

'What on earth?' the driver said as two people stepped in front of his cab. Both wore masks, one the scream mask from the slasher movie, the other a masquerade ball mask. If I didn't know what they were playing, if I didn't know the stakes in the game, I might have laughed.

The driver began to slow and, knowing I couldn't afford for him to do that, I made up a lie.

'There's something on the news about groups of people carjacking.'

'Carjacking?' the driver replied in disbelief.

'Yeah, it's happening all over the city. Don't stop.'

'Don't you worry, I won't.' He put his foot down a little. The car lurched forward and, despite the two in the road waving their arms, he didn't slow. They were forced to run out of the way before he hit them.

I turned in my seat and looked back. They were both flipping their middle fingers up at the car. I could hear them shouting — they sounded so violent, so hateful.

'What is this world coming to?' the driver said to himself, before looking back at me through the rear-view mirror. 'You all right?'

'Fine, thank you.' I returned my gaze to the outside world. As we passed the city centre, it looked like Halloween. So many people were out, so many of them wearing masks. So many wanting to cash in on this golden ticket.

All of them wanting me dead.

I tried not to think about it but I couldn't help myself, so I went onto the DareMe app to see what people were saying. I now had over 112,000 followers. On my last post, I had even more messages of support, of kindness, and of murderous intent. Coming out of my profile, I scrolled the timeline. Most of what I was seeing was from Peterborough. Someone called 'thedaremedude' was streaming saying he had come across from Cambridge for this dare. Another called 'psychobitch' was streaming as she wandered around with what I could only assume was a machete, without a care in the world. The police were out, trying to stop people but were, as they always were, pretty powerless to actually do anything.

As I scrolled, a dark ocean of despair washed over me, each flick of my thumb sending me deeper and deeper into the black. The dare on my life was only forty-seven minutes old, and already thousands were playing. But, I had a tendril of hope, a thin thread that I was holding onto: no one knew who KJ74 really was. I closed my eyes and focused on that. KJ74 was being hunted. *I* was safe. I would be OK. I just had to hide, to wait it out.

I opened my eyes, looked out into the night. In the distance, an orange hue hung in the air. Somewhere there was a fire burning. It was confirmed when two fire engines rushed past. I knew it wasn't a coincidence. The dare, the hundred grand; it was setting the world on fire.

Then, an announcement was posted, an update to the challenge and, as I opened the notification, I couldn't believe what I saw.

And I didn't know what the fuck I was going to do.

Player KJ74's real identity is Cassandra Kim Jones of Peterborough.
Your DareMe challenge stays the same.
Kill player KJ74 (£100,000)
You have 4 hours and 9 minutes remaining.

CHAPTER THIRTY-NINE

10.22 p.m. — 4 hours and 8 minutes remaining

I felt like I was going to pass out. My one thread of hope had been taken from me. The one thing that had made me feel I could survive the night. Somehow, someone had worked out who I was. Had I been sloppy? Did my voice give me away? Had I exposed something that an old friend or ex-partner had latched on to? I had done all I could to cover my tracks, hide everything, so that once I had helped my brother I could go back to being a nobody. How had I become the most wanted person for miles around? I wanted my little life back, where I was a nobody. I wanted to go home, get into my bed, sleep through this bad dream. A hundred grand, to have me dead. To have me killed. It was too much to process, and even though I knew I needed to be thinking of what to do, I couldn't.

Instead, I watched people interact with the update, some saying they knew me. Some posted screenshots of my other social media profiles. Some claimed I had leaked my own name for my fifteen minutes of fame. Being a nobody wasn't an option anymore. And my heart sank to know it might not ever be again. But I didn't have time to worry about being famous. They wanted my head on a spike.

As the Uber crossed the river, my road came into view and, suddenly, I realised that if anyone I knew from work was a DareMe player, they would know where I lived. So, trying to appear calm, I asked the driver to stop.

'Are you sure? It's weird out tonight,' he said, meaning well.

'Please, I need to get some air. I don't feel too good.'

I didn't need to say any more. The idea of someone throwing up in the back of his car was enough to supersede how strange the evening was. The driver quickly pulled over and, as I climbed out, I was violently sick on the ground. I hadn't felt ill until then. It had come from nowhere, almost as if me faking was enough to make my body realise that was exactly what it needed to do. The driver almost got out to help, but when I waved to him, telling him I was OK, he left.

Once he had disappeared into the distance, I dared to move once more. I felt like I wanted to throw up again, but I swallowed it down. I just needed to get home, lock the door and work out what the fuck I was going to do. Thankfully, the streets close to mine were quiet. Few people actually knew where I lived. My life was too small, and I was last seen in Bretton — people were likely looking for me there. All was quiet, but I didn't want to be outside any longer than I needed. I broke into a limping run.

As I got close enough to see my front door, something made me stop. I threw myself behind a van for cover. My front door was open, smashed off its hinges. Someone was inside. Looking for me, waiting for me.

Turning, I kept my head low and walked away. Real panic was sweeping in. I had nowhere to go. I had no anonymity anymore. KJ74 was an idea, a yellow-beanie-wearing concept, but she was now linked to me. My name was out there and, despite me living a quiet life and keeping to myself, Peterborough was small. People would find me. People knew me. Anyone could drive past in a car and alert any number of people to my whereabouts.

I knew there were good individuals out there, those who would help, but I also knew that some people would do almost anything for £100,000. Mia was right, people didn't think it was real. I was like a character on Fortnite, or Call of Duty, the kind of games Sam loved. Killing was fun on those games. Killing gave rewards. DareMe was no different in that way. I knew people would easily compartmentalise it as nothing more than a bit of fun.

I hobbled towards the river, my leg now throbbing painfully. Beyond the council buildings and the unfinished hotel, right beside where I had done my first dare jumping into the river, was the old mill. Its abandoned and derelict building was supposed to have been knocked down and rebuilt, like most of the Fletton riverbank, but it remained due to budget issues. I suspected it would be empty, but there might be some people there, homeless people seeking shelter. I knew none of them would be on DareMe — at least, I hoped not.

Once I was safely behind the old mill and able to see across the river to the theatre, its bar full of laughing, happy people drinking wine and enjoying a night out without a care in the world, I dared to pull my phone out of my pocket. With shaking hands, I rang Mia. It rang, and rang, and then clicked to voicemail. I tried again and again, and on the fourth attempt she picked up.

'Mia, they know my name, they know who I am. Someone is in my house. I don't know what to do.'

The line was quiet.

'Mia? Are you there? I need help.'

Her reply was quiet, so quiet I could barely hear her, so quiet I was almost sure I had heard her wrong.

'I . . . I can't help you anymore, Cass.'

'What?'

'Find somewhere to hide.'

'Mia? Please?'

'I can't. I'm sorry.'

Then the line went dead.

I lowered the phone, trying to take in what had just happened. I watched people in the bar across the water talking, laughing, warm and merry, enjoying the company of friends. And here I stood, alone, cold, and reeling from the fact that Mia, the woman who I classed as family, my only hope, had just abandoned me. My best friend had left me for dead.

CHAPTER FORTY

Wakelin
10.23 p.m. — 4 hours and 7 minutes remaining

The streets of Bretton were in chaos, and as Wakelin and several PCs desperately tried to get people to go home, he couldn't help but think of what he had said to his wife about the comparison between this and the London riots in 2011. Back then, he had been sent to the capital to help with the madness that took place for those few days in August, and which had resulted in five people losing their lives. The police had no power then, and despite these scenes not being as angry, Wakelin couldn't help but feel they would lose control of it quickly. They had to suffocate the flame igniting these people. That whispering spark. The issue was, he didn't know where to start.

A DareMe to kill a person had been anonymously posted. Even though there was a team working on finding the source and arresting whoever was inciting violence on the ground, he had no control over it. He had threatened to arrest some of the people out tonight, but they didn't care — he had even told them that if a person died, they would be charged with attempted murder, but again, they had shown no concern. He could have arrested them all, but the priority wasn't crowd management. Uniformed officers could handle that. His priority was finding KJ74 before someone hurt her.

'What do we do?' PC Peters said as he, like the others, failed to get people to go home.

'Keep trying,' Wakelin said.

Peters nodded but Wakelin could see the glimmer of fear in his eyes. It was justifiable. He could smell the bloodlust in the air. As Peters approached a few kids, none of them more than twelve years old, he headed to a bunch of older teenagers who were out enjoying the spectacle.

'All right, lads, nothing is happening here. It's time to move on.'

'You can't move me,' one of the lads said, the look on his face one of pure petulance.

'I'm only asking, nicely. I know why you are all out here.'

'Yeah?'

'Yeah, DareMe. She was seen around here, right?'

'Was she? I don't know nothing.'

Wakelin smiled. 'You know, if you engage in the dare, you are going to be culpable for a very serious crime.'

'Man, I ain't no player,' one of the kids said. He was a lad no older than fourteen, the age where his body was growing and his brain was awkwardly trying to catch up.

Wakelin flicked a glance down to the ski mask he was holding in his hand. 'Mm-hm.'

'It's cold, innit?' The lad smirked. 'I just wanna see someone catch Cass.'

'Cass?'

'Man, ain't you watching? KJ74's name was released. It was like ten minutes ago. I swear you pigs are getting more and more . . .'

The lad continued to talk, to throw offensive terms Wakelin's way, but he had stopped listening. He bounded towards Peters.

'Boss?'

'Load the app. KJ74's name has been released.'

Peters unlocked his personal phone and saw the latest post. Without speaking, he turned and showed Wakelin.

'Oh, shit!' Wakelin said. 'Put that app on my phone.'

'They are monitoring back at the station. They have a whole team on it.'

'And still I'm finding out from a player. A kid in a fucking mask. Just load it.'

'Sure.'

As Peters installed and created a profile for Wakelin, he dealt with the petulant teen by threatening arrest. It seemed to work. Once he and his friends had moved on, Peters handed the phone back. 'Here. All done.'

Wakelin saw the app icon on his screen. 'I'm going to her place now.'

He fired up his car engine and had to beep his horn several times to make people move out of the way. But they continued meandering, so he put on his siren. Several jumped. There was something about a police siren — when it went off, people moved. Always had, always would.

Wakelin tried calling Cassie Jones as he drove to her address. It rang and rang, but there was no answer.

'Come on, Cassie, pick up,' he said, trying again and again. Each time the call went to voicemail. He put his foot down. As he drove, he pinged her a text, asking her to get in touch. Once he was sure it had sent, he rang Jen at home.

'Jen, all OK?'

'Fine, we are fine. They have released the girl's real name.'

'Yeah.'

'I've seen on the news, it's not just Peterborough taking to the streets, people are angry. Find her, Greg.'

'I will. Ring Tom again, make sure he's still in. Keep the house quiet, OK? Make it look like you're not home. The city is dangerous tonight.'

'I'm getting scared,' Jen said.

'Yeah, me too,' Wakelin replied. 'Just stay in, stay quiet. Talk with Tom. I'll find her.'

Wakelin said goodbye, hung up, dropped the phone beside him and drove as fast as he could.

By the time he arrived at Cassie's address, he knew he was too late. The front door was hanging open. Slapping on some latex gloves to minimise cross-contamination, he gently pushed the door wide open.

'Cassie? Cassie Jones, it's DS Wakelin. Are you here?'

He waited a moment to hear her speak or move. He already knew she wouldn't reply. The house felt empty, cold, but that didn't mean she wasn't there. Nor that there wasn't someone else who was also looking for her lurking in the shadows.

Keeping his wits about him, he stepped over the threshold into her house. The last time he was there, he could tell Cassie knew more than she was letting on. But he hadn't expected the case to turn this way. She was KJ74, the one being hunted for a huge bounty. He didn't understand why. She had torched the car involved in her brother's assault. That would have pissed off whoever that was, but to offer £100,000 for killing her as retribution was disproportionate. He suspected Cassie Jones knew a hell of a lot more than she was letting on.

'Cassie?' he called again, just in case, before stepping into her living room. The place had been flipped: sofas slashed, coffee table thrown, TV slammed on the floor. He had seen this sort of crime dozens of times. Whoever had broken in was likely trying to find Cassie, just as he was, but when they had failed to find her, they'd begun looking for something else, something specific. His theory was confirmed when he walked into the kitchen and saw an iPad on the side, untouched. If this had been a regular break-in, that would have been the first thing to go.

Whoever had come here wasn't after a quick buck — they were after Cassie. And something else. Something far more valuable than a hundred grand to them.

Even though Cassie hadn't replied to his first message, he fired off a second, asking two very specific questions.

CHAPTER FORTY-ONE

10.29 p.m. — 4 hours and 1 minute remaining

The sense of abandonment cut me to my core. Mia had left me to fight this alone. As much as I tried to see it from her perspective, I couldn't. If it was the other way around, I would have been there for her in a heartbeat. I knew I should hate her, but I was too devastated to feel anything other than heartbreak. The hate might come, but not yet.

Everything had spiralled out of control. It had only been a day since I signed up to DareMe. I'd started out hopeful I'd be able to help Sam with some small, insignificant dares, and now I was hiding in a derelict building while hundreds, maybe even thousands of people hunted me. I didn't want to look at the DareMe app. I wished I never had, but it had saved me only half an hour before by alerting me to the player called Hunter, stalking me. I knew I had to open it. As much as I hated it, I now needed it more than ever.

I had two missed calls and two messages. I ignored them and loaded the app. I saw my followers had jumped again to nearly 150,000. A new congratulations banner danced across the top of the screen, telling me I was now in the top twenty most followed players in the country. I knew what I had become. I was that car crash on the side of a motorway that you knew was going to be messy, likely haunting, but you had to slow and look anyway.

I fucking hated what the world had become. Knowing there was nothing I could do about it and, feeling moderately safe, I allowed myself to cry. It was a deep and pathetic sob, and I didn't hold back. Each lungful of air, each guttural wail, helped to shift the bowling-ball-sized knot in my chest that was trying to crush me from the inside out. Each sob offered a little more clarity until I realised something that forced me to get up. I had been so worried about them knowing who I was that I hadn't thought about anyone else.

If they knew my name then someone would know I had a brother.

I needed to move.

I bent and dropped my phone into my bag, and was about to zip it up when I heard footsteps approaching. Before I could react, a man turned the corner and stood directly in front of me. His torch blinded me.

'Ma'am? Are you OK?' he asked, lowering his torch. As my eyes adjusted, I saw he was in a police uniform.

'Oh, thank God. I need help,' I said, a fresh waves of tears beginning to fall.

'Cassie Jones?' he said, shocked to know it was me.

'Please, people are trying to hurt me. I need help.'

'It's OK, it's OK,' he said, taking a small step towards me.

I began to stand, but as I did, he grabbed my shoulder. There was a sharp smack as his hand met my face, sending me crashing to the ground.

CHAPTER FORTY-TWO

10.32 p.m. — 3 hours and 58 minutes remaining

The blow sent stars across my vision. For a moment, it was impossible to know which way was up or down. I needed to find my feet, to run and hide, but my legs wouldn't do as they were told. As my vision blurred back into focus, I saw the PCSO don a mask. With his phone in his hand, he began to talk. He was livestreaming, livestreaming my murder.

'This is stickittotheman and I've found KJ74. I'm about to end this dare.'

He turned the camera to me, and I scrambled backwards away from him. I was desperate to get up, but I had nowhere to go. Behind me was the corner of the abandoned building. I was boxed in. He had pushed me into a dead end, a trap. When he saw that I'd realised this, he laughed, then looked at his phone.

'Wow, Cassie, lots of people want to see you die. There are over ten thousand here with us now. Say hi.'

He turned the camera to me, and I saw the number of live watchers climbing.

'I promise to make this quick,' he said.

'You stole that line from an eighties' movie,' I said, my fear manifesting as contempt, anger. I hated him. I hated all of them playing this game. I hated myself for getting swept up in it too.

'Fine, no cheesy lines,' the PCSO said. He placed his phone on the ledge of a boarded-up window. He then picked up a loose brick from the ground and held it towards me. I thought this would be the thing to end my life, that it would crack open my skull. He saw me think it too and, through the mouth gap in his balaclava, I saw him smile. He didn't come towards me with the brick, though, instead he used it to keep his phone in place. As he had his back to me, I pulled my bag behind me, blocking it from his view, and as quietly as I could, I opened it.

The PCSO turned again and looked at me. A hunter stalking his prey. I needed to buy myself a little time, just a few seconds to distract so he didn't see my hand in my bag. I needed to try and get him talking.

'You are supposed to help people like me. Isn't that your job?'

'It is.'

'Then why are you doing this?'

'I'm new to it, less than a year. Do you know how much someone like me earns? A lowly community support officer? Just over twenty grand a year. That's it. For all the abuse and wading through shit. Just over twenty grand. After my bills have been paid, I can't even afford to go for a meal, or take someone on a date.'

'That isn't my fault,' I said, but he didn't hear me. He was monologuing, sounding off about his place in the world. And, actually, he was doing me a favour. I needed just a little more time. My hand had found the saw from the museum.

'I work like a dog, and for what? For little shits to spit at me in the street, for drunk dickheads to try and fight me because of my uniform? I wanted to help, but all I am is poor and alone. This gives me a way out, to start again, do something with my life. You know, I fucking hate people. I didn't at the start, but in this job, you just get shit on over and over again. For fuck all money and in a climate where the cost of living makes it impossible to stay afloat. I'm done. I've been done for a while, and then I see you, stealing cars and torching them and earning half of my annual wage in a few hours. You know what that told me?'

'What?'

'That crime does pay. After this, I'll leave, go somewhere warm, somewhere else.'

'You need to let me go,' I said, readying myself, tightening my grip.

'No, no I don't.'

'Fuck you!' I shouted.

'Now, Cassie. Be polite, people are watching.'

'Fuck you!' I shouted again. I needed him shocked, angry. He had obviously daydreamed of this moment, planned it even. I needed his fantasy to be ruined, so he would feel less in control. I needed him angry. I needed the game to not be a game anymore. 'You might get that hundred grand, but you'll always be a piece of shit. And I'll fucking haunt you until the day you die.' I knew what to do to put him on the back foot. 'Approximately five foot ten, maybe eighty-five kilos. I can see a tattoo of—'

'What are you doing?'

'Describing you. Everyone's watching, including the police — your employers. A tattoo of a skull on his left—'

'Stop talking!' he shouted, stepping towards me.

'Make me.'

The PCSO lunged at me, his hand balled into a fist to hit me again. I could see he wanted to beat me to death.

Before he could hit me, I pulled the saw from my bag and smashed it around the side of his head.

He staggered backwards, and cried out like a wounded beast. I got to my feet quickly, and hit him again, this time on the back of the head and he went down. He moaned, barely conscious. He wouldn't try to hit me again.

I walked over and took his phone. There were still over 60,000 people watching. Again, people turn to look at a car crash.

'I know the police are watching. You need to deal with this man. He is one of yours.'

I walked over and pulled the mask off my attacker. His was a bloody mess but I knew someone would recognise him.

I ended the livestream, dropped his phone and smashed it on the floor. Then I picked up his mask, stuffed it in my bag and gave him one final kick.

I had to get out of there before anyone else watching worked out where I was and came to finish what he'd started. Walking away from the city, I pulled out my phone and looked at the messages sent. One from Wakelin was top of the list.

I want to help you Cassie. I need to protect you. Let's arrange a safe place to meet. I won't let anyone hurt you, and then, I need you to talk to me. Someone is willing to pay a lot of money to see you dead, and I need to know why.

I'm here to help, Cassie, but you need to come clean. What do you know?

What have you got that is worth so much money to them?

CHAPTER FORTY-THREE

Wakelin
10.37 p.m. — 3 hours and 53 minutes remaining

Back outside Cassie Jones's house, Wakelin waited for Forensics to arrive. Her house was a mess and although he knew whoever had set the dare wanted her dead, they also wanted something else. What that was, he didn't know. He could only hope that they had left a trail he could follow. He needed to find them, to stop the DareMe challenge, and find her. His mind reeled as he tried to understand how a young man being assaulted and his sister being hunted for cash were linked.

His phone pinged. It was Peters, and he said only a few words.

Log in to DareMe. Search KJ74.

Tapping the app icon, he did as Peters said and watched the attack unfold on his phone. The time stamp said it had finished less than ten minutes before. He rang Peters straight away.

'Why am I only just seeing this?'

'I thought you'd be checking the app.'

'No, I'm trying to find her. I thought there was a whole team watching DareMe, and trying to work out where she is?'

'There is.'

'Then why am I not being looped in?'

'I don't know, I'll look into it. Make sure you are first to know. Sorry.'

Wakelin signed. 'No, it's not your fault. Communication has always been shit. Just, keep watching, anything new, tell me first. Ten minutes is too long.'

'Got it.'

Hanging up, Wakelin looked at the video again. Pissed off that someone didn't think to call him straight away. Even the DI should have at least messaged. He'd address that later, and turned his attention to the details around Cassie on the screen. It looked like she was at the river, near to where he was. Watching intently, he walked to his car. He was shocked to see Dean Worthington, a PCSO who patrolled the city centre, be unveiled as her attacker. Wakelin knew him and had always assumed he was a good man. Once the livestream ended, he rang his DI.

'Wakelin.'

'Boss, have you seen the attempt on Cassie Jones's life?'

'I have.'

'Why am I last to know? Boss, I'm on the ground, I need to be first.'

'Take a breath DS Wakelin, we are all stressed.'

'Sorry.'

'Is that Dean?' The DI said.

'Yeah, yeah it is.'

'Jesus. I thought he was one of us.'

'So did I. He's down by the river, I'm on my way. Have we got others attending?'

'Yes.'

'Good. I'm five minutes out.'

'Find him, get him to a hospital, but arrest that son of a bitch first.'

'Will do,' Wakelin said, about to hang up.

'Wakelin?'

'Yes, boss?'

'This is becoming a shit show. I need you to bring that girl in.'

'I'm working on it.'

Hanging up, Wakelin got back in his car and called Cassie. Again, she didn't pick up. Dropping his phone on the passenger seat, Wakelin fired up the engine and drove the few minutes to where he thought the attack had taken place. As he parked and got out of the car, he heard moaning coming from inside one of the derelict buildings.

He pulled out his torch, advancing quietly. He rounded a corner and saw the PCSO on the floor, trying to pull himself to his feet. Cassie Jones had done a number on him, but Wakelin didn't care. He deserved it.

'Dean, it's DS Wakelin.'

'Help me.'

'Help is coming. Why, Dean?'

Dean looked up, regret in his eyes, but he didn't speak.

'You know the shit you're in?' Wakelin said, his voice tight and so full of rage he knew if he spoke at more than a whisper, he might beat Dean unconscious.

'Well, can't change it now.'

Resigned to the fact he couldn't escape arrest, Dean managed to pull himself into a sitting position. Wakelin walked over, placed him in handcuffs, and began to read him his rights. 'You do not have to say anything, but—'

'Yeah, yeah, I know. I never meant to get carried away.'

'And yet, here we are.'

'It's just a game, that's all. It was supposed to be a fucking game,' he said under his breath.

Wakelin walked away. He couldn't listen to his excuses or justifications, through fear he would finish what Cassie had started. 'Sit tight, a medic will be with you soon.'

As he took a deep breath that formed a thick cloud above his head, Wakelin's phone pinged. It was Cassie.

I've got your messages, and your questions, but I won't pick up. One of yours tried to kill me. I don't know who I can trust.

Wakelin called, hoping that because she had reached out, he could show her that he was on her side and wanted to help. He could take her to the station, where she would be safe. But it rang and rang and rang, eventually clicking into voicemail.

'Cassie, it's DS Wakelin. I know you are afraid, but you need to talk to me. You can trust me.'

CHAPTER FORTY-FOUR

10.44 p.m. — 3 hours and 46 minutes remaining

Despite Wakelin saying I could trust him, I knew I wouldn't. People were hunting me, wanting to kill me for money. A PCSO had tried to end my life. They had forced me to hurt someone, and that was something I had never wanted to do. My sadness at Mia abandoning me had been replaced by the adrenaline coursing through my system. I hated her for being such a coward, for running away in my hour of need. The only person I knew I could trust was Sam. I didn't mention Sam in my message to Wakelin, I had to hope everyone was so focused on me, they didn't go looking for him.

I needed to get to my brother. Wakelin had asked me to come in, but I couldn't trust him. I couldn't trust anyone anymore. It was just me and Sam.

Once I had him, I didn't know what I would do next. As I made my way towards the city, hoping to go unnoticed, I had to trust that when I knew he was safe, the next step would reveal itself to me.

Wakelin's question played constantly on a loop in my mind. What did I know that was worth a hundred grand?

But I didn't have the answer. I just had to hope that Wakelin worked it out before someone else found me. So, I messaged him back.

I don't trust you, but if you find out who wants me dead, and stop them, I will.

Hitting 'send', I went on to DareMe and scrolled the timeline. So many people had now moved into the city centre. There was a crowd gathered outside the cathedral grounds. I would have to go through them to get to Sam. I wanted to simply hide away, count the hours down, but Sam wasn't safe. I needed to act, to help him. It was my job, my duty.

As I continued to scroll, my own video came up. There were thousands of replies to my plea. Most were vile. The anonymity of the app meant people could reveal their worst. People said they would hurt me for a tenner, some said they would do it for free. I knew they were just keyboard warriors. What really scared me was the many people who all said the same thing. If a PCSO was allowed to try to kill me, then surely they were allowed to try too. Money was a motivator and now the PCSO was validation.

I pushed past the countless comments, and then found one that wasn't vile or murderous. I found one that was kind. It was from someone called TattooDan. It was one small sentence.

Come on, people, be kind. We all gotta try to help those in need, haven't we?

I knew who this was. Maybe I had one ally in the world. A glimmer of hope flickered.

Feeling slightly more confident than before, and slightly less helpless, I continued towards the city centre. As I drew close to Bridge Street, close enough to hear the growing crowd, I took off my coat and stuffed it in my bag. It would make me instantly identifiable. I pulled the PCSO's balaclava out of my back pocket and put it on. It was wet, and I realised it wasn't water, it was blood. I wanted to vomit knowing it was smearing onto my skin.

Taking a deep breath, ignoring the taste of iron, I walked through the city streets. As I walked past people, some looked at me but no one stopped me. There was a party vibe about the crowd rather than the bloodlust I'd expected. It was almost as if they were using what was going on as an event to have something to do. Even so, if any of them worked out KJ74 was among them, I would be killed. The mob would take over.

As I tried to make my way through the hundred or so people, one grabbed me and spun me around.

'This is insane!' the woman said. Her words slightly slurred. I saw she was carrying a bottle of wine.

'So crazy!' I replied, trying to match her energy.

'Like, I hope she doesn't die. But, if she does, this is gonna get wild.'

'So wild,' I said, again mirroring her. I turned to walk away, and as I did she called out.

'Happy hunting.'

I spun back. 'What did you just say?'

'Happy hunting. It's just a saying, everyone is saying it.'

'But you just said you didn't want her to die?'

'Yeah, but it's just a saying. It doesn't mean anything. DareMe is just a game. Chill out, it's a party.'

Annoyed at my questioning, and my lack of party vibe, she turned and grabbed someone else, who matched her enthusiasm for the party without faking it. *Happy hunting.* Even people who didn't want me dead were still playing, still culpable. It made me sick.

Continuing through the crowd, smiling and weaving, I eventually got through. I pulled out my phone and punched in directions to the city hospital. I wouldn't get in a cab and I couldn't get a bus, so I had to go on foot. Apple Maps said it was a forty-minute walk. Forty minutes of being outside, alone. Forty minutes of Sam being vulnerable. I broke into a jog.

At first, it was fairly easy to run, the adrenaline acting as a fuel in place of sleep and nutrition. About half a mile in, the pain in my leg from where that dog had bitten me started all over again, turning my jog into a limp. However, I knew I couldn't stop. Every minute I was outside was another minute where a player could find me, or could use Sam to lure me in. In a normal world, I would just call the police, tell them to care for my brother. But I didn't trust any of them anymore.

Once I got to him, I had to get him out of the hospital. Somewhere safe, and I could think of only one place where that might be. But it was a long shot. People didn't want to be near the condemned, for fear of being dragged down with them. I was the equivalent of a big red X painted on a door. The plague is here. Come in, try and help, and you will die too.

Hobbling along, feeling alone, I pulled off my mask and, as I did, I felt the tacky dried blood on my skin. I stopped near a puddle on the edge of the road and making sure I wasn't being watched, I lowered to the ground. I scooped up dirty rainwater and washed the blood off my face, scrubbing until the water came away no longer red from the blood. I then stood, dried my face with my jumper, and keeping my head low, pressed on.

I hoped when I got to the hospital, I could get to Sam without anyone seeing me, and then get him out of there in the same way. Again, a long shot but then, when I thought about it, getting out of this thing alive was becoming exactly that.

As I hobbled on, I vowed Sam was getting out of this alive, even if it cost me everything. I was the reason he was hurt. I was the reason we lived as we did. Sam's mistake and my involvement in DareMe was always going to happen, because of what I had done. I had been fated to end up here, and I was ready to face it.

CHAPTER FORTY-FIVE

Jamison
10.54 p.m. — 3 hours and 36 minutes remaining

Jamison stood at his office window, looking out into the night. The tension behind his eyes was now a full and pounding headache, one that threatened to pull his eyeballs back into his skull, blinding him for ever. He wanted nothing more than to close them, rest them, but he knew he couldn't. He had watched the attempted murder of KJ74 over and over on his phone and had felt himself become more and more enraged by the audacity she had to be so fucking resourceful. Most people would have just died. But not her, not Cassie fucking Jones. He'd watched, trying to see if the thing he needed was in her hand. But, as hard as he looked, he didn't see the USB anywhere. He hoped that meant it was gone, destroyed, or was in the river, never to be found again. Yes, it contained a vast amount of profitable information, but he was beyond that now. He could live well enough off the other six he was going to blackmail. There were only two of them to share the bounty now. It was likely gone, but he would not be satisfied until he could search for it himself.

He hated to admit it, but he was mildly impressed by her. She was managing to evade a whole city who wanted blood. She was willing to cause harm. He'd expected her to be the type to roll over, beg, cry, but in the latest video she wasn't going down so easily. She was cunning, violent even. She wanted to live. She wanted to win.

But so did he. There wasn't space for anyone else to be victorious. So, he had to change the rules. And time was running out.

There was a gentle tap on his office door. He composed himself, pushing back his greying hair, and sat at his desk. 'Come in.'

Mike walked into the office, nodded at his boss, and closed the door behind him. 'You wanted to see me?'

He was nervous. Jamison liked it. 'Any update on where she is?'

'No, but the city is getting busier and busier by the hour. Hundreds of people are now playing. I'm watching the streams. As soon as someone has eyes on her, I'll know.'

'What about that PCSO?'

'We went for him, to find out what he could tell us, but someone beat us there.'

'Who?'

'Wakelin.'

'I see,' Jamison said, sitting back in his chair. From what he knew, Wakelin was a good copper. Smart, determined. He didn't like him being so close. As he thought about the next steps, Mike waited patiently.

'It's pretty clear now she won't make this easy,' he said.

'No, boss. The PCSO is pretty banged up.'

Jamison laughed. 'I'll say. She's full of surprises. But we need that USB.'

'It might be gone. Might have gone up in the car?'

'I won't take that risk,' Jamison snapped, making Mike flinch. When he continued, he did so at barely a whisper. 'If she has it and opens it, and someone else sees it, say a certain detective, we are fucked. I need her dead.'

Mike nodded. 'So, what's next? Want me to get out and hunt for her?'

'Instead of hunting for her, let's have her come to us.'

'How?'

'She started all this because she wanted to help someone she loved, right?'

'Yes.'

'So, let's get someone she loves.'

'The brother?'

'No, he'll have police around him. No doubt it's been upped too. Find someone else.'

Mike nodded, and, without waiting to be excused, he left the office.

Jamison stood once more, needing to move. His anxiety at his plan coming undone made it impossible to rest for long. He pulled out his phone, opened the app and typed 'KJ74'. People were getting restless. It seemed she had disappeared.

But that wouldn't be for long. As soon as she saw they had a loved one, she would come to them. If she had the USB he would take it back from her cold, dead hands. Then he could enjoy his future in the sun without a worry in the world.

CHAPTER FORTY-SIX

11.18 p.m. — 3 hours and 12 minutes remaining

I could see the hospital building through the trees that lined the dark footpath. The last of my adrenaline had completely bottomed out, and hunger cramped my stomach. I wanted to eat, to sleep, but I couldn't. There were still over three hours in the game. In that time, I had to find a way to make it stop for good. I had to make sure nobody could put a new DareMe challenge online to have me killed.

Slowing down to regain some composure before I hobbled into the hospital, I thought about Wakelin's question again. What did I know that was worth so much? I still didn't have an answer.

But there had to be something. Or else, why me? This couldn't just be about the car.

As the question rolled around my exhausted brain, I rounded a corner that led directly to the hospital's main entrance. A few minutes, at most, and I would be inside with my brother. I could work out how to keep him hidden and safe. A hospital should be safe enough but they had got to him before. I knew in my gut they could get to him again — if they hadn't already. Plus, it wasn't just them anymore. There were thousands out there who could hurt him.

Ignoring the throbbing pain in my calf, I pressed on. I didn't look, but if I pulled up my trouser leg, I was sure I would see crimson soaking through my sock. I'd have to get it cleaned before it got infected, but only once I knew Sam was safe.

I reached the entrance to the hospital, lowered my head and walked in. People in hospitals were distracted, stuck in their own worlds. I avoided eye contact with everyone. If a PCSO was capable of accepting this dare, then I had to reason anyone would be. A doctor, porter, nurse, anyone — 100,000 different people for 100,000 reasons.

With my leg hurting so much, the lift would have been better, but the lift was a sealed box with no escape. Anyone could be a player. I couldn't risk it. So, instead I heaved myself slowly up the stairs until I reached the second floor. The door onto it was closed. And I didn't want to buzz to be invited in. So, I looked through the glass. It was quiet, and I had to believe that meant no one had come for Sam. A porter stepped out from around a corner, coming my way, and I ducked beside the stairwell. I heard the door open, and looking I watched the porter walk away. I dashed, making it to the door before it closed, and stepped onto the ward. I looked around. The night had settled in and people were asleep. A nurse at the desk ahead typed quietly into a computer. Further down the ward, another nurse walked from cubicle to cubicle. And outside Sam's door was a uniformed police officer. It all seemed calm. If someone had come for Sam, there would have been chaos. My brother was OK, and he was nearby.

I couldn't just walk in, though. I was still in the game, being hunted. The dare still existed.

Hanging back, I watched as the nurse behind the station stood, grabbed a file and left. I stepped back into the stairwell, and slunk down a few steps, lowering myself so I couldn't be seen. I watched as she walked past. A few seconds later, I heard the lift door open and close.

One down.

I looked for the second nurse. I could hear him in one of the rooms. But the police officer stayed diligent. I needed him to leave. I needed a distraction. Looking around, I tried to find something to draw the attention of the officer, and then my eyes landed on a fire alarm activation panel. If I smashed the glass, it would cause panic, chaos.

I did it.

The shrill was instant, and so loud I flinched. Exit lights began to flash and emergency doors began closing one by one. I stepped towards the nurses' station and ducked down as the police officer walked past, no doubt trying to establish what was going on, and see where he could help.

I dashed towards Sam's room, ducking inside just as the nurse stepped out of the room beside his. The room was dark, Sam likely asleep, even with the alarm sounding, but I didn't turn to him. Instead, I looked through the gap in the door hinges to see the nurse walk past and towards the station.

I moved in the darkness towards my brother.

'Sam? Sam, it's me.'

He didn't say anything back, and as my eyes adjusted to the dark, my heart dropped. The bed was empty.

CHAPTER FORTY-SEVEN

11.32 p.m. — 2 hours and 58 minutes remaining

I panicked. Sam was gone. As I turned to try and find him, while avoiding the police officer, I came face to face with the nurse. The alarm had masked the sound of him entering, and the way he looked at me, he knew who I was.

Then the alarm stopped, and the silence it caused hung between us like fog. Without daring to blink, I backed away to the other side of the bed, reaching for the saw that was in my rucksack.

'You'd better get out of my way,' I said.

'No, no. Cassie, it's OK. I'm not playing,' he said, showing his palms in defence.

'Then how do you know who I am?'

'Everyone knows who you are. But you're safe.'

'I don't believe you.'

'After the PCSO, I might not believe me either. But I promise, I'm not playing DareMe. I'm a nurse. I want to help people.'

'That's what you would say. That's what the PCSO said too.'

'I'll step back. I'm not going to keep you here. I'm not going to hurt you.'

I wanted to believe him. I wanted to believe there was some good in the world. But I couldn't let myself.

'Where is my brother?' I demanded.

'I moved Sam out of this room.'

'Why?'

'A police officer called.'

'Who?'

'Someone called Wakelin. He instructed me to hide Sam.'

'He said that?'

'Yes.'

'Why?'

'He said if they're after you then they might come for him too. Cassie, what are you doing here? It's not safe.'

I thought about it, maybe Wakelin was on my side after all. Or maybe he wanted me to think so, so he could lure me in, and claim his prize. 'But there was a police officer outside,' I said.

'Didn't stop someone getting in before, did it?'

'Where is he?' I demanded.

'He's still here. We just moved him along, in case.'

'Where is my fucking brother? Tell me.'

'I will. I promise. I'll take you to him. Look, Cassie, I know you are afraid. But, I promise, not everyone agrees with this. Not everyone wants to play.'

'Take me to him. You walk in front of me, keep your hands up.'

'I'll do one better, I'll stay here,' he said, his palms still raised. 'He's at the end of this ward. The last room.'

I thought about it. It could be a trap. He could have known I was in the hospital. Maybe someone on the front desk recognised me and rang ahead. He could have a friend in the other room, waiting for me with the livestream set up to show my murder. Maybe they would even split the bounty. It was a lot of money. I needed to check.

'Hang on,' I said, pulling out my phone. DareMe was buzzing with people looking for me. Every video on my timeline was someone hunting me. Someone wanting to kill me. Someone wanting to be rich. But as far as I could see, no one was at the hospital. Closing the phone, I looked back. The nurse hadn't moved.

'You'll stay here?'

'I'll stay here.'

'Get on the bed.'

The nurse did as I asked. I turned around and backed out of the room. Before he could pursue, I hobbled towards the end room, keeping the saw raised just in case I needed to swing it again. Outside the room, I stopped. The police officer was still absent. I looked back. The nurse was standing in the doorway to Sam's old room.

'It's OK,' he said.

Keeping my eye on him, I spoke though the closed door. 'Sam?'

Nothing.

'Sam, are you in there?'

Then I heard him speak. 'Cass? Is that you?'

Bursting through the door, I saw my brother on a bed. He looked tired, battered — the bruising on his face was worse than when I last saw him. But he was there. He was OK.

'Sam!'

Dropping the saw, I ran to the bed and hugged my brother tightly.

'Cassie. You're limping.'

'I'm OK. Are you hurt? Has anyone threatened you?'

'No, James moved me. He told me what was going on.'

'James?' I asked.

'Me,' the nurse said, from the doorway. 'Cassie, no amount of money is worth taking someone's life. I want to help you and Sam.'

'Cassie, I've seen what's been going on, what you have had to do,' Sam said. 'Is this my fault? Am I the reason someone wants you dead?'

'No, Sam, no. It's not.'

'But the debt—'

'Sam, this isn't about you, I promise.' I meant it too. This was a chain reaction, the result of a mistake I'd made a decade ago, which had put us in a place where we struggled to get by and were completely alone. If I hadn't done what I had done all those years before, Mum would still be here. Sam wouldn't have gotten himself in this mess to help us get by. This was all because of me. All of it.

Sam nodded and I leaned in and kissed him on the cheek. 'I came here to get you out, get you somewhere safe, but it seems someone else is looking out for you.' I looked at the nurse. 'It's James, right?'

'Yes.'

'Thank you for looking out for my brother.'

'I don't know why the world thinks that this is all OK.'

'It's a game to most,' I said, without a hint of mirth.

'It's sickening,' James said quietly. 'You and Sam, you can stay here as long as you need.'

I nodded, sure that if I tried to thank him again, I would cry.

'Cassie, we need to look at your leg.'

'It's fine.'

'Cassie, let me do my job. You're injured.'

I nodded. 'OK, sorry.'

'Sit. Let me get it cleaned up.'

It was my turn to do as I was told. I sat beside Sam on the bed and I leaned on his shoulder. I was warm, with the only person I knew I could trust, and I was tired. A sudden urge to stop washed over me. If I closed my eyes, I would surely drift off.

'Cass?' Sam said quietly.

'Hmm?' I said, not lifting my head from his shoulder.

'You shouldn't have come here. It was a huge risk.'

'I gotta look out for you.'

'You don't. I'm an adult now, I can look after myself.'

'I know you can, but—'

'When Mum died, you lost your youth. You had to step up and be my carer. I know you feel some sort of responsibility for what happened. But you don't owe me anything.'

I looked at my brother and could see the earnestness in his eyes. It was too much. I had to look away. He didn't know what had happened that night in the car. He didn't know the reason Mum lost control. He didn't know I was the reason her seat belt wasn't fastened. If he did, he wouldn't have said what he'd just said; he might not be talking to me at all. If he knew the truth, he would surely hate me.

James came back into the room with the necessary medical supplies. He pulled up my trouser leg and began to clean, treat and dress my wound. I looked down as he worked. The deep purple bruising from the canine puncture wrapped around my calf.

'This should have had a stitch put in,' he said, focused intently on helping me, without hurting me too much.

'I was kinda pressed for time,' I said.

'Yeah, I guess you were.'

James worked in silence. Once he was finished, he pulled off the surgical gloves. 'Is the dressing too tight?'

Standing, I tentatively put my weight on my leg. It still hurt, but it felt supported. I bobbed a few times up and down, just to be sure.

'It's great, thank you.'

'Sit tight. I'll get you both a tea.'

'Cass?' Sam said as the silence swept in in James's wake.

'Yeah?'

'I don't get it — you paid back the money, right?'

'Yeah. Yeah, I did.'

'Then why is this happening to you?'

'I thought it was because of the car. But that's not worth all this.'

'What else could it be?'

'The copper, Wakelin — he thinks that they must think I know something about them.'

'What is it?'

I sighed deeply. 'I have no idea.'

'Cass?'

'Yeah?'

'Why did you steal their car?'

'In retrospect, I shouldn't have,' I said, trying to smile. 'Opportunity was there. They were watching our house, the keys were left in the car. But also . . .'

'What?'

'Fuck them, that's what.'

Sam smiled. 'I don't think I've heard you swear before.'

'Yeah, well, things change.' I stretched a long, painful stretch and, testing my leg once more, I felt confident the dressing would hold. I almost sat back down again but stopped myself. If I did, I would run the risk of falling asleep, so I paced the small room. Something itched in my mind. Something I had said.

As I tried to work out what it was, I looked out of the window into the night. The room faced the main car park, and at first it looked as quiet as it was in the ward. What had I said that was important? It was something about the car. But what was it? The gun — could this be about the gun?

While I pulled at the thread in my mind, I saw a faint glow of blue in the distance. I knew exactly what that was.

People's phones.

I pressed my hands to the glass, cupping them to see better. Once I had, it became clearer. A dozen people, maybe more, were approaching the hospital's main entrance. They knew where I was.

'Sam, we gotta go.'

CHAPTER FORTY-EIGHT

11.45 p.m. — 2 hours and 45 minutes remaining

'What? What is it?' Sam said, getting to his feet.

I didn't reply but grabbed my phone and loaded the app. Typing my name, I saw new livestreams from outside the hospital.

'They've found us.'

'How?'

No sooner had Sam spoke, than James ran back into the room. 'We need to go, now!'

'Did you do this?' I asked.

'No, no — I promise.'

I looked at James, and felt he was telling the truth. Someone must have seen me coming into the hospital and spread the word. 'Cassie, I didn't do this. Now come on, before they get here.'

Nodding, I helped Sam, who was still uneasy on his feet. As we left, I scooped up the saw and stuffed it back in my bag.

'There is another lift, specifically for staff and post-surgery patients only. They won't come up here,' James said, buzzing us through a door that said, 'Staff only'. We moved quickly.

The lift was slow, and as it reached the ground floor we all held our breath, expecting to see a mob waiting for us.

The doors opened, and the corridor in front was clear.

'Come on,' James said.

Instead of taking us to an exit, he took us to a changing room for male staff. He went to a locker and pulled out two fresh sets of scrubs.

'Put these on. Quickly.'

Sam and I dressed as fast as we could without question, and it was only when we were changed that I understood he was giving us both a disguise.

'Right. Now we keep calm. Just walk past anyone trying to find you,' James said.

We moved through the corridor and into the main foyer.

'Where are we going?' I asked.

'Staff car park. You need to get out of here.'

'Keep her between us,' Sam said to James as we moved.

James started talking about his shift, using terms I didn't understand, hiding us in plain sight. As we walked, a small group of people who were trying to look nonchalant started moving through the hospital. To me, they stood out as people who had violence in mind, but no one else seemed to notice.

They were giggling like children at Christmas.

What a fucking world.

The three of us passed without incident. Once we were outside in the near freezing night, James hurried us to the staff car park. It was a short but exposed two-minute walk. His car was on the second level, and once we were beside it, he handed me the keys.

'Just leave it somewhere safe. Once this is over, come back here and tell me where it is.'

'Thank you,' I said, giving him a hug. I tried to focus on the fact he thought I might still be alive to come back.

He nodded. 'I wish I could do more.'

'You've done more than anyone else, more than even those I thought loved me,' I said, my rage towards Mia fresh and unfiltered.

I fired up the engine and headed towards the ramp that would take me out of the car park and hospital grounds. I looked at James in the rear-view mirror. He waved and, stuffing his hands into his pockets, he walked back where we had come from.

As we turned onto the road, more and more people were moving towards the hospital. Word travelled fast. A minute later, three police cars raced past. I felt for the staff and patients. Inside a place where hardworking people fought to keep calm, several individuals were on the hunt, playing the game, wanting to kill. A place where saving lives was the priority had become a place where people were trying to end mine.

It made me feel sick.

Once we were over a mile away, I dared to look at my brother. He was watching me, concerned. He looked as exhausted as I felt.

'What now?' he asked.

'Now, we find somewhere to hide you.'

'Do you have somewhere in mind?'

'Maybe,' I said. 'Maybe. Sam, take my phone. Google "Lost Time tattoo".'

'OK?' he said.

I flicked a glance my brother's way as he typed into my phone. A few seconds later, he had a number.

'It's a mobile.'

'Ring it. Put it on loudspeaker.'

Sam did as I asked, and the phone rang three times before it was answered.

'Hello?'

'Is this The Man from Lost Time?' I asked.

'Yes?'

'You tattooed me today. A little angel,' I added, hoping he would know it was me speaking.

'Oh yes, yes I did,' he said, hushing his tones.

'I saw your post on DareMe, about kindness.'

'Kindness is key. And I meant it too.'

I hesitated. I was about to take a leap of faith, a huge one, but I wasn't sure what options I had.

'KJ?' Dan said.

'It's Cass,' I replied.

'Cass. I meant what I said. About kindness. Every word.'

Sam looked at me, confused. I took a deep breath. 'Can I bring someone to your shop for a few hours?'

'Of course. When?'

'In about fifteen minutes.'

'I'll be there in ten,' he said, hanging up.

'Who was that?' Sam asked.

'Someone I think I trust.' I put my foot down to get into the city. If I could get Sam inside that tattoo parlour, and it stayed dark inside, no one would ever find him. My gut told me I could trust Dan. He was a friend in this, just like James was. When it mattered, maybe not everyone was a monster.

I just had to hope my gut wasn't wrong.

CHAPTER FORTY-NINE

Wakelin
11.57 p.m. — 2 hours and 33 minutes remaining

Wakelin was tired of chasing, of being on the back foot. He had been late to Bretton, where Cassie had been chased by a player called Hunter, he had been late to Cassie's house, late to the old mill and now, even though he was in the loop first, as requested, due to the roads being in chaos, with fires and street protests and borderline looting, he was late to the hospital, and by the time he pulled his car up at the main entrance, there must have been over 100 people gathered outside, looking for her. The hospital's security was overwhelmed and even though there was a police presence, they too were struggling to prevent their access. People pushed, laughed, pulled, filmed. It reminded him of footage he had seen a few years back from Black Friday somewhere in the US where people had acted like animals scavenging for scraps of meat.

'Fucking hell.' He pushed his way through. Everyone was holding a phone, everyone wearing a mask, and they only reacted to Wakelin when he pulled his police badge out. They created a channel but, to his shock, no one backed down. No one left. They knew that he knew why they were there, and they didn't seem to care. And the way people looked at him, it was like their eyes had glazed over, like zombies. When did it all go to shit? People were once good, kind; they looked after their own and got on with life. Now everyone wanted to be social media famous, showing off their riches, in a time when poverty was at its peak. People still didn't accept they had enough, always wanting more, and more. Wakelin had seen it with his own kid, how he needed the best of the best, how having just enough wasn't enough.

People didn't see Cassie Jones as a person anymore. She was a ticket to the high life. Once this was all over, he would spend as long as it took tracking all of these little shits down and holding them accountable for what they were doing. Then, he reasoned, he would retire. The world just wasn't the same one he'd lived in when he joined the force. It was time to step out of it, find a corner of peace, and stop trying to fix it.

As he finally muscled through the mob and into the hospital, he saw that Peters was already inside. The kid was young, but Wakelin was impressed with his wherewithal in the chaos.

'Hey, Peters.'

'So, obviously, she was here. She arrived about twenty minutes ago.'

'Says who?'

'Says that man there.'

Peters pointed to a receptionist, presently giving a statement.

'And he didn't ring us?'

'Nope. He went online.'

'Of course he did.'

Wakelin walked towards the man and spoke to the PC taking his statement. 'Hey, could you give us a minute?'

The PC nodded, walking outside to help keep back the mob.

'Hey. You're the one who saw her arrive?'

'Umm. Yes,' the man said.

'But you didn't call the police?'

'I — I didn't know what to do.'

'Clearly you did. But you decided instead of doing the right thing, you would go to DareMe and tell the world.'

'I — No, wait—'

'Got many new followers from it? Was it worth it?'

'Wait, I didn't mean to—'

Wakelin cut him off. 'If anyone gets hurt here this evening, it's on you. You know that, right?'

'Hurt? No, I just—'

'Did you do a deal? Is that it? Someone comes and does the dirty work, and you get a cut of the hundred grand?'

'No, no, nothing like that,' the man said, sweat breaking out on his brow. Wakelin enjoyed it. 'I'm sorry,' he continued.

'You're sorry. How will that help that poor woman?'

The man didn't reply.

'What's your name?' Wakelin asked.

'Paul,' he said.

'Paul, if anything happens to that woman, I'm gonna hold you to account. Do you understand? If she is hurt here, because of you, I will hold you culpable.'

'What? I haven't done anything wrong. I wouldn't hurt her.'

Wakelin stepped towards him, wanting to swing and punch him in his weaselly little face. But he stopped himself. If he hit him, like he wanted, he would be taken off the case, and that wouldn't help Cassie. 'You're a piece of shit,' he said. 'Peters, arrest him.'

'Arrest him? For what?'

'Perverting the course of justice.'

As Peters took over dealing with the now visibly shaking, Paul, Wakelin looked around and saw a nurse standing a way down the main atrium. He was watching Wakelin and gestured with a flick of his head for Wakelin to approach. He then ducked out of sight.

Wakelin followed and rounded the corner, away from the crowds. The nurse was standing beside the men's toilets.

'You wanted me?' Wakelin asked.

'Yes.'

'You know something?'

'It's James. I'm the one who hid Sam.'

'I see,' Wakelin said.

'I saw you with that receptionist. You seemed pissed off.'

'Cassie doesn't know who to trust. People like him ain't helping.'

'No.'

'James, I am on her side.'

'Are you?'

'Yes. Why else would I want you to move the kid?'

'People do crazy things to try and get rich,' he countered.

'Yeah, they do,' Wakelin replied, holding his eye. 'Look, James, somehow a normally quiet, kind, loving woman is in a whole world of shit, and unless we help her, she will be dead before the night is done. If you know something, you have to tell me.'

'She was here to get her brother.'

'I assumed as much.'

'You know her brother?'

'I know everything about Cassie now — her friends, where she works. I am the detective in charge of helping Sam too. James, I just want to help her. She needs it.'

James nodded.

'Where are they now?'

'I don't know.'

'They're not here somewhere. Hiding?' Wakelin asked, scrutinising the nurse to see how he responded.

'No. I gave them my car, told them to go. They didn't say where.'

Wakelin believed him. 'When was this?'

'Less than ten minutes ago. I'm sorry, if I had known you were coming, I would have got her to stay. But the crowd started building and . . .'

210

'No, no, it's OK. You were only trying to help her. James, I'm going to need your registration plate.'

'Yes, of course.'

Wakelin took down the make, model and registration plate of James's car and, thanking him, he began to walk away. The crowd didn't know she was no longer there. He wanted to keep it that way, so when he approached Peters, he ordered him to get more officers on the scene and conduct a full search of the hospital. He said it loud enough for one of the players to hear, and word spread quickly. The police would keep people out but his comment would also keep them at the hospital, hoping for a glimpse of the hundred-grand girl.

Leaving, he loaded the app, and scrolled. Most videos were of people either in the city or at the hospital. It seemed the whole app was focused on the small city that most had heard of, but couldn't place. Now, everyone knew where Peterborough was.

On the search bar, he typed 'Cassie Jones', and it took him to a new page where there were countless more videos and posts about her. Most were of people among crowds, streaming their hunt. However, one video stood out for being different. The livestream was of a quiet road, and the person filming seemed to be alone. Wakelin watched as they approached a house, walked up to the living room window and looked inside. The person behind the camera then spoke, calling for Cassie, taunting her. Wakelin stopped walking and watched intently. The camera moved and then filmed someone sitting on their sofa, their head in their hands. They didn't know they were being filmed though their window.

Then she looked up, and, when he saw who it was, he broke into a run and rang Dispatch. He knew everyone connected to Cassie Jones, the faces and names of everyone in her life. This person was unmistakable.

'I need the address of Mia Brown. She's a friend in the Cassie Jones case. Get her address, send it to me, and whoever is closest needs to get to her house, now!'

He went back to the video and watched as whoever was filming smashed the glass in her front door and let themselves in. Then, the video ended.

Someone was about to use Mia to lure Cassie to her death. He needed to get there first.

CHAPTER FIFTY

11.59 p.m. — 2 hours and 31 minutes remaining

Even though my gut told me to trust Dan, I was still wary as we approached his tattoo parlour.

With the city so busy and loud, we opted to park James's car close to the old walk-in surgery. It was close to the centre but, with the building and the pub opposite now empty, there was no reason for anyone to be there. I used to be fearful of these parts of the city, the places that had been forgotten. They were legacies of the world moving into online purchasing and of eating out rather than drinking all night. They were too quiet, too still. Now this little pocket of silence was the safest place I could think of.

The irony wasn't lost on me.

The walk from the car to the tattoo shop was only a few minutes but it meant crossing a main road. Traffic was light. But the city was chaos. People had split into two camps, those who wanted to be in on the action and those who didn't.

It was only twelve hours since I was last here, but it felt like a lifetime. And with the panic of those hours, I hadn't even thought about the tattoo he had etched into me. Now aware, it felt sore. But then so did my leg, and my heart, and my brain, so I ignored it.

Dan's shop was close to Bridge Street, perilously close, and as we drew closer, we could hear the rumblings of a thousand voices from the city streets. I couldn't see how many people were now out partying, wishing one another a 'happy hunting' but I could tell it was a lot more than there had been an hour ago. However, that wasn't my concern. All I cared about was getting Sam safe and out of the way until this was over.

Thankfully, those playing DareMe, those after my blood, didn't know what Sam looked like. This was as good a hiding place as any until I worked out how to end this.

When I was able to see the shop, my heart sank. It was dark and empty. Dan had said he would be there. I had to trust he would turn up soon.

'Stay here,' I said to Sam. He looked pale, his pain medication probably wearing off. He nodded, too tired to argue. Leaving him in the shadows, I walked towards the tattoo parlour, glancing around in case someone approached. I knocked.

At first, nothing happened. There were no lights, no movement, and, feeling too exposed and vulnerable, I was about to walk away and find somewhere else to hide Sam. Then, the door opened.

'Quick,' Dan whispered.

I gestured to Sam and we ran into the dark shop.

'Keep going, out back,' he said.

Sam and I did as he said, fumbling our way towards the back of the shop. Dan closed the door behind him, locked it and followed. As he joined us in the small room, I felt a flicker of anticipation. In the darkness, I looked around for a phone, livestreaming us.

My hand instinctively went into my rucksack and around the stolen saw.

Dan flicked on a light and, squinting, I could see him looking down at my hand. He knew what I was holding. He must have seen what I had done to the PCSO.

'I'm on your side, Cassie, I promise,' he said, holding up his tattooed palms in exactly the same way James had, and exactly how the PCSO hadn't. I let go of the saw.

'Sorry,' I said.

'It's OK, I understand. I'd be the same. I've followed what's going on — I'm not sure I'd trust me either.'

'Then why should I?'

'I guess you can't know for sure.' Dan looked from me to Sam. 'Are you OK?'

'Sore,' Sam said, but as I looked too, I noticed it was more than that. The colour had completely drained from his face. He looked close to passing out.

'Shit, Sam, sit down.'

I went to Sam's side and Dan joined me. We gently lowered Sam onto a tattoo bed. Sam then laid back and, taking a deep breath, closed his eyes. I looked at Dan. He was concerned for my brother. He cared. My gut wasn't wrong.

I walked away from Sam, and Dan followed. When we spoke, we did so quietly as Sam looked close to falling asleep.

'Thank you for helping us.'

Dan simply nodded. 'Is this the person you said you wanted to help, when I did your tattoo?'

'Yes, my brother.'

'It's gotten out of hand.'

'Yes,' I said again. 'I don't know what I've done to warrant this. I only wanted to make a bit of money, to help Sam out of trouble.'

'I've followed you and all this since you came here earlier. It can't be about the car, not for that much money.'

'Nope,' I replied, feeling too tired to try and think of it all again. But Dan was persistent.

'You must have seen something, or taken something, they must think you have dirt on them, or else why offer so much for your . . .'

He trailed off, not wanting to say the word, so I finished his sentence for him.

'Murder.'

'Yes, that,' he said. 'There has to be something.'

'Before the car, all I had done was kiss a bloke, jump in the river, steal that bloody saw and, well, you. Wait, could this be about the saw?' I opened my bag and pulled it out. The old wooden handle was stained with blood, and, seeing it, knowing I had caused that, made me feel sick.

'Hey, you did what you had to do,' Dan said. 'The alternative isn't worth thinking about.'

Pushing down my nausea at the memory, I looked at the saw. Yes, it was from the museum, yes it was old, but it didn't look like something worth a hundred grand.

'It's not this,' I said, dropping it back in my bag. As it landed inside, the metal of the blunted blade hit something metallic. I looked up at Dan and realised I had taken and kept something else.

'What was that?'

'Car keys.'

'Car keys?'

I reached into the bag and pulled out the keys for the Range Rover. 'I forgot I had them.' Could one of the keys be for a lock that was of value? A vault or shipping container of some kind?

'What's that?' Dan asked, reaching over to the bunch. And then I saw it.

'Fuck,' I said. 'It's a flash drive.'

CHAPTER FIFTY-ONE

12.01 a.m. — 2 hours and 29 minutes remaining

'A flash drive?' Dan asked.

'Yeah, it's attached to the keys. I didn't see it before. In fact I forgot I even still had the keys.'

'Shit,' Sam said. He was alert, alarmed by the discovery. 'This has to be it. There must be something on this that they want.'

Dan nodded.

'What the hell could be worth a hundred grand though?' As I looked to Sam and Dan, I could see they were as lost for an answer as I was.

'We need to look on—'

My phone rang, making all three of us jump. I pulled it out of my pocket and looked at the caller ID. It was Mia.

'Aren't you going to get that?' Sam asked, looking like at any moment he might pass out again.

'No,' I said. 'Dan, Sam needs some pain relief, something stronger than the paracetamol I've got, can you help?'

'Yes, sit tight.' He walked into the main shop.

While helping Sam get comfortable, Mia tried ringing again, and again. But I wouldn't pick up. She had abandoned me, and I didn't have time to fix it. I missed her, needed her, but I was too angry, too hurt. One day, I suspected I would forgive her, once this was all behind me — if it would ever be behind me. But right now I didn't have time for forgiveness. I needed to survive. Forgiveness was a luxury.

Dan came back into the room and, helping Sam sit up, he gave him two painkillers and a glass of water.

'It's codeine. Should do the trick,' he said.

'Can I pinch a couple?' I asked, and Dan gave me two without comment.

Sam swallowed the pills and slumped back once more, sleep rushing towards him. I took mine, hoping they would take the edge off the pain in my leg.

'Dan, have you got a computer?'

'Not here, no. We do everything on iPads. But I have one at home.'

'Are you nearby?'

'A ten-minute walk.'

'You live with anyone?' I asked.

'No, it's just me.'

'I need to see what's on the USB. It might help me get out of this mess.'

'Of course. We can go—'

'No, Dan, please. I need you to stay with Sam, keep him safe. I've dragged you too far into this already. I don't want you seen with me. Give me your address, and your keys.'

'Cassie, I—'

'I try not to ask for anything from people, but I'm asking this,' I interrupted. 'I know you don't know me, and giving me your house keys is, well, weird. In any other context it would be ridiculous. But I need a way out.'

'Let me help.'

'You are. And I'm grateful, but I need you to do one more thing. Stay here. Look after my brother, he needs protecting.'

'So do you.'

'No, I need to find out why people want me dead. I need to end this stupid game somehow. Please.'

Dan held my eye for a long moment, and then nodded. 'OK.'

'OK,' I echoed, taking his keys and grabbing my bag. My phone rang. It was Mia again. I declined the call. I needed to focus, to get through town. Dan gave me his address and as I punched it into my phone, Mia tried once more. I declined again.

'I've got another phone, a work phone, if you want?' Dan offered, sensing I was torn and knowing I needed to focus.

'Thank you,' I said.

As Dan walked back into the main shop to get the phone, I opened mine and took down Wakelin's number. I programmed Dan's in as well, and Sam's. They were the only three I needed, and I couldn't help but feel sad for it. My life was in ruins, and the only three people I had were two strangers to me only twenty-four hours ago and my brother.

Mia tried again to call. This time, I turned my phone off.

'Has this phone got DareMe on it?' I asked.

'Yes,' Dan said.

I turned to Sam, who blinked heavily at me, the codeine working fast. 'This will be over, and then we can get you back and get you fixed. OK?'

'Be careful,' he slurred. 'Love you.'

'Love you too,' I replied, giving him a hug and kissing him on the head. I punched Dan's address into the new phone and readied myself to leave.

'Rest up, Sam, I'll be back soon.' I flashed my brother a smile to reassure him. But, in the pit of my stomach, I knew what I was saying might not be true.

CHAPTER FIFTY-TWO

Jamison
12.04 a.m. — 2 hours and 26 minutes remaining

Jamison watched Mia intently. Slumped in her living room chair, he wondered if she might pass out. Every time she slumped further, he slapped her upright again. 'No, no, no, Mia. No sleeping, that spoils the fun.'

He laughed and looked to Mike, but Mike didn't laugh with him. He was wearing a black ski mask, just like ninety per cent of the players out there.

She had taken a beating. She was broken. Cassie would come to save her, that was what she did. But, so far, Cassie wasn't playing properly. She was ignoring her friend's calls.

'Why isn't she picking up?' Jamison asked.

'She's pissed off at me,' Mia said, her voice slow and weak.

'Why?'

'I abandoned her. When the DareMe to kill her was set.'

'My, my, you are a bad friend,' Jamison said. Despite the taunt, he didn't have time for any of this nonsense. Cassie was evading a manhunt, had managed to get to her brother, and because of a tiff between her and her friend, she might not even come here. The plan was obvious — show KJ74 that they were at Mia's and then she would answer the call. She was a woman who wanted to save people, to help people. He'd wanted to use her good nature against her.

It seemed he had underestimated her. Again.

'Is she online?' he asked Mike. He opened the app and looked to see if there was a green icon beside KJ74's name.

'No. Says she was last online twenty-one minutes ago.'

'Ring her again,' Jamison demanded.

'She's not answering,' Mia slurred. The beating she had taken made it almost impossible to move her jaw. 'She's vanished.'

'For your sake, she'd better not have. Ring her again. This time, leave her a message, tell her she needs to call. Tell her to come here. Tell her you need her. Tell her to go to DareMe to see why. She'll come. She'll know what will happen if she doesn't.'

Mia nodded and, with her hands shaking violently, dialled again. It went straight to voicemail. As the phone told her the caller was unavailable and she should leave a message after the tone, Mia looked up at the men in her living room. Despite both of her eyes being swollen to the point she could barely see, and despite some of her teeth feeling loose in her skull, she calmly spoke after the beep.

'Cass, it's me,' she began, forcing herself to keep as calm as she could. 'I'm sorry I wasn't there when you needed me to be. But I am now,' she continued, looking at Jamison defiantly. 'Cass, do not come to my house, do not ring me back. They will kill y—'

'You fucking bitch!' Jamison said, rushing to grab the phone off her. As he snatched it from her hand, Mike grabbed her and threw her onto the ground.

'Don't come here. They will kill you! Cassie, you hear? Don't come to my house!' Mia continued to shout.

Jamison ended the call and stared down at Mia on the floor. 'That was stupid.'

'Fuck you,' Mia said.

Jamison laughed. 'Fuck me? Fuck me? I've worked too hard for too long to have some twenty-something know-it-all bitch stop me. Fuck me? No, fuck you!'

He kicked Mia in the stomach as hard as he could, enjoying the sound of the air being forced from her body.

She moaned, struggling to catch her breath.

Jamison smoothed back his hair, his outburst shocking Mike. 'Right. I guess it is what it is. Best make a little video then, make sure KJ74 sees. If she's gonna fuck about, we'll show her who she is fucking about with. Keep your mask on, no talking. All right?'

Mike nodded. When the phone was set up and recording, Jamison scooped Mia off the floor and sat her back in the chair.

'Tie her up,' he barked at Mike.

Once she was bound, the fight in her fading, Jamison pulled a knife, unlocked it and, without hesitation, comment, or remorse, ran the blade across her throat, opening it up like a yawn.

He wiped the blade on her top, watching her crimson pour.

Then he sniffed, locked his knife, and turned to the camera. 'Her death is on you.'

He ended the recording and cleared his throat. 'Right then.'

He cleaned up in silence. Mike did too, unable to look at his boss.

Jamison noticed. 'Mike?'

'Yeah.'

'You're not having doubts are you, mate?'

'I'm just tired, boss.'

Jamison considered him for a moment, then nodded. 'Soon be done.'

They both left the house where the girl sat upright, her lifeblood covering her motionless body.

From the street, you would never know.

Once Jamison was in his car, he pulled out his phone, opened DareMe and uploaded the video directly to Cassie's inbox. A gift for the girl who had fucked everything up. A message telling her it wouldn't end with Mia Brown. Unless she gave herself up, he would find and kill everyone she loved.

CHAPTER FIFTY-THREE

Wakelin
12.22 a.m. — 2 hours and 8 minutes remaining

It should have taken Wakelin no more than ten minutes to get from the hospital to Mia's house. But the city was in chaos. Pockets of violence had broken out all around Peterborough — protests, people scrapping, flames erupting from burning cars. Looting was widespread, and violence was escalating. People were being assaulted, women who looked a bit like Cassie targeted. Tear gas had been deployed in the city and several people had been seriously injured. Mob mentality was in full force, and people died when the mob ruled.

Wakelin knew, despite the seriousness of needing to get to that address, there was no one to help him. Officers from the Met, Nottingham and Lincolnshire were being drafted in to help control the gangs hiding behind the anonymity that DareMe had created. It had taken a much darker turn. Even with the extra support from other forces, he didn't think it would be enough.

He heard on the radio as he raced towards Werrington that the government were in a COBRA meeting about the situation, discussing bringing the army in. Peterborough was on the verge of collapse. They were talking about putting the city into a temporary martial law state, to send everyone home and enforce a curfew. It would work, but before the city complied, there would be further chaos, just like previous riots in other places. But this one was different. Riots usually happened because of an injustice, which unified people into a contempt for the people in power. Normally, it wasn't about targeting one individual. It wasn't about money. It was about corruption and the powers in place failing to do their jobs. But Peterborough was trying to find and kill a woman named Cassie Jones for nothing other than money. It was a game to them. It made this whole situation more unpredictable, more dangerous.

By the time Wakelin parked his car outside Mia's house and tentatively climbed out of it, thirty minutes had passed. He knew immediately that he was too late. The house was quiet — too quiet. The front door was closed and the street undisturbed. If it wasn't for the broken glass, Wakelin would have been sure he was at the wrong address.

He walked up the front path. The door was slightly ajar. He pushed it open and the hinges squeaked angrily. He called into the darkness. 'Mia? Mia Brown. It's the police.'

He waited for a noise, a voice.

Nothing.

'Mia?' he called once more, advancing into the hallway. He wanted to put a light on, but knew it wasn't a good idea. Over twenty years on the force told him that when you wanted to run into something, it was then you needed to slow down. Despite it feeling quiet, empty, the person he had seen break in on DareMe might still be there, waiting to attack him.

He decided not to call out again.

Slowly moving along the wall, he looked towards the end of the hallway. The kitchen door was open, and light from a street lamp behind the house flooded in, an orange glow wrapping around the kitchen counters, cupboards, and crockery on the draining board. Peering through the small gap in the door to the living room, he could see the furniture was displaced. He placed his right hand on the door, and pushed. It swung silently open.

A coffee table had been upended. The TV had been pulled down, the screen no doubt cracked against the carpet. A living room chair was in the middle of the room, facing away from him. It had been dragged from the corner — the scuff marks on the carpet said as much — and, rounding it, he saw what he had dreaded, what he had hoped to avoid.

Mia Brown's eyes were badly swollen but still open, looking into the fireplace. Fixed, as if she was looking for something, but glazed and lifeless. He didn't need a forensic officer to tell him what had happened. The blood that had ran from the deep cut along her throat, down her top, over the chair and floor said enough.

Once again, he was too late.

'Fuck!' Wakelin shouted.

Unable to control his rage, Wakelin grabbed an ornament from the mantelpiece and threw it. It crashed through the living room window. The sudden noise in an otherwise silent environment killed his need to rage, and, stumbling towards the sofa, he sat, unable to take his eyes off Cassie's friend.

Wakelin felt suddenly done in, exhausted, unable to function. Somehow, those Cassie owed knew everything about her. Somehow, they had not only found out that Mia was a friend, but where she lived too. Whoever it was that Cassie had wronged, they were powerful. He knew Cassie Jones would meet the same fate, and there was nothing he could do. They had found Mia before him. They would find Cassie too. He had been three steps behind this entire time, and he didn't know how he would begin to catch up.

He wanted nothing more than to ring Jen, tell her he was coming home. He wanted to collapse into his wife's arms, bury this in a dark recess of his mind, and never let it see the light again. He needed his wife and so, still looking at the dead girl, he pulled out his phone.

Are you OK? Have you checked in on our boy?

I'm fine, Tom is too. I just FaceTimed him. He says the streets are full of students, partying, but he's promised he won't go out. Are you OK?

Been better.

You have to keep going. Find that girl.

Do I? The whole force is looking for her.

We both know you won't come home, it's not who you are.
Find her, help her, and then come home to me.

I'm tired, Jen. I don't know how to help.

I know you're tired, but we both know you can find her.

You think so?

I know so. Do your job, Greg, and then come home to me.

I love you.

Same x

Wakelin took a deep breath. Jen was right. He composed himself and called the murder scene in. He told them the address and the crime, and then sat back, staring at Mia. He tried to ring Cassie again. Her phone was switched off. She was a ghost — only metaphorically, he hoped.

No sooner had he slumped down, resigned to failing, than the front door creaked. He jumped to his feet, looking for something to defend himself with. Failing even to do that, he balled his hands into fists and waited.

The living room door opened. He took a breath, and then saw who it was.

'Shit, sir, you gave me a scare,' Wakelin said, relieved to see his DI.

'DS Wakelin, are you hurt?'

'No, sir. No. But I was too late. How did you get here so fast?'

'I saw the break-in as well. This city, it's impossible to get anywhere.'

'Yeah.'

'We'll get Forensics in.'

'Anything from the reg of that burnt-out car?'

'We have an owner, but it was reported stolen a few days ago. Not sure why it wasn't flagged. I'm on it though. We'll find out who the driver was.'

'We can't catch a break on this.'

'Maybe they've been sloppy, and we can stop this before time runs out.' He looked at his watch.

'Yeah,' Wakelin said again. 'Boss? Do you think we'll find her?'

'We have to, don't we?'

'We do, before it's too late.' He wished he believed it, but there were less than two hours to go, and, with the end of the dare only getting closer, people would become more and more desperate to win the £100,000 attached to it. Desperate people were the most dangerous.

Looking at Mia's lifeless body once more, he noticed that the chair had been positioned intentionally, and when he realised why, he felt sick. She had been staged. The mantelpiece of her fake fireplace provided the perfect platform for a phone to film it all. They hadn't been able to get Cassie to come to them, so they were going to make her feel so guilty, so culpable that she gave up entirely. He hoped to God she wouldn't feel that her best friend was murdered because of her.

As his boss took in the scene, Wakelin sat in silence, a question playing on his mind.

'Are you OK, Wakelin?'

'Boss,' he began, 'who the hell are we dealing with?'

'How do you mean?'

'These people that want Cassie dead. They know where she lives, they know who her friends are and how to find them. How can these people know so much?'

His boss, his DI, a respected and well-decorated officer of thirty years' service looked at him, and Wakelin waited for him to speculate as he always did. But he simply stared back.

'DI Jamison, who are we dealing with?' Wakelin asked again, and Jamison took a deep breath.

'Someone really bad,' was all he said, pulling out his phone and taking a step away.

CHAPTER FIFTY-FOUR

12.33 a.m. — 1 hour and 57 minutes remaining

Staggering through the city was tough. Violence was everywhere, and everyone was looking for me. Fighting through the crowd, knowing if anyone saw me I would surely die, was the hardest ten minutes of my life. But thankfully, just when I was sure I was about to be stopped and examined, like countless other woman around me, tear gas was fired into the crowd. Everyone dispersed.

Despite it burning my eyes and lungs, I was able to get through to the other side of the masses, and found myself completely alone on Park Road. It was one of the oldest streets in the city, home to a prestigious school and lined with 200-year-old houses that these days must have cost well into six figures. If it wasn't for the smoke from the flares that hung in the sky behind me, and the occasional noise of someone coughing, you could almost believe it was just any other night here. On this street it almost felt safe, but I knew that was my tired mind working on an illusion to encourage me to slow, for my cortisol to dip, and to allow for my overstressed, anxious body to stop.

It was lying to me, to try and save me. Ironic.

Pushing along Park Road, my eyes still burning but thankfully clear enough for me to see between blinks, I looked into some of the houses I passed, with their huge bay windows and soft internal lighting. In one there was a woman sitting by a reading lamp, immersed in a book. My mum would have been around the same age. In another, the news was playing aerial shots of Peterborough on the TV screen. I stopped behind a tree and watched for a moment. It wasn't just the city centre. Bretton was in chaos, as was outside the hospital. Even my street was bedlam. They all knew where I lived. The shot then cut to Birmingham, where there was unrest too. Manchester, London, Cardiff. This thing that had started being about me was no longer that at all. I was simply the excuse. People wanted to rage.

I looked at my watch. Just under two hours to go. I also saw the date. It had passed midnight. It was now the twelfth.

The anniversary of Mum's death.

Again, the irony wasn't lost.

Ten years to the day after I had caused my mum to die, fate had come for me. And even though there was less than two hours left on the dare, I knew it wouldn't end. They would post a new one, and a new one. They would keep going until I was dead.

I would have the same day and month on my headstone as Mum. I didn't see how I would make it through to the thirteenth. I just had to hope Sam would be left alone now. All of this had been for him. I had fixed his debt to clear my own, and maybe — maybe — Mum would be waiting for me. Maybe she would forgive me.

I moved on towards the address Dan had given me. A first-floor flat in an old building that I suspected was once one large house before developers adapted for modern living. When I found it, I climbed the internal stairs, unlocked the door and stepped inside, relief flooding into my bones as I locked the door behind me, sealing me in. I waited for a few minutes, just to make sure I hadn't been followed.

Satisfied I was safe, I walked further into this stranger's world. I wasn't sure what I was expecting of Dan's home, but it was beautiful. Everything was aligned somehow, and as I moved through his hallway into the living room, I felt a sense of calm wash over me. I saw his laptop, exactly where he had said it would be, but I needed water first.

His kitchen was a plant-filled space that seemed more organic than man-made. I ran the tap, splashed my face, cleaned my eyes some more and then drank directly from it. With my thirst quenched and my face cleansed, I felt a glimmer of hope. I had worked out why they were after me, and maybe I would find out how to end this.

I went back into the living room, sat in a leather wingback chair and opened Dan's laptop. I punched in the password he had told me, and once his home screen loaded, I pulled the USB out of my pocket.

This stupid piece of plastic and memory was the reason I was in this mess. If only I had just left it there, or swallowed my indignation, my pride, and not stolen their car. I had done it as a 'fuck you' for hurting my brother, but look at the consequences — I might be killed, Sam too. If only I had done things differently, had thought before I acted. But then, that was the story of my life, wasn't it? Act first, regret later.

The USB felt heavy in my hand, hot. I pushed it into the laptop, then waited for it to connect and load.

'Right, here goes,' I said, double-tapping. The icon opened. There were three files, each entitled with only two letters: EB, HM, OM. I tapped on one, OM, and it opened several documents, PDFs and images of someone called Owen Moore.

'As in MP Owen Moore?' I said aloud.

They had so much information on him. His bank accounts, pictures of inside what I could only assume was his home. There were even audio files of telephone conversations. They knew everything about the man.

Going back, I looked down the list to see if they had my initials — CJ. But they had nothing. About me, or against me.

I exited the file, clicked on EB. Elliot Barnes. The actor. The third, HM, was for a Helen Merrell. I didn't know her but, googling her, I quickly learned she was CEO of a very large company based in Germany.

Whoever it was I was mixed up with, they could access anything and everything on anyone. I went back into the file marked OM, and saw that while at first it looked like they had information only, it wasn't just about that. The MP's financial affairs were interesting, with vast amounts of money coming and going into overseas accounts. There were pictures of him with younger women. Lots of them, and none of them his wife. And suddenly I knew why it was so important to them. This USB held the secrets of three important people. Wealthy people. It was worth a lot of money.

If I found a way to get it back, arranged a safe drop-off location, pleaded my innocence, my ignorance, maybe it would all just stop, and whoever these people were would simply disappear back into the shadows they'd come from. It was a long shot but it was the first clear plan to end this without me dying.

Using Dan's phone, I opened DareMe. I would post a video, explaining I knew what I had done, and how I could fix it, and would ask them to get in touch via my inbox.

When I logged on to my page, I saw there were several messages waiting for me. Most were of people still wanting me to do dares or to give myself up because they deserved to be rich. One message didn't have any words — it was just a video. I tapped 'play'.

At first I couldn't make out what I was seeing as the room was dark. But there was audio, so I turned it up on the phone. The sound was of a woman crying, sobbing. A lamp was turned on, and I gasped, covering my mouth with my hand. Tears began to form, clouding my vision, and I blinked, forcing them to fall. Mia looked unrecognisable, her beautiful face battered, swollen, her eyes barely open. As she moaned, I could see several of her teeth were missing.

'Oh, God. No.'

A man walked into frame, wearing a mask so they couldn't be seen. He pulled a knife and, quick as a flash, he swiped it across Mia's throat. At first, nothing happened, she didn't make a noise, didn't react, and I thought they hadn't hurt her. Then her head fell back and deep crimson blood gushed down her front. She choked for a few seconds, then her head fell forward. The blood continued to pour until she was completely saturated in it.

He then approached the camera.

'Her death is on you.'

The video stopped.

I couldn't breathe. My chest wouldn't function. I fought to draw air in.

Those bastards had killed her. They had killed her because of me. And no matter what I did, they would kill me too. And Sam. And anyone else who got in their way.

I let myself cry until my eyes hurt all over again and my ribs ached. I would never recover from this. Mia's final moments, terrified and alone, were because of me. I knew that every time I blinked, every time I closed my eyes to sleep, I would see her throat being cut, would see her blood pour.

I deserved as much. If this was just about me, I would let them come for me now. But Sam was caught up in this, Dan too. No one else would die because of me. No one.

If I tried to return the USB they so clearly needed, I'd never be safe. I needed them caught. I needed help.

Going to the contact list, I scrolled to Wakelin's number and hesitated. I wasn't sure if I trusted him. But now I had no choice.

CHAPTER FIFTY-FIVE

Jamison
12.39 a.m. — 1 hour and 51 minutes remaining

The best friend was dead. The message had been clear, but still the girl was causing problems. Jamison had hoped that she had lost the USB or destroyed it, but the notification on his phone told him otherwise. Not only did she still have it, but she had opened it. She had accessed the contents. She knew more than she was allowed.

He needed her dead more than ever.

Opening DareMe, he went into the dare he had set for her life. He couldn't change the time, but he could amend one aspect of it to offer more incentive. The city was feral for a hundred grand — adding some more should speed things along. He upped the total and watched as players and watchers engaged with comments on the timeline. Greed was a powerful motivator.

Putting his phone away, knowing the excitement his update on DareMe would cause, he looked back at DS Wakelin. 'Help is coming.'

'Thank you, boss.'

'Don't worry, Greg, we'll find her.' Upping the dare value would do exactly that.

'I just don't know how these people know so much,' Wakelin said again.

Jamison could see that Wakelin was exhausted. The case was now too large for him, and he was broken by it, which was good. He needed him to fade away, for it to become too big for him to manage. He needed Wakelin gone.

'DS Wakelin?'

'Yes, boss?'

'You look tired. Go home.'

'Sir, there are still two hours to go. I want to help.'

'You've done so much.'

'Sir, if it's all right with you, I'd rather stay, even if I'm in the office. I need to do something, anything. Maybe I could try and track down whoever stole that Range Rover?'

'Of course,' Jamison said, knowing full well Wakelin never would.

The DS looked Jamison in the eye. 'How do we stop this, sir?'

'I don't know if we can,' Jamison said.

Wakelin nodded, quietly resigned to the fact that his boss was right.

Jamison took Wakelin by the shoulder, guiding him away from the mess that once was Mia, while another officer arrived at the scene.

'Mike,' Jamison said, 'I'm afraid we were too late. She's gone. From now on, anything to do with the Cassie Jones case comes directly to me. Understand?'

'Of course.'

'DS Wakelin is going back to the station. Wakelin, I'd prefer you to go home, but if you insist on helping, anything that comes through — and I mean anything — you ring me, OK? We all want to find the girl.'

Wakelin nodded and walked towards his car. 'Boss, where's Harry?'

'Dead on his feet. He's resting. Maybe you should as well?'

'I'm good.'

'All right. See you back at the office.'

'Thanks, boss.'

'Is he gonna be a problem, boss?' Mike asked once Wakelin was far enough away.

'No. He's done, he's broken. I'll keep him busy in the office until we find her.'

'Why did you put the prize money up?' Mike continued, still watching Wakelin, who had opened his car door and slumped behind the steering wheel.

'She still has the USB, and she has accessed it.'

'Shit.'

'Yeah. I need her dead.'

'Understood.'

'Make it look like we are investigating in there.' Jamison gestured into the living room. 'Others will be here soon to take over.'

As Mike walked into the living room, Jamison watched Wakelin pull out his phone and speak to someone for a while. He was probably ringing his wife. People did such things after seeing death. But as Wakelin hung up, Jamison couldn't help but notice his energy was less defeated somehow, and as he drove away, he nodded to Jamison.

Jamison nodded back. Wakelin was up to something.

He joined Mike in the living room, not caring too much whether their DNA was found at the scene. If anybody asked questions he could blame it on being sloppy on arrival. They'd get a slap on the wrist at worst.

Mike looked up. Something was clearly on his mind.

'What?' Jamison demanded.

'Boss, I'm nervous. This isn't going as planned.'

'No shit it isn't as planned. But everything will be under control. We are still going to retire in the sun, this is just a blip.'

'What if she . . .'

'What? Mike, what? Talks? Who to? She is terrified, she thinks everyone is out to get her. She's seen the USB, yes, but she has nowhere to turn. She's alone. Have faith. She'll be dead soon.'

'Sorry, boss.'

Jamison nodded. 'It's OK, we are all stressed. Stay here, will you? I've got something I need to take care of.'

CHAPTER FIFTY-SIX

12.47 a.m. — 1 hour and 43 minutes remaining

My call with Wakelin was short. I told him I knew why they wanted me dead and that I had seen what was on the USB. When I told him the details he went quiet, so quiet I was sure the line had disconnected.

'I'm going to ring you back,' he said, and hung up.

I was shocked. He had spent all night trying to reach me, and when I reached out, he hung up. I didn't know what to make of it. In the time since this 'game' began, I had seen the best and worst in people. Some wanted to help, like Dan and James. Some, like the PCSO, wanted to kill. His actions alone had lit the green light for everyone to try — if it was OK for a police officer to want me dead, then it was OK for anyone to.

Wakelin said he was on my side, but was he really? Why would he hang up? Maybe he knew where I was somehow. Maybe he was able to access where I was calling from and had said he would call back, but really he was going to come and kill me. It would explain a lot. The information on the USB was detailed — maybe he had gathered it. He was a detective after all. I couldn't take any chances so, grabbing the USB, I left the safety of the house. If he rang back as he said he would, rather than turning up at Dan's house, maybe I could trust him.

I hid behind a row of garages. The ground was strewn with broken bottles and rubbish. I waited, and as I did, I opened DareMe, just to make sure no one was livestreaming nearby. Hundreds were, but none close to where I was. However, that wasn't what grabbed my attention. There had been an update on the dare, and I opened it.

Welcome, player KJ74
Your DareMe challenge:
Kill player KJ74 (£150,000)
You have 1 hour and 41 minutes remaining.
Do you accept?

They had upped the dare fifty grand more. I was doomed.
The phone rang.
'Cassie?' Wakelin said.
I hesitated. 'Yeah?'
'Are you OK?'
'That's a stupid question.'
'Sorry, I mean, are you hurt?'
'No.'
'I would ask you where you are, but I don't think you'll tell me.'
'You're right.'
'Cassie, the USB. I need to see it.'
'They killed her,' I said.
'I know. I'm sorry.'
'They streamed her death. I watched her die.'
'Cassie, I can't imagine how hard this is for you, and I know it's impossible to trust anyone. But—'
'And the dare is now fifty grand more.'
'What?' He was either the best actor I had ever heard, and in the wrong profession, or he truly didn't know. 'Shit.'
'You didn't know?'

'No, Cassie, it seems I am last to find things out at the moment.'

'I'm just going to ask,' I continued, too tired for any more games, 'is it you? Are you trying to kill me?'

'No, Cassie, I'm not,' he said. 'But I can see why you've asked. The information on that USB, from what you're telling me . . .'

'Yeah. Looks like something only a copper might be able to access.'

'It's why I hung up. I wanted to be alone to talk.'

'Why?'

'You know better than anyone else. People, even people who look like they are good, sometimes cannot be trusted. Cassie, I need to see what's on that USB.'

'I'm not coming in.'

'I wouldn't expect you to. You've done a brilliant job of hiding so far — you need to keep doing that.'

'Then how?'

'Find somewhere to hide it and then get out of there. Once you're gone, message me to tell me where it is, and I'll come and collect it.'

I paused for a moment. His plan was the same one I would demand. But then, it could be an elaborate trap, to make me feel like someone in power wanted to help. I didn't know if Wakelin was the PCSO, or the nurse.

'I've backed it up,' I lied. 'So, if you—'

'I know. Cassie, let me show you I'm on your side. Hide the USB and let me find it. I want to help. Look, I will be honest — the things you've done on DareMe, the crimes, you will have to be held to account.'

'I know.'

'And I will arrest you for them. It's my job.'

'I understand.'

'But this — this thing — this stupid fucking game. I will not let you die, Cassie. You have made mistakes. But you do not deserve this.'

I weighed it up. Without him, I had nothing; no one who could help me get out of this, help me survive. I needed to take a leap of faith.

'I'll call you back in ten minutes,' I said.

CHAPTER FIFTY-SEVEN

Wakelin
12.59 a.m. — 1 hour and 31 minutes remaining

Wakelin drove aimlessly around the outskirts of the city, watching as police fought to control the madness the city had embraced. He knew he should stop, assist, but Cassie was more important. If he could find her, get her to trust him, find out what was on the USB and trace it to the source then he might be able to end a night that would go down in Peterborough's history. So many would be arrested after tonight, and so many would state they had never done anything like it before. It would of course be true — mob mentality was a well-documented phenomenon. But the participants would also all be held to account.

Driving past a street where a bonfire had been built in the middle of the road, he looked down at his clock. Ten minutes had passed and still no call. He began to assume she had got cold feet.

Then his phone pinged. The message was short. Three words.

Dates. Patrol. Rated.

He knew exactly what it was.

He opened What3words, an app that used three words to pinpoint the exact location of anywhere in the whole world. He punched in those three and saw the three-metre-square location was on Burghley Road, north of the city. No sooner had he worked out where to go, another message pinged through.

Rear wheel of the white Mini.

Putting his foot down, Wakelin raced towards the city, fighting through groups of masked-up youths prowling the streets. He almost turned on his siren and blues, but realised it would likely make him more of a target and less of a deterrent.

When he arrived at the location, he found the Mini and, stooping down, he pulled the USB from behind the wheel. Standing up, he looked around. The wind blew through the lifeless limbs of old trees, and carried on the air was the faint sound of the city mobs and the smell of smoke. There was no sign of the girl. She was long gone. Hiding somewhere safe, waiting for the night to be over.

He allowed himself to smile. She'd proved herself to be much more resourceful and courageous than he'd thought when he first laid eyes on her in the hospital.

He turned to walk towards his car and saw another approaching, its lights blinding him. When the car slowed, he was shocked to see it was DI Jamison. Pulling out a key, he quickly scratched the Mini, and walked towards where Jamison was parking.

'Boss?' Wakelin asked, when Jamison got out of the car.

'DS Wakelin. May I ask what you are doing?'

'I'm wired. I needed to drive before going back in. I thought I saw something suspicious, so I stopped.' Wakelin made sure the USB was tightly enclosed in his balled hand.

'I see.'

'Just some kids. I told them to go home before they were arrested. Not that it will stop them of course. I'm gonna head to the office now, like you said. Help where I can.'

'Why were you at the car?'

'That's where they were standing. I think they scratched it. Probably intended to burn it, like they've seen on DareMe.'

Jamison didn't comment but walked over towards the car. Wakelin quickly slipped the USB in his pocket before joining his boss's side.

'Little shits,' Jamison said, looking at the deep scratch in the paintwork.

'Yep. I doubt they'll go home, but they might think twice before doing anything else stupid.'

'Good work,' Jamison said, holding Wakelin's eye a little too long. Wakelin noticed the question in his eyes, but reasoned that he would have one — he was the DI, and Wakelin was behaving oddly, making himself appear like he was hiding something. Which, of course, he was.

'I'll follow you in,' Jamison said, his statement clear. Wakelin was to leave, to go to the office as told, and his boss was going to make sure he did. That worked for Wakelin because the office was exactly where he needed to be.

Wakelin set off, Jamison following as he said he would. He felt terrible for hiding valuable information from his boss, a man he had known ever since he first joined the force, a friend. But until he could see with his own eyes what Cassie had described on the USB, he knew to keep his cards close, just in case. Something wasn't making sense about it all. Somehow, those who Cassie was mixed up with had the ability to get a lot of information. And over the course of the night, Wakelin had been last to find out key information that would help Cassie.

His gut was telling him something. He just hoped what it was saying was completely wrong.

CHAPTER FIFTY-EIGHT

1.04 a.m. — 1 hour and 26 minutes remaining

When Wakelin stood up from the rear of the Mini and looked around, I was sure, for a moment, he could see me. He looked towards the tree I was hiding behind for a long time, and then he smiled. I didn't know what that meant. Then a car approached and another man joined him. I couldn't hear what either man said, and when Wakelin led the guy towards the Mini, I was sure I was witnessing him telling the other man about the USB. However, as the second man walked to inspect the Mini, Wakelin put the USB in his back pocket, without showing him. They spoke a little more and then both drove away.

If he had said anything about me being there, or him having the USB, more would have happened, surely? They would have tried to see me, or made calls to get more police there to bring me in, or something. But both had simply left. That told me Wakelin hadn't said anything to the other man.

I had to hope that trusting him was the right decision. He might have kept the information quiet, because he wanted me all for himself. But again, it was about choice, and I had no other options. If Wakelin was the man he said he was, if he was really trying to help me, he would find out what he could from the USB, and he would find a way to stop this. All I had to do now was survive long enough to see that happen.

I wanted to go back to Sam, to hide with him, but the city wasn't safe for me. And, as Wakelin said, I would be arrested. I would no doubt go to prison for my crimes.

If I survived. Now there was always that caveat.

I had to keep moving.

When I was young, Mum use to take me to Cromer, and we would often explore the little towns around it. I couldn't remember the name of most, but I did one — it was a little village called West Runton. It was right by the sea. There were a few shops, a few pubs, an afternoon tea café, and not much else. People there were kinder somehow, and I remembered that lots were retired. It felt peaceful, quiet, safe. I would go there. If I could.

As I walked, I took out my phone and messaged Dan.

Is Sam OK?

A message came back instantly.

Sleeping, but he's OK, are you?

Maybe.

Can I do anything?

I need a way out of the city. I'm by Town Park.

Leave it with me.

Putting the phone away, I lowered my head and pressed on. I needed to get as far away from people as I could, and then maybe Dan would have a plan. I let myself daydream of a little house, a two-up two-down in West Runton. I would get a job working at one of the pubs or shops. Get a dog. Sam would be there too, definitely working in one of the pubs, and Mia would visit all the—

I stopped myself. Mia wouldn't be doing anything, because Mia was dead. Her blood pouring from her gaping throat was on my hands. The image came back, brighter and harder than when I saw it on the phone, almost like I was in the room with her, watching crimson liquid gush like floodgates had been opened by the steel of the blade.

I felt like I was drowning. I couldn't catch my breath. I stumbled against a tree and lowered myself to the ground, fighting to gain control once more. This is what it must have felt like for Mia, drowning in her own blood as it poured down her throat into her stomach, filling her lungs. She would have felt unimaginable terror, pain. She died knowing it was happening, she bled knowing it was the end, and as I fought to breathe I felt like I was about to join her.

I was so caught up in Mia's final moments, and my guilt, I stopped focusing on my surroundings, and when I finally did, I knew it was too late.

Right in front of me, his features silhouetted by the street lamp behind him, loomed a man.

CHAPTER FIFTY-NINE

1.07 a.m. — 1 hour and 23 minutes remaining

'Are you all right?' the man said, stepping to my side so I could see his profile. He looked like he was in his late seventies or early eighties. Behind him there was a woman holding a dog on a lead.

I pulled myself onto my feet. 'Yes, fine, thank you. It's not safe out here tonight,' I said, wondering why an older couple would be walking their dog at a little after one in the morning, especially when the world had gone to shit — unless they didn't know. 'There are riots. It's crazy, you should go home.'

'Riots?' the woman asked.

'In the city. Have you not seen it on the news?'

'Oh, no. No,' she said.

'You need to go home. People are getting hurt,' I said, hating the idea of these people getting caught up in something that was my mess.

'Why are you out then?' the man asked.

'Why are you?' I replied. 'It's the middle of the night.'

'We always walk this late,' the man said.

'Always have,' the woman added, beaming my way. 'It's so peaceful at night. Are you alone?' she asked.

'I'm just . . . just trying to get to a friend's.'

'Are you sure you're all right? It's just, you look like you're hurt,' the man asked.

'I'm all right.'

'Are you in trouble?'

I hesitated. It was clear they didn't know what DareMe was. So I nodded, hoping that would be enough, and they wouldn't ask why.

'Oh no, is it a man?' the woman asked. I knew what I looked like — middle of the night, alone, injured. I was a woman fleeing, and she had assumed it was from a bad partner or husband. I leaned into it, and nodded.

'Oh, you poor thing. Should we call someone?' she asked.

'No, no, please don't. I just need to get to my friend's, out of the city for a while.'

'We should call the police,' the man said.

'No, please don't. I just need to get out of the city.'

'But, if a man is hurting you . . .'

'Please,' I begged, and the man looked from me to his wife. She implored him too, and he sighed.

'Have you got a car?' he said, thankfully moving the conversation along.

'No.'

The man looked at the woman, an unspoken question passing between them. A lifetime of companionship rendered conversation unnecessary.

'Oh, all right,' the man said.

'Come with us, we live close by,' the woman said. 'We have a car.'

'No, thank you. I don't want to cause any trouble. They — I mean, he is trying to find me.'

'We are literally two minutes around that corner. I can drive you out of the city,' the man said.

I looked at the couple, the earnestness in their eyes, the older generation pull to do good. I weighed up the risk to me and potential risk to them. Their dog, a small Tibetan breed

I couldn't remember the name of, came over and licked my face. It made me smile for the first time since it all began.

'Let us help,' the man continued. 'We are old. No one looks much at the old.'

I nodded, and looking around to make sure we were alone, I followed the couple towards their home.

As we walked, I told them I needed to look at my phone, hoping it wouldn't make me appear rude. I wanted to scroll DareMe, see if anyone was streaming nearby. From what I could see, there was nothing. However, one person streaming close to me, even watching me, could easily be missed. Everyone on the app seemed to be in the city, all the posts about this dare.

I went to my profile. I had over 200,000 followers and a message congratulating me on being the highest-profile player on DareMe.

I closed the phone and relied on my own senses. The wind blew through the trees that lined the street. A dog barked somewhere nearby. The hum of the city centre riots floated over. The smell of smoke lingered. But around me, close to me, all I could hear was the shuffling of feet, the clip of dog claws on tarmac, and my own ragged breathing.

It only took two minutes, as the man said, to reach their house, and as I entered, I sighed. I wouldn't stay long but I felt safe again.

'Take your shoes off, please,' the man said.

'Of course.' I kicked them off. As I did, I noticed blood on my socks, and I quickly pulled them off and stuffed them in my shoes. I didn't want to have to answer the obvious questions. Placing my bag down too, I followed them into their living room. They offered me a seat, after which both of them went through to what I could see to be the kitchen. I perched on the edge of an armchair, the floral pattern as loud as it was inviting. My memories of my nan were hazy — she passed when I was a little girl — but the smell of this living room took me back to a memory of a Christmas before Sam was born. It was just me and Mum and Nana in a room much like this one. In the background, Bing Crosby played, the house warm and cosy. There was a hand-carved wooden bowl on the coffee table, and Mum said I couldn't eat any sweets as I'd spoil my dinner. Nan gave me a mischievous wink and, when Mum left the room, she put one in my hand. I giggled as I chewed the toffee, and Mum saw, but she didn't say anything.

The woman came back in, holding a cup of tea, its steaming top making me realise how cold I felt. She handed it to me with a smile. 'Here.'

'Thank you.'

'Graham is just getting ready to take you where you need to go. Do you need something to eat?'

I wanted to say no, but no sooner had she mentioned food, my stomach growled angrily, speaking for me.

She smiled. 'I'll make you a sandwich for the road.'

'What is your name?' I asked.

'Sally.'

'Cassie.'

'Hello, dear.'

'Sally. You and Graham are very kind, thank you.'

She nodded, smiled again. 'Warm yourself by the heater,' she said, and once more left the room.

With the house being warm, the chair comfortable and the carpet thick, cushioning my aching feet, I let myself lull for a moment. Wakelin had hidden the USB from the other man. He was on my side. I let myself feel hopeful that he would work out who it belonged to and stop them. In less than ninety minutes, the dare would be void. If he could get to them, then they wouldn't be able to post a new one. In ninety minutes, it could all be over. Sam would heal. I would too, and that would be that.

Closing my eyes, I listened to a clock on the mantelpiece, each tick taking me closer to the end of this nightmare. It was comforting, hypnotic, and I felt myself begin to drift. My head slumped slightly, jolting me awake. Knowing I couldn't fall asleep, I stood up.

The house was so still, so quiet.

Too quiet.

There should have been noise, the clatter of a plate as a sandwich was made, conversation. Keys jangling, something. I strained to listen and heard nothing.

I moved towards the door that led into the kitchen and, once my ear was so close it brushed against the wood, I heard Sally whispering from the other side.

'. . . I'm telling you. She told me her name was Cassie, Graham — Cassie. It's her. I'm sure of it.'

CHAPTER SIXTY

1.12 a.m. — 1 hour and 18 minutes remaining

They had tricked me. They knew exactly who I was and what was going on, but what I didn't know was where they sat with this knowledge. Some had helped, some wanted to hurt and, even though they were octogenarians, I didn't want to assume their intentions. So I began to move away from the kitchen, ready to make my escape. I had taken no more than three steps back when the kitchen door opened and Sally smiled towards me.

I didn't know if running into the street would be jumping from the frying pan into the fire. So, when Sally walked in, smiling, I smiled back, pretending I hadn't heard their conversation. I needed a moment, to think of my next step.

'How's the tea?'

'It's great, thank you.' If I needed to, I could throw it in her face and make a dash for it. I didn't want to act before thinking, though. So, I took another sip.

'Thank you again for this. Not many seem to want to help a stranger anymore,' I said, testing the waters.

Sally smiled again and Graham walked into the room, a sandwich loaded onto a plate.

'I've only got ham. I hope you're not a vegetarian or anything?'

'No, no, ham is great, thank you.'

Graham handed me the plate and then took a seat on the sofa opposite me. Sally joined his side, and both watched me intently. The smell of the bread was enticing, and I wanted nothing more than to devour the whole sandwich in one go, but they knew who I was. They knew what I was worth.

I looked around, trying to find a phone streaming, but couldn't. With them watching, I took a small bite, just a touch of the crust. My mouth salivated at the few crumbs I had given it, begging for more. But I couldn't go on.

'You need to eat,' Sally said.

I nodded, taking another minuscule bite.

'You look so hungry.'

'I am,' I said, 'but I feel a little sick. I might need some air.'

'No,' Sally said, too fast. 'No. Graham, turn the heating down. As you said, it's not safe out there.'

I nodded again, putting the sandwich down. 'I'll try again in a minute.' I picked up my tea and hesitated. I didn't know anything about poison. Was it odourless, tasteless? Could it be in the bread, or in my tea? I pretended to sip, fake swallowing.

'Graham?' I said, holding the old man's eye. 'Could we leave, please? I'm worried about dragging you into this.'

'No,' Sally hissed. It startled me, Graham too, and when I looked at her, I could see she was thinking, processing, working out how she could kill me and become rich.

I stared at her, the silence consuming, the clock the only thing telling us that the world hadn't been muted.

Tick. Tick. Tick.

I swallowed and stood. 'I'm leaving now. Do not try and stop me.'

'You can't go,' Sally said, her voice pathetic and small. She tried to grab me, but I pushed her into the sofa.

'Graham, stop her, stop her!' the woman wailed.

I walked towards the door and Graham stepped towards me. I opened my mouth to warn him that I would hurt him, when I saw a knife in his hand.

'Stab her, Graham, do it!' Sally shouted.

Graham raised the knife, and even though I was younger, faster, I knew if I tried to grab him, he would hurt me — then kill me. I needed to stall.

'You're not filming,' I said, backing away into the middle of the room.

'What?'

'You only get paid if you film the event. The dare is null and void without it being livestreamed.'

'She's right,' Sally said.

'I know she's right,' Graham countered. 'Get my phone, will you?'

Sally walked into the kitchen and I backed away further towards the chair I'd sat in, towards the steaming cup of tea. I needed just a few more seconds.

'I thought you were decent,' I said.

'So did I,' he said. 'We did really just want to help you. But then Sally worked out who you are. It's a lot of money. Sally and I could see the world.'

'You'd kill a woman, so you can travel?'

'It sounds awful when you put it like that. But I will die soon — it could be a few years, it could be ten. We never travelled. We raised kids, looked after this home, paid our taxes, voted. We did our part, and for what? To be forgotten in our golden years? To struggle to get by? We deserve it.'

My stalling had worked. As Sally stepped back into the room, Graham looked towards her. I grabbed my cup, the tea still hot, and threw it into his face. He screamed, covering his eyes, and the knife clattered to the floor.

I pushed past Sally, sending her crashing into the wall, and hobbled out into the hallway. She was surprisingly fast. As I went to grab my shoes, and bag, she was there, brandishing the knife her husband had dropped. I left my things and escaped into the cold night.

Sally pursued, but I slammed the door into her, and she tumbled back into the house. Before either she or Graham could get up, or shout for help, I ran.

CHAPTER SIXTY-ONE

1.15 a.m. — 1 hour and 15 minutes remaining

The cold worked its way from the ground into my feet and ankles, making each step difficult, painful. But I pushed the discomfort down and kept running. I didn't think the old couple would pursue, but they might call for help, and then others would come. They would be well fed, they would have slept. They would have shoes and socks on their feet. They would have friends to help.

I couldn't afford to stop.

I saw an orange hue hanging in the sky ahead of me. Fire. There was trouble ahead, and my options were limited. If I turned back, the older couple might be out looking for me, alerting people that KJ74 was nearby. Beyond them was the city centre, which I knew would mean certain death. So, with no choice, I walked towards the fresh glow in the sky, pulling my face mask on to try and blend in until I was through the other side.

It didn't take long to see where the fire was. Ahead, the road was blocked by three cars, the middle one on fire. Around it, people watched as it burned and hissed.

Keeping my composure, I approached a woman who was filming, standing beside a small wall that was someone's front garden.

'Holy shit,' I said, hoping to sound excited rather than terrified.

It worked, as the person next to me, streaming the event, turned and filmed me. 'I know, right?'

'Good idea though. Block the road so if she comes this way, she can't get out.'

'Exactly. So, you playing or watching?'

'Watching, mostly. You?' I said, impressed with myself for being able to hide in plain sight.

'Yeah, same, watching. Unless she turns up. How long is left?'

I looked at my watch. 'Just over an hour. Think she's gonna make it?'

'No way,' the woman said, turning to film as the car popped angrily in the fire. Once it settled, she looked my way again. Then, she looked at my feet. 'Hey, why have you got no shoes on?'

Shit.

I hesitated, not knowing how to answer.

'I said, why ain't you got shoes on?' she asked again, and I began to move. 'Bitch, it's you, isn't it? Hey! Hey!' she shouted as the car exploded, sending a fireball shooting into the sky.

Grabbing her, I pulled her back, covering her mouth. She fought to get free and in the struggle, she pulled my balaclava off my face.

If I didn't subdue her somehow, she would shout once more, and those watching the fire, like moths to the flame, would turn their attention to me. I had to run.

I pushed her as hard as I could into a garden wall. She fell over it, cracking her head on the floor, but not hard enough to knock her out. As I pushed on through the gap between the outside car and the pavement, the heat of the flames hurt my face, but I didn't stop. The car beside me began to catch, and fire ripped through its interior just as I cleared it.

I looked back. The woman was pointing my way, but she wouldn't be able to reach me. The road was now blocked by flames.

I ran. Rounding a corner, I pressed on over a number of streets until I was sure I'd not been followed. I stopped, panting to catch my breath, and then looked back. Three people were there, looking towards me, two men and a woman. They stood together, staring my way, like pack hunters ready for the kill.

'Hey, Cassie.'

I didn't reply, but began to back way. At first, they didn't move. They just watched. Then, they slowly advanced, perfectly in unison. A three-headed monster coming to kill me.

CHAPTER SIXTY-TWO

Wakelin
1.18 a.m. — 1 hour and 12 minutes remaining

Wakelin drove carefully towards the station. All around now, he could see people committing crimes. Stealing, scrapping, even smaller things like smoking a joint in plain sight. Peterborough was a lawless state. As much as he wanted to join the fight, Jamison had more or less ordered him to the station, and even if he hadn't, the USB Cassie had left was burning a hole in his pocket. If she was telling the truth about the contents — and he had no reason to think otherwise — whoever it belonged to had a lot of power.

Wakelin could feel Jamison watching from behind. It niggled him that the boss had followed. The city was in trouble — and Wakelin should have been looking for Cassie. A question began to form, but he quickly dismissed it. Paranoia was contagious, it seemed.

Arriving at the office, he waited for his DI, and both men walked into the situation room together. It was like a ghost town. Where there were usually at least half a dozen officers milling around, even in the middle of the night, there was no one else on their floor. Everyone was out, helping, as he should have been.

Arriving at his desk, Wakelin sat and sighed, waiting for his computer to load.

'Are you sure you don't want to go home?' Jamison asked.

'No, I want to help. I'll keep an eye on DareMe, and if anything comes in, I'll help. Looks like someone needs to hold the fort,' Wakelin said, looking around.

Jamison looked around too, his face unreadable. 'This is a complete shit show,' he said. 'Glad you're with me.'

'Want me to try to get Harry back in, boss?'

'No, no. Let him be.' He tapped Wakelin on the shoulder and made his way into his office.

Wakelin watched out of the corner of his eye and, once his boss was behind his desk, blocked from view by his monitor, he pulled the USB out of his pocket.

Keeping an eye on his boss's door, he pushed it into his computer and the icon leaped onto his screen. He was just about to tap it when he hesitated.

Cassie had accessed the files and, shortly after, the dare on her life went up £50,000. The owner could trace it. If he opened it again, they would assume it was her, and the reward would increase, leading to more violence, more chaos, more likelihood that she would be killed.

Removing the USB, he put it back in his pocket and stood, pretending to stretch in case Jamison looked up. Wakelin didn't know enough about tech to understand whether he could access the files without alerting someone. But, thankfully, he worked for the police, and the police had quite a good tech team. Surely one of them would be in the office, with this crime being directly linked to an app.

As Wakelin began to walk away, to descend into the belly of the station and find someone who could maybe help, Jamison saw. Wakelin approached his office and tapped on the door. 'I'm getting a coffee. Want one?'

As soon as he asked, Jamison's phone started ringing. He looked at the screen and ignored the call. 'No, thank you.'

Nodding, Wakelin left. He heard Jamison's phone ring again and again. He didn't pick up.

Wakelin didn't know why he was keeping the information from his boss, his friend. But his gut told him to. If Wakelin had learned anything in his years on the force, the gut seldom lied.

Walking out of the empty situation room, he took the stairs two at a time and walked into the cybersecurity department. Whereas upstairs was quiet, down with the tech team was anything but. Every available screen had an officer in front of it. Peters had said it was being monitored, but everyone was in, both shifts, working hard to end this nightmare. There was barely room to move in the small space. Every desk was covered in empty takeaway boxes, coffee cups, and the whole team were tapping on keyboards and speaking into headsets. Every screen had DareMe on it, with people analysing the videos, looking for clues to find either Cassie Jones or those trying to hunt her.

In the room, furthest away from anyone else sat the only woman on the team, slightly away from the others, by choice. She was intently focused on her screen, the blue light illuminating her features, softening their edge. Sarah had been in the force for as long as Wakelin, both passing out in the same year. He was at her wedding, was godfather to her first boy. When his gut told him to trust no one, he still trusted her.

He approached and she looked away from her screen and smiled. 'Hey, Greg. Didn't expect to see you down here, what with everything going on.'

'How's it going?'

'You're kidding, right? This DareMe software is impenetrable. Everything is encrypted, even the founder of the app isn't listed anywhere. It was like the devil himself created it, just to piss me off.'

'That good, huh?'

'Yeah, that good. There's a rumour going that you know the girl?'

Wakelin nodded. 'Well, not know her, per se. She's the sister of a victim I was trying to help.'

'What's she like?' Sarah asked, and Wakelin couldn't help but note that to Sarah, Cassie was almost like a celebrity. But then, he supposed she was. Everyone knew who KJ74 was. And the quiet woman he'd met in the hospital waiting room was now gone.

'Terrified,' was all he said. 'Sarah, can we walk?'

'OK . . .' Sarah gave Wakelin a quizzical look and followed him out of the room.

Once out of earshot of everyone, he stopped. 'Sarah, we go way back, right?'

'Too far back.'

'I need a favour, but I need it to be kept quiet. From everyone, even people here.'

'Greg? What is going on?'

Wakelin had another look around to make sure they were alone and then pulled out the USB.

'This was left for me, by her. She says there is some pretty interesting stuff on it. I think this is the reason someone wants her dead.'

'So, look at it,' Sarah said.

'That's the thing — Cassie did, and then the DareMe money went up.'

'Oh, we wondered why they had done that. They must have software on it, alerting them if it's accessed.'

'Do you think you can get into it without them knowing?'

'Please, even my kids can do that.'

'How long?'

'Ten minutes.'

'Sarah, when I say don't tell anyone, I mean don't tell *anyone*. Not even Jamison, OK?'

'What's going on?'

'I don't know. But my gut is telling me to keep it quiet. Find me something. A name, where that amount of money is coming from. I get that it's all designed to be anonymous. But surely it leaves a fingerprint of something?'

'Digital footprint — yeah, everything does, but the security on DareMe is complex. It will take time.'

'We don't have time.'

'All right. Let me get on it. I can get whatever is on the USB to you quickly. With the money and where it comes from, and who has posted the dare, no promises. Everyone is trying to crack it at the moment, and we aren't getting anywhere. But the USB, I'll have whatever is on this on your phone in, like, ten minutes.'

'You can do that?'

'Greg, come on, it's insulting.' She winked, then turned and walked back into the busy room.

'Sarah?' Wakelin called out, and she came back. 'Have you got a spare USB knocking about? Similar to this one?'

'Sure, not identical, but I reckon I'll have one that's close.'

Sarah dipped into her desk drawer, grabbed a similar USB, handed it to Wakelin and then sat back at her desk like she and Wakelin had just been having a gentle catch-up.

Wakelin pocketed the USB and went back upstairs via the kitchen to get that coffee. Back at his desk, he looked at DareMe to see if Cassie was visible.

The app was saturated with things about her, but he couldn't see her anywhere.

CHAPTER SIXTY-THREE

1.21 a.m. — 1 hour and 9 minutes remaining

They didn't run. They didn't shout. They simply followed. I was a dying zebra, and they were the lions. They knew they didn't need to pounce, to charge. They could save their energy, take their time, enjoy the easy meal. Or, in this case, easy pay cheque. They knew I wouldn't run towards people. I would try and hide, and all they had to do was seek. There was no refuge, no base. There was nowhere safe.

Three people. One hundred and fifty grand. The maths made sense. One evening's work for a new car, or an expensive holiday, or money towards a house. Fifty grand could set a person up.

I continued up the road I was on, drawing closer to the college where I had studied Business at sixteen. The road was one I had walked along a thousand times before, in a different life. Back then, I'd had hope. I'd had opportunity. Life was easy and uncomplicated and eternal. If I for a moment could have seen myself as I was now, would I have changed anything? Could I have? Was my life now the result of bad luck, or fate? And what was my fate to be? Was I to die at the hand of a stranger? Or would there be more? Would there be another dawn, another day? Would I see the sun ever again?

I wanted to run, but I was so exhausted, I could barely walk. The wound on my leg was throbbing once more, the painkillers barely helping. My feet burned with the cold. But if I tried to run, I'd get only so far, and then they would catch up. If they were happy to simply walk, it worked for me. I'd find a moment to dash, hide, and hope they didn't find me.

As I drew closer to Queens Gardens, the road that curled around the side of the town park and to the college entrance, I looked down it, wondering if this was the moment I ran, but the road was long and wide. They would catch up fast and I would have nowhere to hide. So I crossed over and kept walking. They did too. Silently stalking.

Ahead of me, on the opposite side of the road, two people were walking towards me. They were young enough to know DareMe, but with no masks I assumed they weren't playing. Ironically, I hoped they were. I hoped that they would be driven by greed, neglecting right from wrong. I hoped that they would see me and want to be rich and therefore fight for the prize. £150,000 between five wasn't as much as between three. If they were playing, if they knew I was KJ74, maybe they, and the three following me would get into an altercation, and I could slip away.

'Hey!' I shouted out. At first they didn't look up. 'Hey!' I said again, and the one closest stopped walking. 'You know DareMe?'

'Yeah?'

'You playing?'

'Why do you ask?'

I took a breath. 'I'm KJ74.'

'Holy shit. It's her.'

They began to cross the road, coming towards me, and I staggered on.

'Hey! She's ours,' one of my stalkers shouted, the one I assumed was in charge as he was in the middle. He broke into a gentle jog, but not towards me, towards the two crossing the road. 'Fuck off, she's ours,' he said again. I turned to look at the standoff I had created, like a Western showdown, both groups looking at one another, waiting for the church bells to toll high noon, when they could draw their guns.

One of the two I had called over spoke. 'Cassie, we ain't playing, but we'll help. Get out of here. We'll hold them back for as long as we can.'

I nodded and upped my pace, walking further away. I didn't look back, not right away, but I heard the two groups begin to argue, and then a fight broke out. Feet scraped on the ground as people lunged, moans sounded when connection of fist and head was made. I needed to get off the road. Half running, half stumbling I made it further away until I reached another junction. Only then I dared to look back. My saviours were outnumbered and losing. Just before I rounded the corner, disappearing from sight, I saw the flash of a knife. One of my defenders was stabbed. He screamed, fell to the ground. As the other dropped to his side to help, my stalkers stepped over them, heading my way.

I looked for somewhere to hide. One of the houses had scaffolding up on the front of it and a skip in its drive. I heaved myself over the lip and landed heavily in a pile of old tiles, plasterboard and broken-up furniture. I tried to land on my feet and instantly regretted it as a shard of glass shot into the bottom of my right heel, sending white-hot pain straight into the grey space behind my eyes. I wanted to scream. But if I did, I would surely be killed. I bit my lip so hard, I felt blood dribble down my chin.

I waited, forcing myself to breathe shallowly so I couldn't be heard. After a minute, the thrum of feet hitting tarmac came into earshot. I froze, rabbit-like, holding my breath.

'Where is she? Where did she go?'

'She must have kept going.'

'She can't have got far. Split up. When you find her, call.'

The thwack of footsteps on the asphalt faded, then disappeared. I looked down at my foot. A piece of glass as wide as a biro was sticking out of my heel, I needed to pull it out, so taking a deep breath, I pinched it between my finger and thumb, and tugged it free. Blood dripped from the cut, and the pain was so intense my eyes watered. Again, I had to push the pain down. I needed to bind it. I looked in the skip and found an old piece of material. It looked like a decorator's cloth covered in old paint. It was filthy but would have to do. I tore off a strip and wrapped it around my foot tightly, tying the knot on the top of my foot so I could move. I climbed out of the skip, covered in plasterer's dust. Limping badly from the cut that throbbed in one foot, and the dog bite that ached in the other, I hobbled away.

CHAPTER SIXTY-FOUR

Wakelin
1.29 a.m. — 1 hour and 1 minute remaining

Waiting for Sarah to message felt like the longest ten minutes of Wakelin's life. He watched the news helicopters above the city, hoping to hear from Cassie, and not to see her on the app. Neither happened.

Just as the ten-minute deadline Sarah had set for herself passed, a message popped up on his phone. It was a notification that a large file was being sent through. He followed the instructions in the message, and when prompted, he typed 'Benjamin', the name of his godson, and waited for the files to load.

A new message pinged through from Sarah.

> *I took the liberty to have a peek. Greg, how the hell has someone managed to find out all this about these people? Do you think it's one of us? Cos it looks that way to me.*

As Wakelin opened the files and read about each of the powerful, wealthy, famous people and their dirty little secrets, he wondered if his instincts were right. He saw the file marked OM. He opened it.

'Owen Moore,' he said quietly.

Owen Moore had been under investigation for over a year. A case had been built, but it was unexpectedly dropped, and forgotten. Wakelin read the file, and then had no doubt.

It wasn't the level of information necessarily that made him feel sure he was dealing with corruption, but the way the information had been stored. It was methodical, organised. Personal information, financial information, home information. Family, associates, friends. The lists on each person were detailed and in order, the same order a detective might use when investigating a crime. He knew, because on this particular case, Wakelin had been involved. The information and way it was stored was identical to how he remembered seeing it as the case was being built.

His gut was right. It was an inside job.

Whoever was behind this had used their police know-how, and likely resources, to dig up skeletons from closets that certain high-powered individuals would want to stay shut away. It was the perfect blackmailing device and Cassie Jones had stumbled upon it by accident.

Wakelin had asked himself time and time again what Cassie knew that would have put such a price on her life. Now he had the answer, but what she had wasn't worth just £150,000. This information was worth millions.

Wakelin looked up towards Jamison's office and studied the man before him. He had known his DI for a very long time, but how well did he really know him? Jamison kept his cards close. He had few friends outside work. He didn't join in on social events. He kept himself to himself.

Wakelin ran through what he did know. Jamison had been the first to join him at the murder site, had followed him here after. He had refused to pick up his phone when Wakelin was in earshot, even in the middle of a crisis. He thought back to when he was at Mia's address. Jamison didn't seem shocked at seeing her dead. At the time, he had put it down to his boss being a seasoned detective, but could it have been something more? When Mike arrived, he had walked into the living room without needing to be told that was where she was. How would he have known?

Could it be them? It made sense — set a dare to have Cassie killed and, when she was, who would have to attend the scene? The DI in charge of murder investigations, that's who. It made sense, being last to know what was going on, the last to make it to a scene, the car registration coming up a dud would have been easy to control if the information went directly to the DI. Everything on this case was going through the DI. Wakelin thought he was failing to do his job, but what if he wasn't?

Wakelin didn't want to believe it. His boss had been in the force for thirty years, a decorated and determined officer. Injured several times on the job, more arrests that Wakelin could count. It had to be someone else.

Regardless of what he wanted to believe, he knew that somewhere in the department was a bent copper, and he needed to flush whoever it was out. Fast. They were in the final hour. Time was running out. Soon it would all be over, one way or another. He had to make sure it went the right way.

Wakelin was a keen fisherman, and he knew that you didn't catch the fish. You didn't chase or grab at it. Instead, you lured the fish to you. Then all you had to do was take it.

It gave him an idea.

Making sure Jamison or anyone couldn't see, he fired off a long message, hoping to God Cassie was somewhere where she could read it, and act.

Then he got up and knocked on his boss's door. Jamison hung up his phone and gestured for him to come inside.

'Boss, I think I will go home. I'm done.'

'Greg, I think that's a good idea.' Jamison noticeably lowered his shoulders as tension left his body. 'You've not stopped since this nightmare began. Get some rest. Tomorrow, once this is all done, I'll need my best people to dig though the pile of shit in its wake. We'll find her,' he added.

Wakelin nodded, said goodnight, and made his way towards his car. As he climbed in, he hit 'send' on the message and made his way to where he needed to be.

CHAPTER SIXTY-FIVE

1.31 a.m. — 59 minutes remaining

I was stuck. No matter which direction I hobbled in I could hear voices, see fires burning. The intensity of the flames sent shadows dancing ominously over what used to be a pretty part of the city. I was boxed into a small patch of the world. If I was seen, there would be no escaping. This patch would become my final resting place, my grave.

My left leg throbbed from the dog bite and now I couldn't bear weight on my right foot. I was incapacitated. There was no more running. No more fighting. All I could do was hide, and hope.

I stumbled into someone's garden and cowered down the side of the shed, in the thin gap between it and their fence, and I fought to keep the cold out of my bones. I wanted to ring my brother, to tell him I loved him, that I was sorry for messing this up. I'd started out on DareMe to save him, and now it was going to cost us everything. I had ruined our lives once already, ten years ago. Now, I had done it all over again.

I was so wrapped up in my own pain, my sense of failure, fear, that when a message came through, I didn't process a single word of it. So, forcing myself to focus, I read it again. This time, the words made more sense, but I was still confused.

Cassie, it's DS Wakelin. I'm messaging you in secret. This is strictly between us. I am working on how to end this. I know you're tired, I know you're hurting, but I need your help. I need you to trust I am trying to save you. You need to go onto DareMe one more time . . . Say the following . . .

I read the message several times, trying to hear his voice speaking to me, to get a sense of whether or not I trusted him. But, I remembered, he didn't show the other man the USB when he could. They would have found me if he'd said anything about me being close. Besides, what choice did I have? I was going to die one way or another unless a miracle happened. I didn't understand why he wanted me to stream and say what he asked me to say but I readied myself to do it anyway. I was tired, I was done. I had nothing to lose. I messaged him back, telling him I would do so.

I opened my DareMe app and pressed the livestream button. My face leaped onto the screen, broken and beaten, my eyes dark, my cheeks hollowed, exposed. No mask, no barrier. KJ74 was no more. Now, I was just Cassie Jones. I hit 'record', and a red light began to pulse, telling me I was live.

'This is Cassie, KJ74. I'm still here,' I said, laughing. A tear escaped. I smacked it away, angrily. 'This message is for those who set this dare on my life. I don't know who you are. But now I know why you want me dead. Now I know what I did that was so wrong. I never intended to take it but I want amnesty. I want to return it. I want my life back. In twenty minutes, I will be at the location that I will send to you privately. I will give it back as long as you promise to end this dare.'

I ended the livestream and fired off a simple message back to the user who had shared Mia's murder directly with me.

Next to the ice rink in Bretton there is a storage unit yard. I just want my life back.

I hit 'send' and lowered my phone, hoping that Wakelin was on my side. The fact he'd said for me to go to a location miles from where I was told me he had a plan. I had to trust it.

My limbs ached. Putting my phone away, I slowly stood. An outside light mounted to the wall of the house flicked on. The back door opened, and a voice shouted.

'Hey, I can see you. Get out of my garden or I'm calling the police.'

Panicking, I began to run, just as a man come to the back patio. I wanted to bolt out the same way I came, but he was blocking my path. I turned to my left and clambered over his fence. I tried to stay upright, but as I applied pressure onto my right foot, I fell and slammed into the ground below. It knocked the wind out of me. Thankfully, the man was all bark and no bite, and he didn't follow. But I was exposed, in the street, brightly lit by LED street lamps.

Heaving myself upright, I began to move. As I limped I couldn't stop the tears. There was not enough kindness in this world. Not enough help. It felt like everyone wanted me dead. People wanted money and fame. Only a few wanted to do what was actually right. I needed somewhere to go, somewhere dark, somewhere quiet and, because of how hard it was to walk, somewhere nearby. And all I could do was hope Wakelin would end this fucking game, before it killed me.

CHAPTER SIXTY-SIX

Jamison
1.34 a.m. — 56 minutes remaining

Jamison's eyes were closed when the message came through. He wasn't asleep but resting. The day had been long, stressful. He was getting too old for it all.

He grabbed his phone, grumbling, and unlocked it. It was Mike. A short, direct message.

She's posted.

Two small words, and yet they acted like a shot of adrenaline straight to his heart. He opened DareMe, searched for KJ74, and the video of her loaded on his screen. It was posted two minutes ago. It was as fresh as it could be without him seeing it live.

He tried to work out where she was, but nothing stood out. Turning the volume up on his phone, he watched her speak, unblinking. She looked tired, sore. She was scared for her life, and she wanted amnesty. He watched it again, then looked in his inbox.

The ice rink. It was quiet, far enough away so that players wanting to kill her wouldn't be there. He couldn't work out if she was clever for it, or stupid. She knew what he was capable of. Mia was proof. He wondered if she was planning an ambush, and quickly dismissed it. Cassie Jones was all alone. She was also a type to live in hope — she wanted it to all go away, for her life to go back to what it once was. Small and pathetic. She also wouldn't know he knew she had accessed the files. She would likely plead she didn't know what it contained, but he knew the truth.

Cassie Jones didn't have a plan. She wasn't going to ambush him. She was broken, and broken people beg.

Closing the app, he rang Mike.

'Boss?'

'She's going to the ice rink.'

'I'll head there now.'

'I'll meet you there.'

'Boss? Is that a good idea?'

'I want to look her in the eye. This is personal now. Bring your balaclava. We need to look like players.'

Hanging up before Mike could say any more, Jamison grabbed his coat. In the pocket was the mask he would wear as he snuffed the light from her eyes.

Approaching the office door, he looked into the silent office. It had been his home, his prison, ironically, for the best part of thirty years. Once that USB was back in his hand, he would be on the home straight. This shitty race would be over, and a life of warmth, decadence, loose women with tight asses would be waiting for him. One day, sipping a whisky with his feet dipped in a pool, he would think of this day, of how close he came to losing it all, and he would laugh. It would be a good story to replay in his mind, a brilliant chapter in the memoir of his life. Cassie Jones would be a footnote. Nothing more.

He looked at his watch. She would be there in sixteen minutes. He needed to be there first, to case her, before he killed her.

CHAPTER SIXTY-SEVEN

1.36 a.m. — 54 minutes remaining

I couldn't stop thinking about zebras now. About how I was a dying one, being stalked. I once saw a David Attenborough documentary in which a zebra tried to run from a pack of lions. It bucked, wanting to ward off the attack. It paced and turned on itself. And then, it simply stopped. The lions approached and it didn't move. I remembered thinking any minute now, it will bolt. Any minute now it will kick out. But it didn't, it just waited to die. The animal knew there was no escape. As violent as the attack was from the lions, I wanted to believe that the zebra was at peace, reflecting on its life on the savannah. Thinking of its family, its children perhaps. My mind romanticised it into being OK. Now I knew that was bullshit. The zebra didn't want to die. It wasn't reflecting. It was in shock, its brain shutting down in an attempt to spare the poor beast from the pain it knew was coming.

I had stopped running too. My body wouldn't go on, and the will to make it move wasn't there either. I was perched on someone's garden wall, my head low. I knew I should get up, keep moving. Wakelin was trying to help, and maybe that was why I'd stopped. They say the last mile of a marathon is the hardest, just when the end is in sight. There was a possible way out of this and, because someone had taken control of that, my responsibility was diminished.

Of course, that wasn't true. I was surrounded, all around the city. Thousands upon thousands wanted me dead, moving in packs, waiting to kill the beast when it realised there was nowhere else to go.

Pulling out my phone, I didn't go to DareMe. Instead, I went to my camera roll and began scrolling through the thousands of pictures stored there. Pictures of me and Mia, of Sam. Pictures of Mum. If the hunt really was over, I needed to make sure I left without any regrets.

Once I had scrolled enough to feel a shimmer of peace, I rang Dan.

'Cassie? Are you OK?'

'Is he awake?'

'No, he's still sleeping.'

'Could you wake him? Please?'

'Hang on.'

The line went quiet for a full minute, and then Sam's sleepy voice came onto the phone.

'Cass? Where are you?'

'It doesn't matter. How are you feeling?'

'I'm OK,' he said, and I had to cover my mouth to stop me crying. 'Cass?'

'Sam, I have to tell you something.'

'Cass? What's going on?'

'Just listen, please,' I said, my voice a whimper.

'You're scaring me,' Sam said, his grogginess gone. 'Where are you? I'll come to you.'

'Sam, please, just listen!' I shouted, and he fell silent. I took a deep breath, not knowing where to start. 'Sam, when Mum died . . .'

'Cass, what are you doing? Mum? She's gone. It's you that we need to think about. Please tell me wh—'

'I lied to you about it.'

'What?' he said.

'I lied about that final moment. There was no other car.'

'What do you mean?'

'There was no other car. It was just me and Mum.'

'Then how?'

I closed my eyes. I didn't want to relive it, but the lions were close.

'I wanted to go to a rave.'

'Cassie, I don't understand.'

'Mum said I couldn't. She said I was too young, said she would worry that someone would try and spike my drink. I argued I was nineteen, an adult and I could decide for myself. But she still wouldn't let me. I got angry, I felt Mum was being unreasonable. I argued louder. She did too. I lost my temper and threw my phone.'

'Cass, stop.'

'I didn't mean for it to hit the dash and come back at Mum. I didn't mean to hit her with it. It then landed on the floor and Mum undid her seat belt to reach it. But I kept shouting at her, calling her a bad mum, telling her I hated her. She lost control, and the car crashed into the tree.'

'There was no other car?'

'No. Sam, it was me,' I said, crying, through relief at finally telling the truth, crying because saying it aloud, for the first time in my life, made me completely culpable. 'Mum is dead, because of me.'

The line was quiet, so quiet I was sure he had hung up. I wouldn't blame him either. I deserved so much worse. I deserved the lions.

'Cass,' Sam said quietly, and wiping my nose, I looked up to the sky. The clouds floated past, obscuring the pale moon as they travelled, without a care in the world. They could look down, see what was happening here, to me, but they simply moved on. No judgement, no comment. Just a curiousness that didn't linger.

'Cass, are you there?' Sam said.

'Yeah.'

'Did you mean for the crash to happen?'

'No, no, I swear. I was just angry. I made a mistake. I wanted to throw my phone, my final protest and then sulk. I wasn't going to go to the rave. I was just upset. I swear, Sam. I swear.'

'Why are you telling me this now?'

'I want your forgiveness.'

'But why?'

'Because I'm going to die tonight.'

'Cass, where are you?'

'I'm sat on a wall.'

'What do you mean you're sat on a wall?'

'They will find me soon.'

'Cass? I need you to listen.'

'Please forgive me.'

'Just fucking listen!'

'OK,' I said, ready for him to tell me I was a monster, a murderer, that he hated me, that he wished me dead. I was ready. I had been ready for ten long years.

'You need to get the fuck up.'

'What?'

'Get the fuck off your ass and move. You didn't kill Mum. It was a horrible accident and I'm sorry you've carried this for so long. You should have told me a long time ago.'

'Sam, if I hadn't shouted at her, if I hadn't thrown my phone . . .'

'Life is full of what-ifs when it doesn't go the way you hoped. Shit happens. I miss Mum. I do, but she is gone, and you don't deserve to die because of it. So, move your fucking ass and find somewhere to hide until this thing is over.'

'Sam, I—'

'Shut up!' he shouted. 'Don't you see? You've carried this burden for ten years, you've supported me single-handedly into adulthood, you gave up your youth to do so. You don't owe the universe shit.'

'Sam, there is nowhere for me to go.'

'Don't give me that bullshit. You are the toughest person I know, and you're gonna give up now? Fuck that! You want me to forgive you?'

'Yes.'

'Then I need to see you to do so. I'll forgive you tomorrow.'

I heard a noise, a cough somewhere nearby, and saw one of my stalkers approaching. A heavy-set man. I froze.

'Cass? Are you there?'

The man looked up, sweating so hard his head steamed in the winter air. He saw me, and began to shout. 'Hey! Hey! I found her.'

At first I didn't move. I just sat, looking back. 'Sam, someone has found me,' I whispered.

'Cass, you need to get up now. I know you are tired but listen. If you want my forgiveness, I'll give you it face to face. You need to get through this, and then you and I can talk about what happened to Mum.'

'Sam, please, I just need to hear you say you don't hate me.'

'I don't, but I will if you give up. Now move.'

Slowly I stood, as the man drew closer and closer. 'Sam, promise me we are going to be OK?'

'You need to be alive for that.'

I nodded. 'OK.'

'OK?'

'OK,' I said again, as a fresh wave of energy began to flood into my limbs.

'Fucking move, Cass.'

'I'll see you soon, Sam. I love you.'

I hung up before he could say it back. I wasn't strong enough to hear it, not after spilling my secrets.

Putting my phone away, I looked towards my would-be murderer.

'Hey, Cassie,' the man said, his voice light and melodic, as though he was speaking to a child.

'Fuck you!' I shouted and began to run.

I lost him quickly. As soon as he couldn't see me, I took off my coat and dropped it into a bush, hoping he would assume I had climbed through it and look for me the wrong way. Town Park was ahead of me and, as I limped on, I couldn't help but feel this would be the end of this story, one way or another. Town Park was where that photo was taken of me and Mum that I looked at every morning. Town Park was the bookend to all this. The place I remember the most about my mum, on the anniversary of when I lost her. Running hurt — everything hurt — but this zebra wasn't dead yet.

CHAPTER SIXTY-EIGHT

Wakelin
1.40 a.m. — 50 minutes remaining

It was difficult to know who to trust. But Wakelin did know someone he could turn to for help — PC Peters. The kid had been in the thick of it. He had shown he was tough, hardworking. He'd wanted to help stop the chaos. Wakelin couldn't see him having caused it.

After a brief phone conversation, Peters said he would leave the hospital, where he was still fighting to control the mobs, to join Wakelin near the ice rink. Wakelin had asked him to keep it quiet, to not tell anyone where he was going.

By the time Wakelin arrived at the car park, Peters was already there, alone. He had passed the first test.

Getting out of their cars, they shook hands.

'How are you holding up?' Wakelin asked.

'I'll be ready for bed,' Peters said, forcing a smile to hide his exhaustion. 'DS Wakelin, there is a rumour that a friend of KJ74—'

'Cassie. Call her by her name, she's a real person.'

'Sorry. A friend of Cassie's was murdered.'

'Yeah.'

'Shit.'

'That's why we're here. I've spoken with Cassie Jones.'

'You have?' Peters was unable to hide his surprise.

'Peters, I don't know who to trust, but I'm trusting you. Something's going on.'

'What?'

Wakelin told him everything he knew about Cassie ending up with the USB, about the information on it, and how when it was accessed the DareMe total shot up. He said how he thought it belonged to a copper, a detective, because of the information stored. When he mentioned the word 'corrupt' Peters reeled. He had passed the second test. Peters was not involved.

'Shit,' he said again.

'Yeah, shit.'

'Who is it?'

'We are about to find out.'

His gut was drawing closer to a conclusion, one that would shock the force and become the talking point of the country after the dust settled. His profession would be dragged through the mud again. All of them would be bent because of one man, but he didn't care. A life had been taken, another at stake.

'Cassie messaged the people who killed her friend. Only them. They are coming soon.'

'Have we got backup?'

'It's just us,' Wakelin said.

Peters nodded. He was a little afraid, Wakelin could tell. 'All right. Let's get this bastard.'

Wakelin smiled and began to walk. The storage units were through a small patch of woodland between the trampoline park and the ice rink. As they fought through brambles and nettles, neither man spoke, until the trees thinned, exposing a fenced-off compound with line after line of shipping containers that people rented for storage.

'OK,' Wakelin whispered. 'They are supposed to come to these gates.'

Peters looked, then nodded.

'I want you to hang back, don't be seen. Even if it is a bent copper, we don't know who else is involved.'

'But what about you?' Peters asked.

'It's OK,' Wakelin said. 'Hang back, and as soon as someone arrives, film it all. We need to see who it is. We need to hear their voices. OK? I'll tell them I'm not alone, that if they hurt me, it'll be captured on video.'

'But if they are capable of killing . . .'

'It's gonna be all right. If anything goes wrong, call it in. Help will come. But you, stay out of sight.'

'But, sir—'

'Just do as I say, OK? Once you have them on film, once you know you have enough, call it in. Get backup here.'

'This is risky,' Peters said.

'Don't worry, I've got a trump card up my sleeve. This isn't complicated — this is all about money, nothing more.'

Peters nodded and Wakelin moved off. Wakelin came to the edge of the trees, and, seeing he was alone, quickly ran from the cover across a road and around the far side of the fenced-off area. From where he stood, he couldn't see Peters anymore, but he could see the main road and the gates to the storage facility. When the person they were waiting for arrived, Wakelin could watch him, listen and then stop the DareMe challenge on Cassie's life.

CHAPTER SIXTY-NINE

1.43 a.m. — 47 minutes remaining

As I turned into the park, I hoped that the heavy-set man didn't follow. I looked over my shoulder. He wasn't close, but he was still pursuing. I'd not been able to shake him.

I looked at the time on my phone. The glow of the screen temporarily blinded me. I was still forty-seven minutes from the dare being over. Forty-seven minutes to try and survive. To hide away, and not get caught. But even if it ran down to zero, even if the dare ended, would they stop? They wanted blood. I had come to be a symbol of hatred, of everything that was wrong with the world. I was someone to blame for the shitty lives most people had. I was now the cheap celebrity, the fifteen-minutes-of-fame whore. I was an escape from the mundane. I was a glimmer of hope that life might get better.

If they caught me, if they killed me, they would be rich. It was enough to start again, try again. And, I had learned, people wanted that a lot more than anything moral. Altruism didn't exist. My life had less meaning than the bounty placed on it.

There was no way it would be over. But I wanted Sam's forgiveness. My brother needed to see that I wouldn't give up. I couldn't give up.

'Hey. I just saw a light. I think she's in the town park somewhere,' a voice shouted, somewhere nearby. Cursing, I locked my phone and put it in my pocket.

I hoped I'd done enough to not be found.

I hoped I had been smart enough to not be caught.

I was wrong, because when I heard him shout, I knew he was close.

'We know you're here. No point running anymore.'

Looking around, I hobbled further into the park. I passed the café, searching for somewhere to hide. In the middle of the park stood a huge willow tree, surrounded by a circular patch of grass that in spring boasted daffodils and bluebells. I rounded the tree, wondering if I could climb it, but knew I would fail. My body was too tired, my bare feet too sore and numb. I knew if I tried to put too much pressure on my wounds, my legs would buckle. So, I pushed on, in more of a limp than a run.

Finding a copse off the main path, I pressed myself into it. It was mostly brambles and bush, but in spite of the spikes digging into my skin, I lowered myself to the ground to take the pressure off my aching feet. I fought to keep my breathing calm and quiet. I hoped they would come through, assuming I'd left via the south side of the park, their search fruitless.

Time would tell.

As my breathing fell into a steady rhythm, in and out, I heard a voice calling, and my breath snatched.

'Come out, come out, wherever you are!'

Then, silence. I counted in my head. *One, two, three, four, five, si—*

'No point hiding anymore,' he called again, a little closer, and I could hear the excitement in his voice.

I huddled into the brambles, fighting the cold that had seeped deep into my bones from a night out in the sub-zero temperature. I kept as still as I could and waited to hear him speak again, to see if I could work out where he was — before he worked out where I was.

But everything was quiet. He didn't call out again, and that told me he was closer still.

Hiding wouldn't help. I had to move.

Across the park, near the café I had hobbled past, a man ran out of the darkness and stopped under a street light. He turned on himself, scanning to find me, and the knife shimmered under the artificial light above his head. As he caught his breath, it fogged above him, like dragon steam.

'We know you're here. Come out, come out, wherever you are,' he taunted.

We. He had said 'we'.

The lions had arrived, and no sooner had he finished shouting, two more people ran to his side. The heavy-set man who first saw me was panting hard. Beside him was a slight woman, her breathing steady. They all stood close, searching in the gloom. A pack of lions, ready for the hunt. Ready for the kill.

I backed further into the copse, the brambles doing their thing. Shielding my phone, I dared to look at the time. There were still forty-three minutes to go, forty-three long minutes.

'Come on, you may as well give up now. We promise, we'll make it quick,' the man called out again, and his accomplices laughed. 'It will make you even more famous, Cassie. Isn't that what you want? Isn't that why you've done all this?'

The lead man whispered to his accomplices, who nodded and they then split up, going in different directions to try and flush me out. If I stayed, they would find me. If I stayed, I would be murdered on a livestream, like it was all just a fucking game.

I had to make a run for it.

Taking some deep measured breaths, I looked down at my bare, bloodied feet and my injured calf, and hoped they would carry me for just a little longer.

'Is there any sign of her?' the man shouted.

'Nothing,' the woman called back.

'Maybe she ain't here.'

'She's here. Keep looking,' the first man said.

Drawing in one final breath, I quietly freed myself as best I could from the thorns, ready to launch into a sprint. Ahead of me, around 100 metres away, was the gate. If I could get to it without being seen, I could lose them in the warren of city streets, could hide in people's gardens until the time ran out.

If I could get to the gate, I might just stay alive.

I began to count down.

Three.

'Cassie, we are going to find you.'

Two.

'Come out, you bitch. There is nowhere you can hide.'

One.

Pushing off the tree, I ran as fast as I could towards the exit, hoping I wouldn't be seen. But hoping was foolish, for less than halfway along I heard the lead man call out.

'There she is, get her. Get her!'

There was no way I could hide now. I had to run, run for my life, run for my forgiveness. Knowing it was as simple as that: run and maybe live, not run and most certainly die, I found new strength, new purpose. Even with that purpose, I carried injuries and, not being able to see underfoot, I stood on a stone. The mass of it dug into the wound from the glass. I screamed and fell to the ground as white-hot pain flooded into my leg.

I could hear Sam in my head. *Get up, Cassie. Move your ass.*

I forced myself upright and kept running, but the woman was fast, faster than I would be if I was fully well, and she got so close I could hear her, feel her breathing down my neck. She grabbed my hair, tugged hard and my head snapped back.

Before she could do any more, I turned and with a balled fist I swung wildly, catching her in the ear.

She let go of my hair as she staggered back, dazed from the blow.

I ran again and, reaching the boundary to the park, I ran in front of a car, its front bumper barely missing me. I turned into a quiet road, not seeing it was in fact a dead end.

CHAPTER SEVENTY

Wakelin
1.49 a.m. — 41 minutes remaining

The wait was impossible. With each minute that passed, Wakelin became increasingly sure they hadn't taken the bait, and his mind began to race as to why. Maybe they had worked out that he was on to them. Maybe Sarah had messed up and they knew he had accessed the USB. Maybe he'd got this all wrong and Sarah was in on it too? Or perhaps Jamison, if it was him, had been following Wakelin. After all, he did turn up just as Wakelin collected the USB. Maybe this trap was one for himself.

He thought of Sarah again. Had she told Jamison? She was a single mother, working hard to bring up her two boys — maybe she had had enough of the hardships of working for the police. He wanted to dismiss thoughts of her possible involvement, but his prime suspect in all of this was someone else he would have, until today, thought incapable of such a thing. The questions rushed at him. He was unable to answer any of them and the silence outside his head hung like static. There were no cars, no people talking, only the faint hum of the electric cable above the railway line 100 or so feet away. No one was coming.

Wakelin went onto DareMe, hoping to not see Cassie anywhere. He wanted to watch the city becoming increasingly frustrated at the time slipping away. It seemed almost everyone was, besides one stream from someone called 'hundredgrandman'. He had posted a short video, streamed live minutes before. It turned his worry into a consuming dread.

The video was from what looked like the town park. It was dark, the image grainy, but there was no doubt it was of Cassie, limping away, pursued by more than one person. The video stopped when she turned out of the park. The pursuers no doubt realised if they continued to stream, more would come, and their bounty might be taken from them. Wakelin was sure if this wasn't somehow stopped, Cassie Jones was about to die.

He felt torn. Town Park was maybe ten minutes away. If he left now, he could get there and help her. But, in that time, those who wanted the USB might come, and then leave again. Worse, maybe they were watching DareMe too, and knew that this plan to trap them was all a lie. There were too many variables at play. Too many plates spinning, and not enough time to catch them all.

Stay and hope they arrived. Leave and hope to get to Cassie in time. Hope, too much hope. The plates were about to fall.

But only one needed to continue to spin. One. Wakelin couldn't watch her die. He needed to act. He would get to her, hide her from the world, until he could think of a new way to end it.

Just as he was about to run, headlights approached.

Stepping back into the shadows, Wakelin closed his phone and watched. The car pulled up just shy of the gates, and a man got out. Mike.

'Son of a bitch,' Wakelin said under his breath as he watched him look around, making sure it was quiet before pulling a balaclava over his face. He then sat against the bonnet of his car, waiting. A minute later, more headlights shone towards the storage units. Even though he had suspected it, Wakelin's heart still sank when he watched his boss, his mentor, his confidant, climb out of the car and also pull on a mask.

'Duck outta sight, would ya? I don't want her seeing you,' Jamison said.

'But, boss?'

'Don't worry. When I get it back, we'll kill her, finish the DareMe challenge. And while you disappear and finish what we started, I'll investigate the murder. With so many wanting her dead, we'll never find out who did it.'

Wakelin hoped that Peters was in a good position to film it all, because if he was, all of it — their faces, vehicles and that brief but smoking-gun conversation — would now be evidence. If Peters had been successful, there would be proof that DI Jamison, a well-decorated, well-respected police officer was the one who had caused the chaos of the DareMe challenge, which had resulted in violence and murder.

It was time to play the game. He had saved his trump card for when he needed it, and now it was time to stop the dare on Cassie.

Taking a silent, deep breath, he stepped out of the shadows, and he and Jamison came eye to eye.

CHAPTER SEVENTY-ONE

1.51 a.m. — 39 minutes remaining

By the time I realised I was limping into a self-made trap, there was no way out. They knew it too. At the end of the road, the three who were stalking me came together and stopped running. Once again, they walked slowly and ominously towards me.

I looked around for something I could use as a weapon. Nothing leaped out, so I kept moving backwards, deeper into the dead end, hoping I would see an old piece of metal, a loose brick, anything that I could attack one of them with.

And still, slowly, they approached.

'Nowhere left to go, KJ74,' the lead man spoke, his voice sing-songy, taunting, as before.

'Fuck you,' I said, walking up to someone's front door. I banged on it, hoping someone would come, let me in, but the house stayed quiet. Across the road, I saw someone, a man wearing a black hoodie, at their open window, and I called out, 'Help me, please.'

They didn't reply, and then I saw they were filming, but they weren't playing. At first I wondered why, and then, with a sickening twist, I realised it was to boost their own social media following.

'Fuck you too,' I shouted.

Still, they didn't speak. Maybe they were the grim reaper, silently waiting for me to die so they could take me away.

'You're not gonna make it easy for us, are you? Problem is, KJ, time is running out, so we can't tease you anymore.'

Still backing away, I bumped into a low wall and almost toppled over it. Behind was a house, the end of my dead end. There was nowhere else to run and, still, I had found nothing to defend myself with. They knew it too.

The heavy-set man pulled out his phone, and began to livestream. 'Hey, followers. This is it, we have her, the DareMe is almost complete. We are gonna be rich,' he said to his fans, giddy and childlike, before turning the camera to me. 'Anything you want to say?' he said, his tone harder. 'Anything that isn't "fuck you", that is.'

The others laughed too quickly, too loud, too forced. The stress was getting to them, and it made me realise they hadn't done anything like this before. Yes, I had watched the lead one stab another person, but that was reactive, in the heat of the moment and fuelled by adrenaline. They hadn't intentionally walked towards a person to murder them.

But I had been here before — by the river, with the PCSO. I had defended myself from attack. I had fought, I had survived. Even though there were three of them, and I was outnumbered, injured and exhausted, it gave me a slight advantage. I couldn't win, I knew that, but if this was going to be my final stand, if this was going to be where I died, and if the world was going to watch the spectacle, I wasn't going to go down without a fight. Millions might see, but this wasn't about them, this was about Sam. I needed him to know that I got off my ass, that I kept trying, that I didn't give up. He had reason enough to hate me. I didn't want this to make it easier. Sam would see me fight for my life and when I lost, he would know I tried.

I. Fucking. Tried.

Knowing I was about to meet my end, suddenly everything became clear to me. My life was fleeting, full of regret. I wished I had more time, wished I had been braver, wished I had confessed to how Mum died years ago and had allowed myself to move on. I wished I'd let myself laugh more. I wished I'd realised that bills were just bills, and that the world was beautiful and finite and what I should have been paying attention to. I wished I'd had a family of my own. Sam would have been a great uncle. I wished I'd danced on a night out. I wished I'd kissed that boy. I wished I'd fucking *lived*. Really fucking lived, and sacked off fear, and fought for my little slice of peace, of happiness — which wasn't a privilege, but a fucking birthright.

But now wasn't the time for wishing. Now was the time for action.

The three continued to advance, slowly, carefully. I took a step forward, raised my hands, balled them into fists, for what they were worth.

They hesitated for a split second, before smiles beamed though slits in cotton face coverings.

'You really ain't gonna make it easy,' the smaller man said.

'Shit,' the large man said. 'There are already almost three hundred thousand people watching!'

'Well, let's give them a show,' the woman said.

I didn't reply. Knowing through my encounter with the PCSO how hard it was to fight off one attacker, I needed to save my energy. Then, I hadn't been sleep deprived, wasn't exhausted and hungry, wasn't injured as much. That time I'd had a weapon. The saw which now sat in the hallway of an older couple who also wanted to kill me. It didn't bode well. I looked to my left. In the upstairs window, the grim reaper watched on.

'Right then,' the heavy-set man said, handing the woman his phone to continue the stream. 'Let's get on with this and kill the bitch.'

He bounded towards me, and I hobbled away from the wall into the middle of the road. I could see he didn't know what to do, whether he should grab me or hit me. He bobbed around, emulating a boxer. He looked ridiculous, comical even, but I could see the desire, the hate in his eyes.

He made a lunge for me, and I sidestepped. I wanted to swing and hit him, but he was out of reach and, with my badly hurt foot, I would have stumbled and fallen, and it would have been over. So I stepped back, waited for him to lunge once more.

I dodged his attempt to grab me again, his hands clambering and missing. Foolishly I sidestepped closer to the other two, and the second man snared me from behind, pinning my arms behind my back. I struggled to free myself, but he was too strong. The heavy-set man walked towards me, confident as I was now caught. Too confident. Because when he was close enough, his guard low, I kicked him as hard as I could between his legs.

He screamed as he crumbled to the ground. I tried to flick my leg backwards, to kick the other man there too, but he was faster than me, and managed to turn his hip so I only brushed against his leg. He pushed me hard and I stumbled forward, falling over the moaning man and landing heavily.

Rolling over, I tried to get to my feet, but before I could, a fist flashed towards me, catching me on the side of the head, sending me back to the deck once more.

'How'd you like that, bitch?' the woman shouted, the camera catching the action in high definition. No doubt to the bloodthirsty delight of 300,000 sets of eyes, maybe more.

I managed to regain my composure, but before I could get up, the lead man stepped closer and grabbed a handful of my hair. He pulled so hard it lifted me upright and tore a huge chunk of it from my scalp. As I screamed, he hit me in the mouth, sending blood spluttering over my left shoulder and dislodging one of my teeth.

Then he clasped his hands around my throat, squeezing so hard my eyes felt like they would pop right out of my head.

I fought to get him off, but he was too strong, and I couldn't free his grip. My lips began to tingle, and my limbs began to feel detached, hollow, and no longer mine. My vision blurred.

This was it. This was how I was to die. As I struggled to focus, I saw the phone come towards my face, filming my death in close-up — a high-drama moment that would no doubt have everyone watching unable to blink.

'Holy shit, there's almost half a million watching this!' the woman said excitedly.

Half a million people about to watch me die.

Sam would be one of them, and even though I knew it was over, I needed Sam to see I had tried as hard as I could. So I let go of his hands that I was desperately trying to prise off my throat, and reached to his face. I slapped my fingers against it, until I found what I was looking for, then I jammed my thumb into his eye.

He staggered back, screaming like a wounded animal, releasing his grip, and I dropped to the ground again, gasping for air. No sooner had I landed than the second man hit me, an open-handed slap right across my temple, making stars flash and my teeth wobble in my skull.

I hit the ground, my face smashing into the asphalt, the taste of grit and blood in my mouth. I tried to move, tried to see clearly, but my vision swam, and my legs wouldn't work to get me upright. I fought to stay conscious, barely managing to, but when my vision came back all three of my attackers, my soon-to-be murderers, were standing over me. In the lead man's hand was the knife I had seen when the two strangers tried to help, its blade shimmering under the street lamps above. All three of my attackers were panting, lusting for blood, and over me, to my left, the grim reaper filmed on.

'You getting this on film?' the lead man said, still panting heavily.

'Oh yeah,' the woman replied. 'And our numbers are climbing by the second. Man, we are famous.'

'Turn the camera to me,' he replied, and she did as she was asked. 'Hey, everyone, this is hundredgrandman, and after four hours and forty-two minutes of the DareMe challenge, we are about to complete it. At our feet is KJ74.'

I tried to stand one final time, to run, to hide, but as I began to move, the second man kicked me back to the ground. I rolled over. Then, somehow pulling myself into a seated position, I began to scramble backwards on my hands and feet, closer to the wall I had almost fallen over, closer to the wall that would be my final resting place.

This was it. The fight was done. I had tried, and I knew that Sam would know that, and that was enough.

It had to be, because I had nothing left.

The game was over.

CHAPTER SEVENTY-TWO

Wakelin
1.55 a.m. — 35 minutes to go

Jamison recoiled in shock. Wakelin watched as the cogs began whirring as his superior tried to find a way to explain the situation they found themselves in.

'DS Wakelin,' Jamison said, looking around to see if he was alone, 'are you here for the same reason as me?'

'And what would that be, DI Jamison?'

'To stop those trying to hurt Cassie Jones.'

'It's over. The only people who knew to come here were the people trying to hurt her.'

'Then how, might I ask, are you here? Did you do all this? Are you the one who is trying to kill her?'

'Enough. We both know the truth. I set this up with her, with Cassie, to catch you.'

Mike stepped out of the shadows, his balaclava still on. He looked towards Jamison first, and then Wakelin.

'Hello, Mike.'

'Greg, I can explain,' Jamison began.

'Save it. I know.'

'Do you?'

'End the dare. She doesn't deserve this.'

As Wakelin spoke, Mike took a step towards him.

'I'd stop there if I were you,' Wakelin said. 'You think I'd come alone? You think I wouldn't have backup? Right now, you are being filmed. You've been being filmed since the second you arrived. We have your faces, we have your conversation about killing her. There is no way out of it for you. If you do anything to me, you're all fucked.'

Jamison's mouth turned into a snarl. Wakelin didn't blink.

'I do, however, have a deal on the table.'

Jamison looked around, trying to find someone hiding, filming, but Peters was out of sight.

'I'm not bluffing — all of it is on film.'

'Greg. Just pause for a second, OK?' Jamison said, his hands up in defence. 'Aren't you sick of this?'

Wakelin didn't reply.

'The abuse, the stress, the long hours, the lack of being able to have a normal life? Aren't you sick of how much they take? I will stop the dare, but I need that USB.'

'End the dare.'

'I will, once I have that USB.'

Wakelin pulled the USB out of his pocket, the one he had asked Sarah for, and partially concealed it so that Jamison couldn't see it wasn't an exact match. 'I want to offer a deal.'

'Go on,' Jamison said, unable to take his eyes away from the USB.

'End it now, and it's yours.'

'Yeah, all right. Don't you think I know what entrapment is? I'm a detective, for Christ's sake.'

'I know,' Wakelin said. It was time to play his trump card. 'But you haven't listened to my deal.'

'Go on then, I'll bite.'

'You just asked if I was sick of it all. Yeah, I am. I am so sick of this shit. End the dare. Let her live. I know you are going to use the information on this USB to blackmail some important people. Cut me in. Then the corruption, the bribing, the murder, it all goes away.'

'What about those who are filming us right now? Unless you were bluffing?'

'No, not bluffing. They are with us too. End it, and we can all be rich, but if you don't, I'll release this video, and you'll go down for all of it. Simple as that.'

'How much do you want?' Jamison asked.

'Thirty per cent.'

He laughed. 'No way, I've worked for years on this. Ten.'

'Twenty.'

'Fifteen.'

'All right, deal,' Wakelin said.

'Well played.' Jamison pulled out his phone.

Wakelin was stuck. He needed to time this perfectly. Time was of the essence to save Cassie's life, but he needed to delay also, hoping Peters had called it in as instructed, and help was coming. If he delayed ending the dare, Cassie might die. If he didn't, he probably would.

He reckoned she had suffered enough. 'Hurry up.'

'I'm doing it, see?' Jamison said, flashing the phone screen. On it was a cancellation of dare notice, and a button under it wanting confirmation.

'Tap it, and I'll throw you the USB.'

'Throw it first.'

'It ain't working like that. Come on, boss, let's leave this city, this shitty job, and be rich.'

'Fine, then, get your other people out here,' Jamison said.

He was losing control. Wakelin was winning. He nodded. 'OK. Peters, come out.'

The was a snap of twigs, and PC Peters stepped out. 'I've sent the video to our other person. As you asked,' he said, and Wakelin inwardly smiled.

'Now, end it. Once it's done, the USB is yours, and that video that Peters has sent to our third man disappears. All of it disappears. And we can all get the fuck out of here. DI Jamison?'

'I'm thinking.'

'Let me make it easy. You can't kill us, as the video will go out. You can't deny it — we have proof. All you can do is end the dare and give me my cut.'

Jamison didn't move.

Wakelin felt a bead of sweat run down his back. This plan hinged entirely on Jamison not calling his bluff.

'My offer isn't on the table for ever. Tick tock,' he said, his voice unwavering, despite his fear.

Jamison held Wakelin's eye for a long while, deciding what to do.

CHAPTER SEVENTY-THREE

1.59 a.m. — 31 minutes to go

The wall was cold against my back. I knew that soon I would feel nothing else, ever again. I scratched my back against it as hard as I could. The abrasion was painful. My last memory would be of that. Pain. Intentional pain. In the absence of being able to control anything else, at least I had that.

My three killers drew closer, the knife in the lead man's hand pointed towards me. The woman was still filming, as was the silent, ever-watching grim reaper to my left. I wanted to cry, to beg, to plead that I had value, but didn't. Sam couldn't see my end being one where I pathetically begged. He needed to know I was OK with it, because I needed him to be able to heal, properly this time. Not like with Mum.

'Fucking get on with it then,' I said, trying my best to sound like I was taunting. I forced out a laugh, bitter and broken, before spitting blood at the shoes of my soon-to-be killer.

'Once this is all done, you'll go back to being a pathetic little bitch,' I said. 'No amount of money will change that.'

'You got balls, I'll give you that.'

'One of us has to,' I said, and he laughed.

I laughed too, and I could see it unsettled him. I wasn't trying to delay — things were beyond that. I just needed to go on my terms, my way. Slowly, I began to pull myself up the wall, dragging myself to my feet.

'See, Sam, I got off my ass,' I said, looking down the lens of the camera.

'Do it! Kill her!' the second man said, and the lead man took one more step. He was close enough to strike.

'Wait,' the woman called. 'Look.'

The lead man turned back, but the knife stayed trained on me.

I tried to see what she was telling him to look at, but he was blocking my view. He turned back to me and, this time, I couldn't see the same hatred in his eyes anymore. All three looked different somehow. Smaller. Afraid. I glanced to my left. The grim reaper had stopped recording and was closing their window.

The lead man put the knife away.

'Oh shit.' He pulled off his balaclava. 'Oh, God.'

He looked at me, and he started to cry. The large man began backing away and the woman stopped recording.

'I—' the lead man started, and then stopped. 'It was just a game, right?'

'What?'

He opened his mouth to speak again, hesitated, and then his words came out, small and weak. 'I would stay, to help but, you know, I don't want the police to know I was here. I hope you understand?' He then lowered his head, ashamed, and backed away.

Confused, I pulled out my phone. I logged on to DareMe and saw that the game had been updated.

Your DareMe challenge has been updated.
The dare is now null and void.
The DareMaker has rescinded their offer.
There is no financial reward for any harm caused to KJ74. All those who have played will be fully prosecuted.

EPILOGUE

Seven months later

'See you, Kim,' Arthur, my resident one-pint-a-night customer said as he headed out the door.

'See you tomorrow, Arthur.' I gave him a wave before continuing to clean the beer taps. The rest of the customers at the bar got on with draining their half-full pints, ready to go home themselves. There was no rush. There never was.

Time was different for me now — everything was. Starting with my name. For weeks after that night, everywhere I turned, every time I went online, Cassie Jones was all anyone was talking about. That night was analysed, discussed, dissected by the whole world, and compared with old psychological experiments from the fifties, sixties and seventies, experiments like the Milgram experiment, and the Stanford Prison experiment. Apparently, what happened that night, now labelled the DareMe Crisis, wasn't new. People had been abusing power through anonymity for centuries. I was just the unlucky epicentre of the latest occurrence.

In the wake of that night, over 300 people had been arrested for acts of violence, vandalism, hate crimes, and the list was growing. Four were charged with attempted murder

— the PCSO, and three stalkers. Two detectives in the police force were charged with murdering my best friend. A third was still at large. Once that went public, the focus shifted from me to the corruption in the force, and I was grateful for it.

We'd buried Mia. My friend who refused to help those who wanted me dead, my friend who died warning me not to come. The crematorium in Bretton was full. Hundreds came, press hounded for pictures, but Wakelin helped keep them out. He was a good man. That night, he managed to convince those who wanted me dead he wanted in on the deal, and once the DareMe was stopped, he played along until backup arrived and then arrested the detectives behind it all. He then raced to find me and take me to Sam.

DareMe was taken offline. The founder, a tech genius from America, felt remorseful for what had happened because of his app, one that was supposed to be about fun. It was reported he'd made tens of millions from it, most coming that night. But now other apps had been developed. There was one called Challenges, another called Risk, a third called Quest. Quest was quickly becoming even bigger than DareMe had managed to be, despite DareMe being linked to the murder of my best friend. And, I asked myself again, what had the world come to?

Money was money, and people wanted to make it, whatever the cost. It was big business. The new apps emulated the philosophy of DareMe, but I didn't have them. My phone had no apps at all. From now on, you could call or text. That was it.

I still had nightmares. I guess I always would. The scars from that day would stay with me for ever, both physically and mentally. But, with Sam's help, I'd fought to move on.

Once Mia was gone, I knew I couldn't stay, and there was only one place where I could think of to go. That night, when I tried to escape the city, there was only one place that came to mind. The east coast.

I bought a little two-up two-down cottage in West Runton, changed my name, taking my mum's, got a little Jack Russell called Barney, and found a job in a quaint little pub.

I was anonymous once more. Happily anonymous, and happily cleaning beer taps.

Sam didn't come with me when we sold the house. He took his share and moved to London. He too had changed, and was making something of his life.

'Need some help?' Connor, the landlord, said, and I smiled.

'If you want.'

Connor joined my side, and we worked together to clean, cash up and say goodbye to the regulars.

'You OK?' he asked.

'Yeah, fine. Just thinking.'

'About what?'

'Nothing much.' I walked around the till to stack the chairs on the tables so that the cleaner could get to the floor easier in the morning. Connor helped too, working in silence. I liked him a lot. He was a quiet soul, simple in his needs. He owned the pub and ran it, but really, Connor was a fisherman at heart. He wanted to be on the sea, and sometimes, recently, I had gone along with him in his little boat. If Connor knew I was really Cassie Jones, he didn't let on.

I might tell him, one day. But I didn't feel like I needed to. That woman was gone. I was someone new, and maybe I should just be that person. No longer living in the past, no longer looking over her shoulder. Maybe I could just be Kim, now and always.

With all the chairs stacked, we both headed outside, the summer air carrying the smell of the sea. I waited as he locked up.

The streets of West Runton were quiet, peaceful and as we walked away, our steps in unison, I felt his hand brush against mine a few times. When we turned onto the main road, Connor hesitated. 'Would you like me to walk you home?'

'No, it's OK.'

'Well then, I'll see you tomorrow?' he said.

'Yeah, see you tomorrow.'

He held my eye for a second too long. I felt that tingle of knowing he wanted to kiss me. But, he didn't. 'Goodnight then,' he said, as he turned and walked away.

I turned to walk away too, but only made it a few steps before I stopped. Life was short, and wonderful and hard and fragile — and meaningful. If I let it be. Happiness was a right. But you had to choose it.

I walked back towards him and, sensing me coming, he spun and looked me in the eye. He took a breath to speak but, before he could, I placed a kiss on his lips.

At first he did nothing. Then, he kissed me back.

When our lips parted, I held his eye. 'See you tomorrow,' I whispered.

Connor was too stunned to speak.

I walked home, unable to stop myself smiling.

By the time I reached my front door, he had messaged.

I've wanted to kiss you for months.

Me too.

I opened my front door and walked in, closing it with my foot.

'Barney?' I called out. He usually charged towards me when I came home. 'Barney!' I called again, and still he didn't come.

Confused, I took off my jacket and headed into the kitchen. It was quiet. Normally he would run around, excited to see me, his little claws tapping on the kitchen floor. But I didn't hear anything.

I flicked on a light and gasped.

Blood smeared the walls. The back door had been smashed in. Walking around the counter, I saw my little dog was dead.

On the side lay a note with my name on it — my real name.

It was a piece of paper with a QR code and a simple instruction underneath for me to scan it. It said the password was 'KJ74'.

With shaking hands, I opened my camera and scanned the QR code, which took me to the loading page for Quest. I put in the password, and it took me to a profile page that had been created for me.

I thought I was going to be sick.

There were two messages in my inbox. I opened the first and almost dropped my phone.

'No! *No!*'

I began to cry. It was a picture of my brother with his hands tied behind his back, lying on a dirty mattress in a room that was concrete and cold. His eyes were open and staring at the camera, and afraid. Unable to look at it, to process what I was seeing, I closed it.

Barely able to breathe, I opened the other message in the inbox.

Welcome back, player KJ74
Do you really think that everyone who lost out that night was arrested?
Your Quest challenge:
Find your brother (before he dies)
You have 10 hours remaining.
Do you accept?

THE END

ACKNOWLEDGEMENTS

A couple of years back, I was having lunch with my friend and fellow author John Marrs. We were chatting about the usual subject; where we get our ideas from. During that conversation, I told John about *The Price*, the novel I was working on and as I told him the bases for the idea, he made a suggestion as to what I could do with the story. For that novel, I didn't listen. However, the idea stuck and the app DareMe, and its function, stems from that conversation over a pizza and diet coke, so, John Marrs, thank you.

Writing *Dare Me* is in the truest sense of the word, a team effort. Without the countless words of encouragement, many conversations, hundreds of 'what if' moments, none of this would happen. But I want to thank my son, Ben, next. Even though he is only ten, he is the person I sound my ideas with the most, and we discuss those 'what if' moments. And I need to credit him too; the final moments of the last chapter were, entirely his idea. The book was finished, and as I was talking through the climax, he added a final 'what if'. The words you see are, in fact, his. So, as always, thank you Ben, you amazing, clever and creative boy. I'm so very proud.

To my editor, Siân Heap, thank you for coming to this idea mid-way, and running with the bat shit crazy concept I wanted to explore. I can't imagine it was easy, but your kind words, great editorial work and easy nature have made this a dream process. Thank you to the whole team at Joffe Books, to Kate LG, and Kate B, and the whole marketing team. I love working with you!

To my agent, Lisa Moylett. I am the luckiest author I know. In the short time we have been working together, everything feels different. Everything feels possible. And to Zoe Apostolides, thank you for all your notes, feedback, time and kindness. I really do have a dream team at CMM.

To my lovely friends, John M, John S, Lisa and Darren. This past year has been challenging beyond the words; you have kept me propped up, and moving. I also want to mention Kim. You've been such a champion of late, and you are very dear to me. Thank you for being there, and for helping when I've been stuck. I'm glad I know you.

To you lovely readers, from NetGalley, to Goodreads, from blogs and vlogs, to you who post on Instagram, and engage with online book clubs. To everyone out there who takes the time to read, and comment and speak about my stories. Thank you. Without you, none of this would exist. What you do for authors, has by far the biggest impact on whether or not a book does well and all of my success so far, is down to the tireless work you do.

And finally, back to my son, Ben. Without you, there is no motivation, no determination, and no inspiration. And I will forever try to repay you for this.

THE JOFFE BOOKS STORY

We began in 2014 when Jasper agreed to publish his mum's much-rejected romance novel and it became a bestseller.

Since then we've grown into the largest independent publisher in the UK. We're extremely proud to publish some of the very best writers in the world, including Joy Ellis, Faith Martin, Caro Ramsay, Helen Forrester, Simon Brett and Robert Goddard. Everyone at Joffe Books loves reading and we never forget that it all begins with the magic of an author telling a story.

We are proud to publish talented first-time authors, as well as established writers whose books we love introducing to a new generation of readers.

We won Trade Publisher of the Year at the Independent Publishing Awards in 2023 and Best Publisher Award in 2024 at the People's Book Prize. We have been shortlisted for Independent Publisher of the Year at the British Book Awards for the last five years, and were shortlisted for the Diversity and Inclusivity Award at the 2022 Independent Publishing Awards. In 2023 we were shortlisted for Publisher of the Year at the RNA Industry Awards, and in 2024 we were shortlisted at the CWA Daggers for the Best Crime and Mystery Publisher.

We built this company with your help, and we love to hear from you, so please email us about absolutely anything bookish at feedback@joffebooks.com.

If you want to receive free books every Friday and hear about all our new releases, join our mailing list here: www.joffebooks.com/freebooks.

And when you tell your friends about us, just remember: it's pronounced Joffe as in coffee or toffee!